FEB 03

DATE DUE

JUL 0 8 2003			
NOV 2 9 '06			
GAYLORD			PRINTED IN U.S.A.

HOW TO
COOK A TART

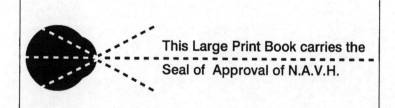

This Large Print Book carries the
Seal of Approval of N.A.V.H.

HOW TO COOK A TART

Nina Killham

Thorndike Press • Waterville, Maine

Published in 2003 by arrangement with Bloomsbury USA.

Thorndike Press Large Print Women's Fiction Series.

The tree indicium is a trademark of Thorndike Press.

The text of this Large Print edition is unabridged.
Other aspects of the book may vary from the original edition.

Set in 16 pt. Plantin by Christina S. Huff.

Printed in the United States on permanent paper.

Library of Congress Cataloging-in-Publication Data

Killham, Nina.
    How to cook a tart : a novel / Nina Killham.
      p. cm.
    ISBN 0-7862-4897-1 (lg. print : hc : alk. paper)
  1. Women cooks — Fiction. 2. Gastronomy — Fiction.
  3. Cookery — Fiction. 4. Large type books. I. Title.
PS3611.I45 H6 2003
  813′.6—dc21   2002190706

For Andrew

Chapter One

What a disastrous start to the day, Jasmine March thought as she stared down at her husband's nubile lover, dead on her kitchen floor. Jasmine held her breath and surveyed the vivid crime scene. Her special marble rolling pin lay six inches from the girl's bashed temple. Blood pooled in a rich raspberry hue. On the counter, tinfoil balanced askew over the plate of Jasmine's homemade chocolate brownies. Jasmine winced. One of the brownies was stuffed into the girl's mouth. As Jasmine gazed down at the young woman's willowy waist, she was sure of only two things. One, her husband's birthday dinner was ruined. Two, her rolling pin, thank God, was not chipped.

It was two months ago to the day when it all began to go wrong. When Jasmine woke that morning she'd been dreaming of breakfast. Not cornflakes or melba toast, skim milk and a sorry slice of apple. No, Jasmine was elbow deep in creamy oatmeal slathered with brown sugar and hot cream. Next, a plate of eggs Sardou: poached eggs nestled sweetly in the baby-smooth bottoms of artichokes and napped with a blushing spiced hollandaise sauce. Jasmine stared up at the ceiling, her mouth a swamp of saliva as she mentally mopped the rest of the hollandaise sauce with a crust of crunchy French bread before taking a sip of nutty chicory coffee and reaching for a freshly fried beignet so covered with powdered sugar it made her sneeze.

Closing her eyes, she tried to burrow back into the warm scents of hot sugar and caffeine. Her skin flushed pink at the thought of it. But the dream eluded her. Jasmine swung her legs off the bed. She gave the heavy fold of her backside a good scratch as she stepped across the room and sat down at her desk. And started to work:

First heat one tablespoon butter in a flame-proof casserole. Brown the meat over medium-high (in batches if necessary). Using a slotted spoon, transfer the meat to a bowl and set aside. To the casserole now add onion, garlic, chili, and paprika . . .

'Jasmine!'

Jasmine stopped typing. 'What?'

'We out of yogurt?' Daniel called from the kitchen downstairs.

'Look behind the deviled testicles.'

'The what?'

'The duck testicles.'

'Jesus.'

Jasmine heard her husband rummage through their extra-large steel-encased refrigerator, then the door slam. She continued. She erased *one tablespoon of butter* and typed *three*. As far as she was concerned, the more butter the better. There was no substitute for butter. Fresh, creamy butter. She shuddered at the current trend of blaming all ills on food. Food didn't kill people, for God's sake, people killed people. With their harping, and criticizing, and careful living. Show Jasmine a skinny woman and you'd be showing her a mentally deficient being. Weren't neurotics invariably skinny? Wasn't it the scrawny, hungry soul who created the most havoc in the world?

Don't get her started.

Jasmine licked her finger and flipped through her notes: Smoked Chicken with Pureed Spiced Lentils, Hot Ham and Bacon Biscuits, Cassoulet Salad with Garlic Sausages. After three cookbooks, she was finally finding her voice. She had discovered her future lay in rustic, not structure. Oh, she had tried the nouvelle rage. Who could forget her Breast of Chicken on a Bed of Pureed

Grapes, her Diced Brie and Kumquat Salsa, her Orange and Chocolate Salad with Grand Marnier Vinaigrette? But her instincts had rightly moved her closer to large portions. She hated the increasing fad of so much visible white plate. She preferred mounds of gorgeous food and puddles of sauces. Jasmine kneaded her heavy flesh and smiled. She had finally found her term. She was going to be a gastrofeminist. She would be Queen of Abundance, Empress of Excess. No apologies of appetite for her, no 'No thank you, I'm full,' no pushing away her plate with a sad but weary smile. Her dishes would fulfill the deepest, most primal urge. Beef stews enriched with chocolate and a hint of cinnamon, apple cakes dripping with Calvados and butter, pork sautéed with shallots, lots of cream, and mustard.

Jasmine smiled with satisfaction. She couldn't imagine a world without cookbooks. A world where a haunch was slapped on the fire and deposited partially grilled, bloody, and smelly on the plate. No sauce, no perfectly planned accompanying vegetable. Oh, a root vegetable perhaps, boiled beyond recognition. And that was only if the cook of the house was familiar with chemistry. No, life without cookbooks was unimaginable. Like Christianity without a Bible.

Jasmine had her mission: to lead the others to the Big One, the most delicious mouthful they'd ever consumed. It was not a vocation for the fragile. Her stomach was heavy with tasting. Her tongue charred from impatience. Her hands shredded from the testing of recipes. All that scraping and slicing and tearing. And then, of course, there were her wrists, always on the verge of seizing up with stress, so quickly, so immediately did she try to relay her message. But a prophet suffers and suffer she would if it meant one more decent meal on the public's table . . .

'Jasmine!'

'What!'

'The bran.'

'You ate it all.'

The moan of a self-impaled man came from the kitchen.

'There might be a spare box behind the semolina.'

Jasmine still remembered the first time she saw a cookbook. Fourteen and in urgent need to rid herself of her virginity, she had just offered it to one seventh-grade boy before finally withdrawing the offer after twenty minutes of his ineffectual groping. As she flounced downstairs from his bedroom, she caught sight of his mother's book-

11

case filled with brightly colored cookbooks. She sat right down as if struck like a gong and began to read, amazed at the heaven before her.

She read the cookbooks like novels, each recipe a chapter. The list of ingredients was the beginning, the instructions the complications of the story, the presentation the climax, and the optional substitutions, if any, the dénouement. She would then take up her own pen and paper and try to create recipes that had never seen the light or palate before: masterpieces like Potato Chip Salad, Squash Strudel, Baked Mustard Custard. Her problem, she knew from the beginning, was that she lacked regionality. Washington, D.C., was not known for its culinary tradition. She had grown up with no regional cooking and so could not whip up the homey, nostalgic cuisines of her mother's mother's mother. No genetically ingrained cream and flour sauces in her family for fourteen generations. She couldn't even claim a familial authentic New England clam chowder or a southern fried succotash. She was a culinary orphan and as such would have to invent herself.

Never one for baby steps, Jasmine threw herself into beef Wellingtons, bouillabaisses, even Bocuse's signature onion soup with its puff pastry top. Instead of clothes like the other girls, she saved her money to buy truffles, forking over her precious dollars and scurrying home with a fraction of an ounce of the fragrant fungus. Her mother, whose only cooking adventure had been sour cream instead of plain potato chips on her tuna casserole, was nervous. The whole teenage obsession reeked of impropriety, though she couldn't exactly explain why. She couldn't in a million years ask Jasmine to refrain from cooking because she feared she was becoming a vassal to the devil. Instead she began sitting down to dinner every night a bit fearfully, picking through the food like a land mine.

'What's that?' she'd ask suspiciously.

'Parma ham.'

'Ham? Why are you covering the melon with it? Shouldn't you save it for sandwiches?'

Sometimes she said nothing at all, just opened her eyes in stunned gustatory orgasm and stared religiously at her daughter.

'Wow,' she'd finally say.

'Uh-huh,' said her daughter.

Her mother feared it was an oral thing. But for Jasmine it was the discipline. She had found great comfort in the rigid discipline of cooking. It was a food military.

There were rules and regulations. Provide a service and clean up after yourself. Do your job well and you're rewarded. Not a job everybody wants but, boy, they sure want somebody to be doing it. Jasmine was a food marine. She was proud of it.

In those days, her heroes had been large men like Paul Bocuse, whose eyes twinkled above the sensuous slab of his ample cheeks. Jasmine herself was becoming a vast young woman. Oh, she was earth itself, flavor and richness and strength. At night she bathed to candles scented with vanilla and creamed palmfuls of olive oil into her rich dark skin, making sure to slide the grease over every patch. In the morning, she was as soft as silk and as fragrant as a Milanese trattoria. She piled her thick hair high on her head, letting the rowdier curls descend coquettishly around her face. She wore billowing white artist smocks and tied red or black bandannas at her throat. Her legs held firm from her excess energy. Her full lips burnished with a fuchsia lipstick set off her milk-white teeth . . .

'Jasmine!'

'What?'

'Are we out of OJ?'

Jasmine sighed, clicked shut her laptop, and went down to join her husband.

Daniel sat at the kitchen table, comparing the number of fiber grams on cereal boxes. Every morning he reread, recomputed, refigured the grams of fiber to the grams of salt and fat. He had become obsessed with eliminating. For Daniel eliminating had become tantamount of breathing. Fresh air and a fresh colon, that was his motto. His body was a battlefield between fiber and the raging toxins which hid like Vietcong in the jungle of his intestines. He would be Rambo, ferreting them out, garroting them mercilessly, his weapon of choice Fiber One, which scrubbed the walls of his gut like Ajax.

Jasmine strolled into the kitchen and opened the refrigerator. 'Manuscript is off to Garrett's today. Six months of testing, retesting, tasting, retasting. I must have eaten enough to feed a small nation.'

She perused the stacked refrigerator shelves. 'I'm starved.'

After a couple of aborted decisions she finally decided on a large slice of leftover tarte Tatin. She sat on a stool by the counter, took a big slurp of her steaming café au lait, and tucked in.

Daniel raised his eyes.

'Fiber One is the best.'

Jasmine shrugged. 'It tastes like sawdust.'

'Maybe, but you never eat it, so what do you care?'

'I'd hate you to spend the best years of your life eating sawdust.'

'Why is this so difficult for you?'

Jasmine's eyes flicked over to him.

'You want Fiber One, I'll get you Fiber One.'

'Thank you.'

He poured his skim milk over the fiber-deficient cereal and began to crunch. He eyed Jasmine as she followed her last mouthful of tart around the plate with a spoon. She cut off its escape with her other hand and popped it into her impatient mouth. He watched as she sucked the life out of it before swallowing. He turned his eyes away.

When Daniel had first seen Jasmine at the American Café in Georgetown seventeen years ago, he walked right into the wall. It was her way with the tarragon chicken croissant in her hands, her intense concentration, her closed, rapturous eyes, the large salad and double chocolate brownie at her table patiently waiting their turn. After salvaging his tray, he grabbed his veggie sandwich, overflowing with righteous sprouts, and sat as closely to her table as possible. He sipped his Perrier and watched while the vision before him sucked like a Hoover at her straw of Coke. She wetted her finger and dabbed at the flaky remains of her croissant. She took a deep, satisfied sigh and looked up, catching him staring at her, and smiled. He, with a mouthful of cucumber, tomato, avocado, and whole-grain bread, nodded back. She then actually smacked her lips and drew forth her salad. Daniel watched in amazement as she forked her lettuce into her mouth as economically as filling a trash bag with trimmings. Finally, she stopped and began to chew, grinning over at him, her eyes mere slits left in a face enlarged by two busy cheeks. Daniel noticed by now that he was not the only one who gawked. Whole tables chewed silently, breathlessly watching as Jasmine, her salad a mere memory, paused. She sat up straight and rolled her neck around to release any tension. She hiked up her shoulders to her ears one at a time as if getting ready for strenuous exercise. One last roll of her head and a beatific smile for the waitress who swerved by her table to grab her two exhausted plates. Jasmine then reached for her dessert and drew it close. She gazed at it, contemplating the melting ice cream flowing down to moisten the side of the decadent chocolate brownie, the thinning line of chocolate sauce which pooled into the white cream before disappearing to the bottom of the plate. She picked up the fork, mumbled something Daniel didn't catch, and began to slide the bites of drenched brownie methodically into her increasingly warm and chocolaty mouth.

She met his eyes as he approached, licking her lips. Without a word he sat down before her. She chewed on her lower lip and said nothing. Daniel reached over and gently removed the fork from her hand.

'I hope you saved some for me,' he said.

She smiled, her teeth brown and white like a Jersey cow.

Within a month he had it all: gourmet cook, maid, and sex slave. Well, maybe not sex slave, but she was certainly enthusiastic. The best thing about it was, it was all her idea. She'd been staying with her mother and was bursting to get out. She extracted him from his group house and set them up in a reasonably priced one-bedroom apartment in Northwest. He could have done without the cheerleading cockroaches who watched him make toast every morning and the bathroom the size of a toupee, but other than that he could absolutely not complain. And the food. Oh, the food. Jesus, the food.

Veal with a crab sauce. A lamb roast studded with so much garlic he couldn't get near his boss for days. Fried calamari with a chili and honey sauce. Duck breast with sautéed peaches. A beef stew with a sauce so good he wanted to rub it all over his body; rich, meaty, sweet, and oniony.

One night, after a ragged afternoon at his day job, he walked into the apartment and smelled the breath of angels. Italian angels, sweet and pungent and herby with a splash of white wine, exuding a perfume that curled around his nose like a tickler. He strode to the kitchen to find seafood simmering in the pot over which Jasmine bent, swirling and sprinkling like a witch. Daniel was born again at that moment. Life gained meaning. The future sat up and beckoned. Marriage, a word he had never uttered without a twang of abject fear, became a gripping desire. Love, lust, and an incurable gluttony poured from him in the form of an unintelligible proposal, to which Jasmine sweetly smiled and which she sealed with a garlicky smack on the lips.

These days, though, Daniel had to watch out. Not that he was going to stop eating. Hell no. When you're living with a maestro you don't turn down the volume. But he'd read the books: a clean colon was the key. A clean colon banished not only excess weight but irritability, drowsiness, forgetfulness, anxiety, indecisiveness, even hostility. Daniel sucked in his gut and gave it a good internal squeeze. It was clean as a whistle and he intended to keep it that way.

Daniel grimaced at the review on page C$_3$. 'Tired, derivative'. Asshole. Who gave critics so much power anyway? They knew how to write. So what. Did that give them the right to print garbage? Years ago, Daniel had imagined himself the next Robert De Niro, but Washington, D.C., was a hard place to leave. He had said to himself that he wanted to go to New York when he had the money. On his own terms. He didn't want to pound the sidewalk, wait the tables, so he had had to scale down his ambitions a bit. He became an acting teacher and the director of a 'small but energetic and promising', according to the local rag, theater group down on Fourteenth Street. He had some friends who had gone to L.A. One had made it. Really big. Sitcom big. But none of them had families. They dated younger women and then complained about their stupidity.

But it was important what he did, he reminded himself. How many people could say that? He was his students' lifeline to their future. He never let them down. He was a teacher. Nothing more honorable in the world. Look at Aristotle, Socrates. No one dared say to them that teachers teach what they can't do. In his opinion, it was those who can't teach who must resign themselves to doing. He was the shape changer. He changed his students' focus from stereotype to deep character. From first notion to several choices back. From imitation to life. From students who knew no more about real drama than bricks in a wall to those who saw drama in the everyday moments, who could stand back from a rejection, a failure, even an exquisite joy and say to themselves, 'I can use this.'

So yes, Daniel had stayed. And now his acting career was over and his theater was six months in arrears. Now, every morning, he peered at his future, a dingy, airless space filled with mealy reviews, ungrateful students, responsible, civic behavior, and in the end, an obituary under the heading NOBODY. He stared into this abyss, his body leaning dangerously close, his crushed toes skimming the edge.

Daniel sighed. Jasmine was everything he wasn't. Optimistic, giving, patient. And lately, the more giving she was, the more patient she acted, the crankier he got. Nothing to do with her, he told himself. Just time, familiarity, restlessness. Life, he figured. So he tried to be happy. Really. He kept reminding himself he had a wife he loved. Yes, he loved her. She cooked like a goddess. He had a daughter who was the prettiest in her class. He had his world. Of course, he wouldn't mind a couple hundred thousand bucks. And maybe a new car. Bigger house. An expensive trip somewhere. Maybe Tahiti. The beach. And breasts. Brown breasts. Round brown breasts.

Daniel put down his spoon.

'I'll probably be late tonight.'

Jasmine glanced at him.

'Again?'

Daniel shrugged.

Jasmine looked away. 'Do you know what you want for your birthday?'

'Nothing,' he said. 'I want nothing for my birthday.'

Jasmine had other plans. She surreptitiously glanced at her notes. She crossed out *daiquiris* and jotted down *bellinis*. Added *bruschettas*. Ah, an aioli. Yes, fresh salmon and cod, artichokes, carrots, beets, mushrooms, and fennel. That's an idea. What else? Oysters? Why the hell not? Might liven things up. Now, the main course . . . here, she was stumped. She wanted something very special for Daniel's birthday. She wanted to create a recipe just for him. As musicians create arias, symphonies, and fugues for presents, she wanted to create the most sumptuous dish. A dish for a king. Something male and hearty. She had thought red meat. Dark rich sauce. Potatoes, mushrooms, onions. But weren't those old hat? Good, yes. But she wanted something different. For weeks she'd been toying, her notebook now worn from so much scratching out. She had considered Asian beef noodle or strong Italian baked pasta, but wasn't that just ordinary in another language? She was hoping that if she carried on, it would come to her in a flash of inspiration. But so far the idea remained perched just beyond the edge of her mind, refusing to dip into her consciousness.

Jasmine collected the dishes Daniel had left and carried them to the sink. When Daniel had introduced himself that fateful day at the American Café, he wasn't Jasmine's type. He was thin, for one thing. Scrawny, her mother pointed out. But he had the soul of a fat man, Jasmine soon learned. His body weight was genetic, not psychological. He adored food as much as she did, matching her appetite and orgasmic murmurs. Unusually for a man who liked to eat so much, though, Daniel could not cook. Couldn't make rice, couldn't even boil a decent ten-minute egg. So after a brief honeymoon of small French cafés he escorted her to and paid for, Jasmine began to cook for him. It was the last she was to see of the inside of a restaurant she didn't have to pop for. But what did you expect, said her mother. 'The guy's unemployed.' No, he's an artist, Jasmine corrected her. Repeatedly, she had to correct her.

But what he lacked professionally he made up for elsewhere. The second night they met, he led her back to the group house he shared with two Moroccan cabdrivers. He sat back on the bed and pulled her down onto him. He smelled of lemons. Here was a man intent on making her happy, making her shudder. 'It is my pleasure to give you pleasure,' he whispered into the crevice of her sweating breasts. Such a thin man but with so much power and energy. And when he had finally come and kissed her tenderly he slid out of bed and poked his head out the door and yelled down to one of the cabdrivers. Jasmine froze, clutching the sheets to her chest. But when the man trotted up the stairs it was with two glasses of ice water laced with crushed mint. Daniel grinned his beautiful smile and thanked him. He handed the cool, icy glass to Jasmine and stood drinking his in big gulps as he stared down at her, fingering the little curl of hair just below his belly button. Jasmine took a long drink, then lay back in a daze. The room contained one double bed, a chest of drawers, a broken chair. Daniel's clothes hung from a pole mounted across one corner of the room. Daniel took back her glass and placed it with his on the chest of drawers.

'You comfortable?' he asked.

Jasmine smiled yes, though she wondered whether it would be better for her to leave than to sleep in a house full of unknown men, wondering briefly what the Moroccan brothers ate for breakfast. She reached for the covers kicked to the bottom of the bed, for she was now starting to chill, but Daniel grasped her hand and slid himself on top of her again. He smiled down into her confused eyes. 'The first time was a necessity. Now we have time for luxury,' he said. He reached back and, gathering the covers over his head, began to explore her body.

When he was finished, she was his. She had thought herself in love a couple of times, once with a young French man who liked to rub his member in snail butter for Jasmine's gratification, but that affair seemed like a short sticky night compared to the force with which she and Daniel coupled. When she woke in the morning with Daniel every cell in her body stood up, armed and ready. She was ready to kill to keep their union. Daniel had become hers and would remain so. She thought of him the same way she thought about a bouillabaisse: rare, precious, inexplicable, a gift from God.

After breakfast, Daniel stared into the mirror and grinned, examining his teeth. He was vain about his teeth. As he grew older, they remained his best feature. He therefore treated them properly like an investment, flossing with religious fervor, having them professionally cleaned four times a year, and never forgetting to brush after eating. It was a dental hygienist who had scared the living daylights out of him three years back. After peering into his mouth and grunting, she had snapped open her face guard and fixed him with a stare. Daniel had smiled back, used to hearing dentists fawn over his perfect teeth.

'You guys are the worst,' she said.

'Excuse me?'

'You guys with good teeth, you're the ones who end up losing them first. You get all cocky thinking you got no care in the world, then whammo, they all fall out. I've seen it happen.'

Daniel's hand flew up to protect his teeth.

'Wh— what can I do?'

'I don't know if you've got what it takes.'

'Tell me.'

'It takes commitment.'

'Yeah . . .'

'Daily, no, double daily commitment. Are you up for that?'

'It's that bad?'

'It's that bad.'

'OK, shoot.'

She held up the floss container like a badge.

'Meet your new friend.'

Daniel shrank back.

'Oh, no.'

'Oh, yes. You want teeth, you got to pay for them.'

Daniel grimaced as she approached, pulling the floss tight between her two hands like a garrote.

'Here, let me show you.'

After five minutes of pain and blood flow equivalent to a slaughtered pig's, Daniel got the message. He stumbled home with his complimentary box of floss and dug into it every day, chanting to the mirror, 'Chicks don't dig dicks with no teeth.'

Today, Daniel squeezed his thighs, noting reluctantly that they were not as rock hard as they used to be in his days of intramural soccer. He'd played fervently with the same league to great local success from the time he graduated from college until two years ago, when he was tactfully (how can anyone do this tactfully) asked to make way for a younger, fitter competitor. It was the saddest day of his life. He put down the phone after an exaggerated belly laugh with the captain and walked out the door. Jasmine called after him, worried, but he kept walking, straight to the car, which drove him straight along his favorite road, MacArthur Boulevard, straight out toward Great Falls. It was either a brisk walk along his old haunt or an endless round of drinks at a bar. He chose the first, at the beginning, and only later when he noticed the five o'clock hour on his return did he veer from home toward the Hecht's parking lot for a thick, tall margarita at Houligan's. When the tears started flowing after his third shot he retired to the parking lot and snuffled in his parked car like a schoolboy.

Jasmine, bless her, had been sympathetic when he came home, wiping the amused grin off her face and acting like a mild-mannered geisha for the rest of the evening. She did the only thing she thought would help: she fed him. She rushed out to the extravagantly priced Sutton Place Gourmet and returned with two bags full of goodies that she proceeded to turn into bite-size works of art. As he watched an old Truffaut movie on television and downed a bottle of icy Rose d'Anjou, she fed him cheese tarts and olive crustades to begin, before clearing away the crumbs and practically wiping his mouth, and returning bearing poached salmon and wild rice salad. She finished off her feat as if she were an acrobat about to take her bow with a double-bean vanilla ice cream drowning in amaretto. Daniel scooped it all into his mouth, never taking his eyes off the TV screen. When he was finished he was overwhelmingly full, impossibly drunk, and sadder than when he started.

Jasmine stood towering above him, her hands on her hips.

'What are you thinking?' she asked.

'I'm thinking what an absurd life I lead.'

'What's that supposed to mean?'

'It all goes so quickly, doesn't it? It's over before you even know it's begun.'

'People live a lot longer these days . . .'

'So do pigs, but we still make bacon out of them at the same age.'

'You don't look old to me.'

'That's because you're my age.'

'What's that supposed to mean?'

'It means what it's supposed to mean, that we're both forty.'

'Not yet.'

'This year. Face it, we're old. We don't look like we did ten years ago, we don't act it either. I guess you could say we're acting our age. I'm just surprised, that's all. I thought I'd have it beat.'

'You think I look old?'

'You look like you should look at your age.'

Jasmine's eyes grew cold. She picked up his dishes and walked back to the kitchen. As he heard her clanking loudly around the kitchen, Daniel smiled for the first time since the phone call. He wasn't going down this path alone. He was taking her with him.

Chapter Two

Sixteen-year-old Careme gripped her hipbones, which protruded against her jeans, and nodded approvingly. Her chest, she noted with satisfaction, was a relief of ribs. She gazed into the mirror, her eyebrows arched. She balled her fists. She was a culinary terrorist. An antifood guerrilla.

'Careme! Dinner.'

Careme rolled her eyes. She strode to her desk and snatched her notebook. She had to make a battle plan. Her first battle was obvious. She would approach the battlefield — i.e., the dinner table — stealthily. With quick precision she would neatly cut off the enemy — i.e., her mother — by refusing any portions.

'Careme!'

If portions were heaped upon her — she smiled — she knew her enemy's tactics, she would spread them thinly upon her plate.

'Careme! Now!'

Careme stood and squared her shoulders. She wore a gray hooded top and Gap button-front jeans she'd painted with white clouds and silver stars. Her straight blond hair was cropped just below her ears and fell conveniently in front of her face. She had light brown eyebrows, gray-green eyes, and a long, waspish neck that she was in the habit of stringing with thin leather chokers. She was all elbows, collarbones, and implausibly long arms and legs. A veritable lowercase *l* in the alphabet of the human genus.

Careme admired those collarbones, which stuck out like stovepipes, before shrugging on an extra sweatshirt to disguise them. A guerrilla had to wear camouflage. She opened the door. A wave of rich meat sauce hit her between the nostrils. She stepped back, placing a firm hand on her growling belly.

'Careme!'

'Coming!'

Downstairs, Careme paused at the kitchen door. Her mother smacked shut a drawer with her heavy hips. Careme winced.

'Oh, there you are,' her mother said. 'Gimme a hand with the béchamel, will you?'

'I thought dinner was ready.'

Her mother stopped and turned to look at her. She continued to watch as Careme walked quickly over to the saucepan and began dolloping in the butter and flour. Careme tried hard to not touch the butter.

When it oozed over her finger she ran to the sink and scrubbed furiously.

'Oh, for God's sake,' huffed her mother.

'It's gross.'

'Here.' Her mother handed her the milk. Careme grabbed a paper towel and took the cold, slimy carton, pouring with an expert if disgusted eye just the right amount for the sauce. She held her breath as the huge casserole of meat and tomato sauce was laid beside her. She turned her head away until just the corner of her left eye could survey the proceedings and dumped the béchamel as quickly as possible all over the meat.

'Easy!' barked her mother.

Careme tossed the béchamel pan into the sink, scrubbing quickly, then lathering her hands well over her elbows. Her mother eased the moussaka into the preheated oven.

'I'll come back when it's ready,' said Careme.

'No, sit down. I want to talk to you.'

Careme slumped in a chair, all knees and elbows. It was her mother's turn to wince.

'Here, have a cracker.' Her mother deposited a bowl of cheese crackers, her favorite as a kid, on the table. Careme jerked back as if avoiding a shark's bite.

Her mother wiped her greasy and meat-stained hands on her apron.

'Careme, this can't go on. You've got to eat.'

'I eat.'

'No, you don't. Look at you.'

Careme looked down at her stick legs, secretly pleased at the lack of fat on her thighs, and shrugged.

Her mother tried another tactic.

'Your father is worried about you.'

Careme looked up, curious.

'We both are.'

Careme shrugged again, stared a second at the cheese crackers, then switched positions to turn her back on them.

'You need to see a doctor.'

Careme laughed. 'I'm healthy.'

'That is not healthy.'

'Do I ever get sick?'

'You are sick now.'

'You know, that is so . . . you know, food is not the answer to everything. Eating doesn't make you well. That's just some bullshit they shovel at you in the magazines.'

'What . . . ?'

'You believe everything you read? All that four-food-group crap? That was a USDA conspiracy to get us to eat their excess cows. Everybody knows that.'

'Careme . . .'

'The problem with you is that you think

34

the answer to everything is food! Well, it's not. You know, other people should be able to live the way they want without making pigs of themselves. You know, you should respect the way other people live. You think you're such a liberal, but that's a bunch of bull. Because you eat like a pig you want everyone else to . . .'

'Careme!'

'It's true! Everything in this house is eat, eat, eat! It makes me sick . . .'

Careme was feeling great. Her campaign was working beautifully. There's a lot to be said for taking the offensive. Her mother stared at her hopelessly, her mouth slack, her hand still in the cracker bowl.

'I mean, half the time they come out with studies ten years later about how the food they've been telling you is soooo good for you is going to give you cancer. So the only real thing to do is to not eat. I mean, is that so stupid? No! Buddhists don't eat very much and they live to be a zillion years old. I'm probably going to live past a hundred because I won't have any excess weight on me. In their eyes, I'm perfectly normal. But it's only in this household that I'm a freak. Do you know what it's like to be a freak in your own household?'

Her mother stared at her a second, then

tipped her eyes down to her watch. She sprang out of her chair and ran to the stove, where she drew out the hot, bubbling, browned moussaka. Careme sat back with a smirk on her face.

'Food of death,' she said.

Jasmine had conceived sixteen years ago on the night she saw three black crows sitting in their oak tree. They tipped the branch lower than usual and she watched from the window of the kitchen as they cocked their heads back and forth, their caws like laughter. Jasmine opened the back door and stood outside in the magnolia-scented heat. She was not one for omens, but she couldn't get it out of her mind. How strange it had been, the three of them staring down at her, like spectators. So when she realized she was pregnant she thought perhaps they had been messengers of some sort. Before the ultrasound she worried she might be having triplets. But no, a single birth, perfectly placed in her waiting uterus, its heart a small white beating dot in the middle.

The longer she was pregnant, the more convinced she was that God was a man. Pregnancy was just a series of indignities. She burped incessantly, she farted like a firecracker, she smacked loudly and urgently when confronted with food. Daniel said that living with her while she was pregnant was like living with Henry VIII. She remembered the first vague motions the baby made inside her. She'd lie in bed at night with her hand pressed against her belly. At the merest beat she'd clamp Daniel's hand on the site. He'd lean close to her belly button and speak to his child. 'Hello in there,' he said. 'This is your father speaking.' As if the child was supposed to stand up and salute.

But she hadn't expected the love she'd feel for her newborn daughter, Careme. The sensual need to touch her baby's flushed, moist skin, the ecstasy of her hot milk breath, the poetry of her explosive bodily functions. She remembered the quiet of those long nights when she had banished Daniel to another room to rest. She had lain, fairly hallucinating for lack of sleep, watching Careme's busy cheeks as she latched painfully to Jasmine's breast, and staring wide eyed with wonder at the distortions and emotions that ran like ripples over her sleeping daughter's face. She learned sweet selfless love for the first time, knowing now that love ran down rather than up the family tree.

The happiness in the home in those days

was palpable. So thick you could, if tempted, cut it with a small butter knife. It would have come away rich, thick, and frothy. It would have tasted sweet, their happiness, but not too sweet. Daniel would reach over at breakfast time and with his hand gently slide his thumb around her cheek. Careme would gurgle and burp and dribble all her love with a toothless smile.

But now it seemed their bliss had evaporated. Life was now about maintaining. What, she wasn't so sure. Slowly, imperceptibly, their home had ceased to be a home. It had become a railway station, and her family busy travelers impatient for that train that was to take them away. Daniel would arrive back from work a complete stranger, not her husband but another man unsure of whose home he had walked into. Careme stalked around the house like a wounded animal, snarling, dangerous, impossibly hurt. And it seemed the more Jasmine tried, the more they pulled away and Jasmine was left standing there, swaying, her heart so full and so useless.

Back inside the sanctity of her bedroom, Careme stroked Medea, her pet python, which she kept in a large glass tank next to her bed. She thought having a snake for a pet very Zen. Medea produced no noise, little waste. Careme told her mother that watching Medea was the perfect antidote to the stresses of daily life. Her mother said she was glad her daughter had finally found kinship with someone like her, a cold-blooded reptile.

Careme lay on her bed and stared up at the ceiling, gazing at the bits of plastic which had once been magical glowing stars. She remembered the night, it must have been five, six years ago, when her mother turned off the light and yelled, 'Surprise!' as the whole ceiling faded away and became a starry, starry night. She was always doing things like that, her mother. Trying really hard. And lately, the more she tried, the more Careme just wanted her to go away. Didn't she see that the world hated someone who tried? It hated peppy cheerleaders. After all, what the hell did her mother have to be so excited about? She was fat, her husband was never home, her books didn't make much money, she wasn't nearly so well-known as Stephen Lane's mother. Careme felt a pang of guilt as she remembered all the picnics her mother used to take her on when she came back from school. Other kids went home to store-bought cookies and a glass of milk. Careme got a picnic basket full of homemade brownies, double brownies they were called, with chunks of hazelnut and milk chocolate. And there would be a cheese plate garnished with a perfect mound of purple grapes and a thermos of lemon tea all laid out on a plaid blanket in Rock Creek Park overlooking the Potomac River. That had been before Careme stopped eating. That was when she was also fat.

Careme tossed her old worn teddy bear up as high as she could, trying to smash its face into the plaster. It hit its nose first. After that her arms grew weak and she tossed it across the room. She lay a second before scrambling up and snatching it back into her arms.

She tried to be a good person. Every morning she woke up with the greatest intentions. Like she was going to study really hard that day, or write a thank-you letter to her father's mother, who had sent her ten measly dollars a hundred years ago now, or even, gasp, be nice to her mother. But by breakfast something would have gone wrong, mainly her mother would say something snide and well, if the day wasn't going to be perfect why even try? And so she would just tell herself tomorrow, tomorrow she'd start.

Don't get her wrong, deep down she was nice. Really nice. She just didn't get to express it a lot. It was tough being popular. You had to have this façade. Otherwise everyone wanted a piece of you. And she felt suffocated by it. She didn't trust anybody. Everyone lied to everyone. It wasn't as if she didn't have friends. She had plenty, but she wasn't sure if she trusted any one of them, not even Lisa. How could she? Everyone would do anything so that the right guy would talk to them, even if it meant telling your best friend's secret. Lisa had told Jason about Alessandra's throwing up after eating. Alessandra didn't know. She didn't see him sticking his finger in his mouth every time her back was turned. And everyone giggled. Alessandra didn't know why everyone giggled and she walked off crying yesterday. Careme wanted to tell her why, but she knew it would crush her even more than the unexplained giggling, so she didn't and just watched, sadly, thinking tomorrow, tomorrow she would do something about it.

Chapter Three

The next morning, Betty Johnson, Jasmine's neighbor, peered over her quivering girth at the scale: 182 pounds. Oh, heavens, she thought, puckering her rosebud lips into a pout. That's it. No breakfast. No lunch. And a slim shake for dinner. As she tiptoed back to her bedroom on small feet that cowered under her elephantine belly like two frightened mice, she warmed to her subject. Food was treacherous. Meals were land mines. A fat-laden sauce could explode in your body and destroy in seconds weeks of self-imposed starvation. She'd read the books. She knew the score. She had to be tougher with herself. She had to be vigilant twenty-four hours a day, seven days a week, yes, 365 days a year. And then some.

Betty padded past her husband where he slept, taking up more than his fair share of their king-size mattress, to her closets filled with a range of clothes from size 12 (on a good day — last good day, five years ago, May 17) to size 18 (on not such good days, which, she had to admit, had been more frequent lately). She picked a dark blue and white striped velour tunic and pants suit. The vertical stripes, the saleswoman had assured her, made a person look thinner, at least two whole sizes. She stood in front of her mirror and let her wrath descend upon her permed hair, which lay in unruly clumps around her face. She pulled them back in a bun. No, too much the fat librarian. She pulled the front portion back in a barrette. Too much the aging fat schoolgirl.

Nope, not a bite would pass her lips until six-thirty that night. Just water. Gallons of water. Well, maybe a glass of fruit juice. Mango-Banana Splash. Mmmm. From deep within her a petulant growl escaped. And a grapefruit for breakfast. Didn't it use more calories to consume? Oh, no. A memory seized her, bringing hot tears to her eyes. Donuts. Jelly and cream cheese donuts. She had bought a box of them yesterday in a nanosecond of weakness and now they waited for her in her kitchen like long-lost family. Betty sucked in her cheeks. One. She could have one. OK. She knew herself. Two. Her lips involuntarily smacked at the thought of the sweet jelly encased in the rich thick cheese. Just two. And then nothing. Absolutely nothing. Not a thing until her diet shake at dinner. Cross her fingers and hope to die.

Jasmine looked at her watch, the band of which was beginning to bite into her wrist like a silver piranha. Late again. It was her one vice. She was a bit like her cooking, really; taking her time, getting it right. She often wondered why on earth the world was in such a hurry. Ah, but there they were. She could see them through the bookshop window. Her public, all five of them. The numbers were not high, yet they were of a caliber other authors only dreamed about. They were discerning, faithful, astute, and above all, book buyers. She liked to think of herself as the William Styron of cookbook authors. Her disciples, adherents to the concept of good, heavy food, were rabid in her defense. Rotund and confident, they held her latest book in their hands with the fervor of communists holding Mao's little red book. Less numerous, perhaps, but possessing a much better sense of humor.

When she breezed in, flashing her trademark fuchsia smile, they pushed forward. Her publicist clicked forward in a short black dress from which two beanpole legs jutted out. Really, Jasmine thought, if the girl would

44

just eat and put some meat on those skull bones she called cheeks, perhaps she would get Jasmine some real publicity in magazines or television rather than these paltry gatherings which no one even heard about.

'They've been queuing for hours,' Susie, the publicist and mistress of the overstatement, said.

A corner table was piled high with her cookbooks. Jasmine eyed the chair, a bandy office number that would curtail any thought of comfort. Susie snapped it away and returned rolling the large swivel chair of the protesting manager. Jasmine murmured 'Coffee, lots of cream and sugar,' and settled down to the most enjoyable aspect of her job, communing with her people. The first in line stepped up.

'Mr Dupree, how delightful to see you.'

'Mrs March.' Mr Dupree radiated supreme pleasure. He carried his heavy flesh high and firm. Fat encased his neck like a boa. His corpulent hands pushed forth the cassis-colored book. Jasmine opened it crisply to its title page and scrawled her usual motto. 'To feast well is the best revenge.'

'And how is Mrs Dupree?' she inquired.

'Passed on.'

'I'm so sorry.'

'Oh, she died happy. A recipe of yours on her lips.'

'I'm so glad.'

'I can't wait for your next book.'

'Working as fast as I can, Mr Dupree.'

And on it went for a half hour. Moments of connection, a trade or two of culinary secrets, an encouragement, all the while her pen never stopping, the red ink flowing like chicken blood.

Across Key Bridge in Arlington, Virginia, an alarm shrilled in a run-down apartment block peopled by those waiting to become someone. From under rumpled sheets, a hand like the tentacles of an underfed octopus searched to destroy the source. Tina Sardino, in the throes of her late twenties, sat up. Skinny with bony cheeks, long, thin red hair, and the hungry, ambitious look of a jackal, she blinked at the mess around her. Empty champagne bottles. Empty Chinese cartons. Two empty wineglasses. There had been one hell of a party, but now, as usual, Tina was alone. She held her pounding temples and climbed out of her wrinkled bed.

When she walked into the kitchen, a trio of cockroaches glanced up at her in midbite. Tina stomped on them without wincing and then whirred together three raw eggs and carrot juice and gulped it down while absentmindedly grabbing her belly for any excess fat. There was none.

She was late again. For acting class. Where she worked on her voice, her delivery, her presentation, her method. Where she mostly schmoozed with the other acting students. They formed somewhat of an informal therapy group, urging each other on, telling each other little white lies about how good they were, how inspired, how it was just a matter of time before they were discovered. But in Tina's case, she was absolutely sure they were right. You only had to look at her, she told herself. She had star quality written all over her perfectly sculpted face. She had talent. She had the looks. And so she accepted their fawning as her due. It was just a matter of time, she remained certain, before she made it, before she appeared on the big screen and the covers of magazines, before she forgot all their names and insisted on an unlisted number.

Tina closed her eyes to the dreariness of her cheap apartment. She paid for the place with the proceeds from her part-time job as a legal secretary. She naturally hated this day job but didn't mind its facilities. She used the Xerox for flyers for upcoming performances, the mail frank to send out her head shot and résumé. Even, she'd die if anyone knew this, their Federal Express number, if she was in a real rush. But ambition was not polite. Anyone knew that. Those who made it did anyway, she thought smugly. They also knew that it was The Look that mattered. Oh, sure, acting technique helped, but in the end, if you didn't have the goods, forget it. Meryl Streep got lucky. It was the Pamela Anderson Lees of the world that really ruled. Tina valued her body as the temple it was. She nurtured it, communed with it, offered it sustenance like a high priestess before the altar. Her priest? Dr Sears. Or Dr Zone to the world.

His guidance was simple but strict. Potatoes and rice were death mongers. Protein was the gift of life. Tina carried his book around like a bible and checked with it religiously before letting any food pass her lips. His mantra was so obvious, she couldn't believe she hadn't seen it before. She had been floundering, an undefined, lackluster being, until Dr Sears provided her with a molecular definition of wellness. He had reached out from the shelves of Crown Books and showed her a place where physical, mental, and spiritual perfection met. He beckoned her from page 1 and brought her to a place where her body and her mind worked together at their ultimate best. The rest was her department.

Careme stood on the edge of the basketball court of her high school with her two best friends, Lisa and Alessandra. Lisa's mother was the second lady's press secretary. Alessandra's father was the Venezuelan ambassador. The school, with its stonehouse headquarters perched on top of a hill above Wisconsin Avenue, was an eclectic and hipper combination of private school students than the more establishment halls of the boys-only St Alban's and the girl's-only National Cathedral School. Careme knew that financially she had no business being there, but her parents had saved and took few vacations so that she could learn her letters in the company of the upper middle class.

'Did you see that jump?' Lisa's arms squeezed the books she was holding against her chest closer.

'He's soooooo cute,' moaned Alessandra, who tossed yet again her long dark hair behind her shoulder and stood straight as a toy soldier.

Careme said nothing, just nodded, never taking her eyes off Troy's arms, which were long and muscled in a light mocha hue that shimmered in the sunshine. Troy was handsome, smooth, a B+ student, and, Careme hoped, the man who would take away her virginity.

Troy's eyes glanced to where Careme stood on the side. He jerked back his head in greeting. She grinned slightly and looked away.

Lisa nudged her. Careme frowned. Lisa was being so uncool. Alessandra flicked back her hair again and turned her back to the court.

'So what do you want to do? Get a pizza before class?'

'Yeah.'

'Let's take my car.'

They jumped into Alessandra's dad's cast-off BMW and drove to Armand's and ordered a spinach pizza to share.

Lisa nudged Careme again. 'I can't believe you want to do it. It is so last year.'

'What are you talking about?'

'Didn't you hear? Virginity is in. Nobody puts out anymore. Not to mention the fact that men are dying out. In twenty years they won't even be a species anymore. We've surpassed them in everything. Why screw around with them?'

'Hello, they're sexy.'

'Do you believe everything the media says?'

'Lisa, you are so full of shit sometimes.'

'It's your life.'

Alessandra tore her eyes away from the men making the pizzas. 'I like to do everything but. That way you lose nothing.'

'Now that's like in the dark ages,' said Lisa.

The cashier pushed the pizza box through the window. Lisa opened it to reveal a bright green and creamy pie. Alessandra leaned forward to sniff deeply.

'Heaven,' she murmured, addressing her slice like a lover. 'Come here, you delicious thing.' Alessandra shook more Parmesan cheese over the already heavily cheesed pie. She added a good douse of dried chili. She brought the slice to her mouth and slid it in.

'Well, I think you should go for it,' said Alessandra with a full mouth.

'You just want to hear about it,' said Lisa.

Alessandra didn't answer. She was shoveling in her pizza as fast as she could, as if she feared it would suddenly jump from the box and try to dash away.

'My mother says you should do it with someone who turns you on,' continued Lisa.

'Your mother told you this?' asked Careme.

'No, I heard her with her girlfriends once.

Girls' night out. Only they were in, drinking a case of wine.'

'Did she do it with someone who turned her on?'

'No. Some guy she thought her mother would approve of. Says she's regretted it ever since.'

'Did she marry him?'

'No. It was just the first time, she was nineteen or something.'

'Then why . . . ?'

'I don't know. Weird.'

Careme picked at her pizza, nibbling at the crust. She was torn in her decision. She was dying to lose her virginity, it weighed around her neck like a bowling ball, but she did want to make sure it was the right guy. She had been tempted to draw up a questionnaire, a Take My Virginity Away application, and hand it around to a couple of choice applicants. They could list their strengths and weaknesses. What drew them to the sex field? Where did they see themselves having sex in the next five years? In truth, she didn't know exactly what to ask and her two best friends, equally virginal, had been no help at all. But she did know that he had to be smart, sexy, and experienced. And according to rumor, Troy was very experienced. Very.

Alessandra, who had finished her two slices and was sucking the life out of her Coke, ogled Careme's uneaten slice of pizza.

'You not going to finish that?'

'No, you want it?'

'You never eat.'

'God, you sound like my mother.'

Careme tossed her pizza into the trash. Alessandra and Lisa looked at each other but said nothing.

Alessandra looked at her jeweled watch and gasped. 'Oh my God, it's one.'

'Oh, shit.'

'Hurry!'

'Wait! I have to go to the bathroom . . .' Alessandra cried.

'We don't have time,' said Careme firmly, and pulled Alessandra down the street by the wrist.

In the late afternoon, Jasmine paused at the front door. She took a deep breath and made a quick panty-line check before grasping the gold pineapple knocker.

'Jasmine!' shrieked the large woman who opened the door. This was Sally Snow, a cookbook author who specialized in low-fat cakes and pastries. She also had her own column in *The Washington Post*. (Heavily edited, according to a mutual friend on the staff.) The party was to honor her latest book, *No Cal, Sal.* A stack of the books lay on the table in the hall, a pen ready for signing and a small box ready for checks.

'Oh, come in.' Sally threw two kisses in the vague direction of Jasmine's cheeks. 'Miranda's here. And so is Karen. Pam's going to be late. Oh, you shouldn't have,' she said as she grabbed the plate of caviar canapés from Jasmine's hands.

In the kitchen, a dozen women gathered around the increasingly laden table. They picked and chewed with studied eyes. Jasmine had been professionally linked with these women for ten years. They met fairly frequently at meetings of Les Dames d'Escoffier, a culinary society for professional cooking women. They attended each other's book parties in dreadful need of having them appear at their own parties. They seemed to clump together according to book sales. As Jasmine's books never made one reprint, she felt a bit out of the loop.

'Help yourself to the wine,' Sally urged Jasmine as she swatted her large ten-year-old son away from the dessert table. 'Shoo. You can have some later.' Her son swiped a brownie and raced out the door. Sally stepped up on a stool, clinked her wineglass, and waved at the room for attention.

'My kinsmen, my clansmen, my fellow foodies. It is so kind of you to come honor my latest book. Of course, many other congratulations are in order. Our own star, Miranda Lane, is here. Her latest, *Jamaica Going Japanesa*, has hit the *New York Times* best-seller list!'

There was tepid applause. On the other side of the table, Miranda Lane, a scrawny robot of a woman, smugly popped organic blue corn chips into her mouth.

Sally continued. 'Now, there are a few copies of my book out in the hall. One-time-only discount. For my friends. Twelve-fifty. I take Visa and MasterCard. Don't be shy.'

Jasmine filled a large glass and examined the table, which looked like a *Bon Appétit* layout. Every item was ranked Difficult to Make. Savory tartlets with homemade pastry, a peppercorn pâté, a three vegetable terrine, her own flaky napoleons filled with smoked salmon and caviar. Jasmine reached for the pâté. She smoothed the rich pork paste over a cracker and tasted, picking up cognac, a hint of nutmeg, even caraway underneath the strong peppercorn taste.

Across the room, *The Washington Post*'s new food editor, Missy Cooperman, in her yellow Chanel suit, sipped her glass of champagne and listened with half an ear while Sally tried to interest her in a story idea about low-fat cakes by color. The Food section, which had been voted the best in the country three times in a row under a former editor, was now floundering. Too many difficult recipes, the readers complained. Too many mistakes. Too many datelines from Paris.

Jasmine stepped up. Jasmine had often written for the *Post*, but now Missy always acted like she was doing her a favor by printing her articles. She made Jasmine write long query letters and then often killed the articles a week before they were set to appear. As far as Jasmine was concerned, the woman knew as much about good food as a horse about phosphates, but she did have the power to introduce your cookbook to the world, so Jasmine made the effort.

'Hi, Missy.'

Missy smiled vaguely at her.

'Jasmine March. I wrote about pickled fish.'

'Oh, yes. Jasmine.' Missy held out her thin hand. 'How good to see you.'

'I thought this week's section was great. I loved the article on Lot Valley cheeses. Can you get them here?'

Missy's smile tightened. 'No, apparently not.' She turned to Sally. 'I must be going.'

'Well, it was mighty nice of you to come,' gushed Sally.

Missy waved vaguely to the rest of the room. 'This was lovely,' she said, and disappeared. Sally looked after her as if the queen of England had stepped away and she wasn't sure if she should continue to curtsy. She finally excused herself to fuss with her table.

Miranda Lane sidled up to Jasmine. Her thin schoolgirl pageboy fell over her face, skimming her greasy lips as she reached for a cheese tart. 'Don't touch Sally's Luscious Lite Lingonberry Pie,' she warned. 'Tastes like Xerox paper.'

'Congratulations on your book,' Jasmine offered. 'You must be so proud, all that work . . .'

'It's selling like hotcakes. I've had to hire a bunch of professionals just to tell me what to do with all the money.'

Jasmine's taste buds turned sour. It was well known that Miranda stole recipes, never giving attribution. But still she wanted to be encouraging, a good colleague.

'Working on another one?'

'Toying with some ideas. Mainly trying not to answer the phone, it's ringing off the hook with publishers.'

Jasmine sucked her tongue to discover a desert of gritty envy in her mouth.

'Wine,' she croaked and moved off, peering into Sally's bookcases crammed with cookbooks as she went. As she stepped closer to examine a classic and was camouflaged by the large potted ficus, Miranda sidled up to Sally, who was busy restocking the truffled deviled eggs. 'Did ya hear about Jasmine?'

'No. What?'

'Days are numbered.'

'You're kidding.'

'Nope. Heard it from Garrett. He's just read the proofs of her latest. Too much fat. Disaster. He's pulling her contract.'

'Bastard.'

'No one buys her books anyway. And certainly not with all those excess calories.'

'That's harsh.'

'Harsh business.'

'Poor Jasmine.'

'He's open to proposals.'

'How do you spell "Garrett"?'

Quickly, quietly, all the blood in Jasmine's body froze to a sluggish ice. She was being cut loose. Set adrift. A cookbook author without a publisher. She was like pastry without butter. Not only unsavory but completely useless. Her oblivion stood before her, a scythe waving, black robe billowing. She choked on her cracker and had a huge coughing fit that left her with tears in her eyes. She could hear the sudden hush just on the other side of the tree. A long pause, then Miranda's bright voice, 'Have you had Jasmine's napoleons? They're absolutely great.'

Jasmine dashed into her home and made straight for the kitchen. She sat down in front of her open pantry and breathed deeply. She reached forward and patted the large clear jar of dried flageolet beans. She pawed the ten-pound bag of basmati rice, sweet and fragrant. She kissed the chick-peas, haricot beans, dried wild mushrooms. Ah, yes, even the dried cèpes. Oh, she felt better. And look, her vinegars, balsamic, sherry, white and red wine, cider, raspberry. And the oils. So many oils. And so many marinated vegetables. She marinated them herself, picking the freshest, finest baby veg-etables, adding extra-virgin olive oil, and enclosing them in beautiful jars. Ah, and look, she smiled. Walnut oil peeked from be-hind a linen bag of fresh walnuts. She could make a goat cheese salad at any moment. She took a deep, restorative breath. She fin-gered the labels of the canned smoked oysters, the mussels, the herring, and the boneless skinned sardines in olive oil. She could make a sardine pâté in seconds. And best of all were her vacuum-packed French-style crêpes, which she kept in case of emergencies. A flip of the wrist and she could sit down to a feast of crêpes oozing with fruit syrup and slathered in whipped cream. She closed the door and heaved a sigh. She needed that.

It took her three tries to catch Garrett, but finally his thin, impatient voice breathed into the telephone line.

'You got more fat in that book than a McDonald's deep fry. Our fact checker added up the calories and nearly had a heart attack. How many times do I have to tell you, fat is out. Those two grotesque ladies on motorcycles made everyone lose their lunch.'

'Their recipes were fabulous.'

'Who cares?'

Jasmine held on to her packet of crêpes for support. 'But nothing has any taste any more,' she said. 'Put some taste back into food and people won't have to go on noshing frantically to satiate themselves.'

There was a pause on the other end. Jasmine could hear crunching.

'Listen,' said Garrett. 'I give the public

what it wants. And it wants lots of food and no aftermath. And that means less calories.'

'Then why is everyone so fat?'

' 'Cause they eat too much, for crying out loud. They buy cookbooks to lose weight.'

'That's crazy.'

'Jasmine, take it from me. There are three ways to sell cookbooks. One, be a celebrity, and honey, you're no celebrity. Two, teach 'em how to use a new appliance, and nothing's been invented since the microwave. Now if you can figure out a way to cook on the Internet, gimme a call. And three, low-fat cooking. Can't keep 'em on the shelves.'

'What about good food?'

'Good food they can get at Roy Rogers. You need to sell them something new. Like your pal Miranda Lane. Her book is a publisher's wet dream: trendy, bright, sellable in one sentence: Japanese-Caribbean. Recipes outa this world: Jerk Sushi, Red Pepper Tofu, Plantain Tempura . . .'

'They're disgusting.'

'Watch it, Jasmine, your jealousy's showing.'

'I still think the public would love a good book on delicious food.'

'Have you thought about toxins?'

'Excuse me?'

'Toxins are big. Everyone's trying to get rid

of them. You come up with a low-fat, low-toxin cookbook, I'll give you a contract.'

Click.

Jasmine replaced the telephone gently on its receiver. She sat quietly at the kitchen table. Almost afraid to move, so shattered she felt. She took long, careful, deep breaths.

All that creating, all that testing, all that writing and rewriting and retesting and no one listening. All that work and no one cared. Why did I bother, she cried. It was the anguish, she knew, of artists everywhere. But all Jasmine had wanted was to make her readers happy. Make them smile with every bite. All she had wanted was to give love. To give food is to give love. She had offered her services. A scout who would barrel ahead and lead the others through the thicket of bad food to paradise. But it seemed no one wanted her services, no one trusted her sense of direction. Or maybe they just didn't want to go where she was going. Jasmine looked around at her kitchen, her pots and pans, her tongs and spatulas, her ladles and rolling pins, her army, and felt she'd let them down. She laid her head on the kitchen table and cried.

Betty from down the street came over to cheer Jasmine up.

'The cavalry's here,' she announced, barging in, holding high a box of Entenmann's fat-free chocolate chip cookies. She perched herself precariously on a bar stool at the kitchen counter, an obese angel on a tiny pin, and began describing her latest diet.

'See, it goes like this,' Betty said, her fist deep in the box of cookies. 'On Mondays you can only eat melon. That's it, that's all you can eat. Breakfast, lunch, dinner: melon. Tuesdays, broiled chicken. And it's got to be broiled. Something about using more calories to chew, or something. I don't know, anyway, Wednesdays . . . let's see. Oh, I remember, Wednesdays it's radishes. That's the one that takes more calories. And Thursdays you can eat raw cabbage. I know. Pee-yew. Luckily Richard travels a lot. Friday, canned pumpkin. I don't know. It's something to do with the way the chemicals react together. But the best part is that on the weekends, Saturday and Sunday, you can eat what ever you want. Anything. And as much as you want. Because, you see, all week you're prepping your body to lose weight and it continues through the weekend even if you eat lots. Isn't that great? And you know, the guy who wrote the book is a diet expert. He's a Ph.D., so he's got to know what he's talking about.'

Jasmine regarded the blurry image of herself in the reflection of her refrigerator. Her richly colored skin had paled. The ample flesh of which she had once been so proud slumped like a teenager. It had become, truth be told, more than ample. But unlike Betty, who thought the second coming would arrive in the form of a fail-free diet, Jasmine had no use for diets. First of all they didn't work. She'd seen too many women yo-yo up and down, each girth expanding as the dieter shelled out even more money to professionals. Professionals who assured them in velvety, soothing tones that this time the diet would surely work, after all, they were dealing in chemistry here, and no need to write out the name on your check, we have a stamp.

Second of all, life was too short.

Jasmine heaped two spoons of sugar into her cappuccino.

'Betty, when was the last time you had a really good meal?'

'Good meal?'

'Something that absolutely fulfilled you. Left you satiated, happy, complete.'

Betty nibbled at her cookie.

'Does cheating count?'

'Why does it have to be cheating? Why can't you just eat?'

Betty grinned at her, horrified, as if Jasmine had just suggested oral sex.

'It won't kill you.'

'No,' sighed Betty, 'but it'll start me down a slippery slope.'

'To where?'

'You know.' Betty puffed out her cheeks.

'What if it didn't make you fat?'

'I'd eat till the cows came home.'

Jasmine leaned close.

'You know what I say?'

Betty's eyes opened wide.

'No, what?'

'I say eat till the cows come home, you're fat anyway.'

Betty's hand sprang back from the Entenmann's box as if bit. She set down her Crystal Lite and stood up, pulling her pantsuit down over her folds with as much dignity as possible.

'I think you should stay away from sugar, Jasmine, it makes you real cruel.'

Jasmine was sad to see Betty go. After all, Betty was a good friend. They'd hit it off almost immediately when Jasmine and Daniel first moved into the neighborhood. Betty had been the only one to knock on their door and say welcome. But it was what she carried in her hands that really cemented the relationship: a six-inch-thick guacamole–cream cheese–cheddar cheese–salsa–black olive extravaganza and a two-pound bag of tortilla chips. Jasmine and Betty barely managed to reach the living room before they were tearing open the chips and eating for all their worth, talking with their mouths open, waiting, somewhat impatiently with a chip held high, for the other to finish scooping. It was then that Jasmine realized she'd found a true friend.

After Betty left, leaving behind three empty bottles of Lime Crystal Lite and an empty box of Entenmann's, Jasmine pushed herself up from her chair. Her eyes fell upon her knives, which she had neatly laid on the counter for inventory. There was her boning knife, with a smooth molded handle which fit her hand perfectly; her bread knife, with its fluted edge; her butcher's knife, blade shaped like a scimitar; her versatile Chinese cleaver, which could mince, slice, bone, flatten, chop, even crack through chicken bones and meat joints. Her chef's knife's gently curved triangular blade. Her Japanese knife arched like a samurai sword, her oyster knife with its short pointed blade, and her slicer to cut cold meats into even, thin slices. And last, her filleting knife for boning and skinning fresh fish without damaging the flesh.

Jasmine had strong opinions about knives. They had to be heat resistant and nonslip. The tang had to be full, extending all the way to the end of the handle. The blade had to be riveted to the handle, not glued. For the kitchen, Jasmine had chosen high-carbon stainless steel. Much more expensive than the regular-carbon steel, but they resisted discoloration. She had her knives sharpened three or four times a year by a specialist. They remained her most cherished possessions. Handled well, Jasmine thought, a good sharp knife was more useful than beauty.

She opened her pantry and leaned on the hinges. What, what, what did she want? Mashed potatoes? No. Would take too long. Pasta? No. How about cheese? Something cheesy, gooey. Grilled cheese sandwich. Oh, yes. Let's see. Butter, cheddar, grainy bread, and a frying pan. So simple, so delicious. She slathered butter over the bread and cut the slices of cheese extra thick. She hopped from toe to toe as she pressed down on the spatula, willing the cheese to melt faster. Finally the cheese began to run and she whisked the sandwich and herself to the table. She wolfed down huge mouthfuls, her taste buds sinking in and dissolving in each rich cheesy bite. Oh, happy, happy taste buds. Jasmine sat at the kitchen table methodically licking and munching her way through her snack. She breathed in deeply, took a long cool drink of milk, and resumed.

As she let the sandwich comfort her soul, she searched it. And she discovered she had been right. Garrett was wrong. His public was wrong. They might not know it but they were sick of low-cal. What they needed was something that would stick with them, that would nurture and comfort them. It was a hard world out there, no loyalty, no conscience. No substance. What they needed was weight. The weight of tasty, rich flavor.

Jasmine banged her spatula on the table. He couldn't cut her off now. She had a public to nurture. She thought of Mr Dupree in his lonely house with nothing but a low-cal, no-toxin cookbook to sustain him. Why, it was practically euthanasia. She would not be party to that. No, in fact, she was going to let loose. She was going to give the public what she knew deep in her heart, deep in the inner chambers of her stomach they yearned for. She was going to bring fat back to America. Fat, glorious fat. Heavy, rich, soothing fat. Unctuous, delectable fat. And most importantly, fat without guilt. The world would sink a little lower from the weight of all those plump, happy people. Heaven, she was sure, was full of fat folk.

Chapter Four

Daniel studied Tina's face. He took in her slight overbite, the clear white of her eyes, the Titian glint of her hair, her lips, slightly chapped under a layer of gloss. He balled his fist against his gut.

'From here. I'm not getting it from here.'

'But . . .'

He grabbed her hand and, crushing it into a closed fist, shoved it against her belly.

'Now say it.'

'What?'

'Your dialogue.'

'How c-could you do this to me? I . . .'

'What is she saying to him?'

'She's hurt.'

'Yes, I know she's hurt, but what is she saying to him?'

Tina stared at Daniel. 'She's saying . . .' Tina stopped, at a loss.

'Think about when you find out someone is sleeping around on you. What do you want to say to them?'

'I don't know.'

'You don't know.'

'No one's slept around on me.'

'That you know of.'

Tina shrugged.

'What would you say if they did?'

'I'd tell them to fuck off!'

'That's it! Right there.'

'What?'

'Fuck off! You're pissed. Not hurt. Hurt is for later. Hurt is when you're alone licking your wounds. Right now you want to slit his throat and pull out his tongue through the hole. Am I right?'

Tina leaned over and kissed Daniel on the cheek, close to his lips. Her breath smelled vaguely of synthesized garlic.

'Oh, Daniel,' she sighed. 'You're so good.'

She gave his lips a long, slow smile before making her way back to her place among the chairs at the foot of the stage. Tina liked to eye Daniel when he gave his acting lectures, her bare legs thrown casually over the next seat. She nibbled at the end of her pen and let her eyes travel up and down his body. It wasn't bad for a middle-aged guy. Wiry, tense, slim under tight jeans and a polo T that he wore casually stuffed into his pants so that it hung over at the waist emphasizing his slim hips. He wore his black hair shock short, which highlighted the increasing gray. She remembered hearing about Daniel almost ten years ago when he was D.C.'s golden boy. He was in everything, then, everywhere: Kennedy Center, Arena, Folger's. Tina had been so thrilled to be granted a place in his class. Though she tried to ignore the fact that the class billed for twelve had only nine students in it and maybe it hadn't been so competitive after all. Still, he was brilliant, a legend, and Tina scribbled down everything he said. She fully planned to mention him in her Oscar speech.

She watched his thick lips wondering how he kissed. Dry, wet, hard? Was he happily married? He couldn't be. He was always at the theater, never home. One of those marriages gone sour. Tina wrinkled her nose. That would never happen to her. When she married it would be for passionate love. She and her man would have similar interests that they would talk about endlessly over takeout, after exhausting each other physically. They would support each other's careers and yet know deep in their hearts that the most important thing was their pairing, their union. Her man was going to be super-masculine, yet strong enough to let his feminine side show too. Naturally, he would have a better day job than she and make enough money so that they could live in one of those elegant art deco apartment houses in Adams Morgan. He would make heads turn but only have eyes for her. Above all he would not mix proteins and starches.

Of course she had yet to meet anyone remotely like that and so made do with a small stable of married men who wined and dined her and then jumped on her bones like she was the last piece of pie. She was beginning to long for a real bona fide boyfriend, someone who would call her up and make her laugh. Someone she could depend on to be there on a Saturday night. She wanted to do that cozy boyfriend-girlfriend thing where you fell out of bed, slapped on your jeans and T-shirts, and walked to brunch at Timberlake's to gorge on eggs Benedict, sauce and egg yolks on the side, and the Sunday *New York Times*. She wanted, OK, she was ready to admit it . . . a husband. Her own. Anyone's would do. But it had to be more permanent, more legal. She wanted, so to speak, the deed to the ranch. She shifted her legs so that her calves arched. She saw Daniel glance at them. She chewed listlessly at her pen. Problem was he probably wasn't available for Sunday brunch either.

At home after work, Daniel avoided the kitchen and walked straight upstairs. He was going to take the longest, hottest shower and think the dirtiest thoughts and probably not do anything about them. He didn't have the energy. He caught sight of his daughter through her bedroom doorway. She sat with her back to him on her bed, her small skull clamped under her headphones, her head bopping up and down to a screeching tune that leaked from around her ears. He glanced about her teenage room. Instead of filling it with posters of musicians and actors like a normal teenager, she had chosen entrepreneurs and Fortune 500 CEOs. Warren Buffett stared down from a prominent position above her bed. She wanted to be an investment banker when she grew up, she had announced pointedly over breakfast six months ago. Something real, she said. Not fairy tale.

Daniel laughed at the thought. It caught in his throat and he ended up coughing. Careme turned to look at him. She got up, headphones still on, and walked over to the door. With an enigmatic smile, she closed the door in his face.

Betty sat with her knees pressed together, trying to take up the least amount of space on the chintz couch. Jasmine handed her a cup of slimming tea sweetened with two packets of Equal.

Betty sniffled into her tissue. 'This is so nice of you to come with me, Jasmine.'

'What are friends for?'

'I just go to pieces.'

Betty had called her in a panic and Jasmine had come dashing to drive through the late-afternoon rush hour and to keep her company on her appointment. Oh, sure, they had their tiffs, but the undercurrent of their friendship was strong and true.

She patted Betty's hand. 'Drink your tea, it'll make you feel better.'

Betty glanced over. She could see them. The doctor, in her immaculate white coat, her assistants. They were waiting. They were trying to be patient. But their professional smiles were growing firmer, like day-old fudge. Outside the window, Betty could hear cars drive by, birds sing, even the wind caress the trees. All blissfully unaware of the trial she now faced. She felt very alone. Very vulnerable. But stoic. She must be strong. Betty took a fortifying sip of tea, then nodded.

'Good for you, Mrs Johnson,' said the doctor. 'It won't take a minute.' The accent was crisply British.

The doctor clicked to the back room on

tall white heels. A murmur. Then she re-appeared at the door and held out her hand. Betty followed her obediently, looking not unlike a large, expensively dressed sheep-dog. Inside the room, two attendants awaited. White gloves. Hair pulled back in nets. They nodded encouragingly. Behind them a curtain. Behind that, Betty knew, stood the contraption. She tried not to think about it as she wiggled free of her Henri Bendel size 20 suit.

'Lovely color,' said the attendant as she hung it up.

Betty would have liked to peel off her slip too but didn't want them to see her cascade of fat rolls.

'All set, Mrs Johnson?'

Betty nodded.

They pushed back the second curtain to reveal the scales.

'When you're ready, Mrs Johnson.'

Betty shuffled over as if shackled. An attendant held out her hand to help her ascend.

The doctor looked down at her chart.

'I see it's been two weeks since your last appointment, Mrs Johnson. I thought I put you on everyday check-in.'

'Yes, you did.'

'It's for your own good, Mrs Johnson.'

'Yes, Doctor.' Betty's lip quivered.

'All right, up you go.'

Betty teetered on. The scales jiggled like a small earthquake beneath her. The doctor peered over her glasses for a reading. She did a double take.

'Oh, my,' she said and scribbled into the chart. She glanced up quickly.

'Don't look, Mrs Johnson.'

But Betty already had.

She staggered. A roar filled her head, a sudden crack, and her head exploded with stars and dancing Twinkies.

'Oh, dear,' said the doctor, a.k.a. weight-control-clinic administrator, peering over her fake half-rimmed glasses, 'the old cow has fainted.'

Later that night, Jasmine stood at her stove and thought about Betty and the waste, the waste of money, the waste of worry, the waste of one woman's life. The doorbell rang and Jasmine groaned.

'You got that, Jasmine?' called Daniel from the bathroom.

Jasmine put down her glass of wine and clicked over to the front door. JD and Sue Ellen stood, smiling tightly, Jasmine was sure, on the other side of the door, thinking, no doubt, that if Jasmine didn't open the door fast enough they would be mugged right there on her Georgetown doorstep. She wondered how long it would take for them to go away. They'd been friends and neighbors of Jasmine and Daniel's for years. They had had first babies together. A strange bonding that. The friends you make though you have nothing more in common than that you both happen to have procreated at the same time, both filled the planet with yet one more being. Their first conversations had been filled with dissertations on baby's sleep problems, baby's digestive tract, baby's first foods. It progressed to stair gates, first bikes, and now teenage horrors. No, my teenager is much more of a pain in the ass than yours. It was loyalty that Jasmine felt toward these two, never great love or interest. JD was a banker, Sue Ellen a part-time businesswoman who had set up a stenciling and interior-painting business from her home and catered to the Republican set.

Within minutes they sat in her living room, Sue Ellen in a Washingtonian conservative forest-green knit sweater and skirt set. Her pumps matched the forest green perfectly. A midlength pearl necklace matched the pearl studs. The appropriateness and boredom of the outfit was breathtaking. Sue Ellen's mousy brown hair had been lightened, streaked, and teased into a neat blond football helmet. JD sank back into the armchair, his blue slacks crossed at the knee, expensive leather shoes gleaming. He held up his glass to the light, then gave it a sniff.

'It's got peach, oak, vanilla, lots of vanilla, Sue Ellen loves her vanilla . . .'

'Love the vanilla,' Sue Ellen jumped in. 'I just can't stand that grassy stuff.'

Jasmine put her nose dutifully to her glass of the wine that JD had carried in with him, holding it up like a chalice. He and his wife had recently bought a stake in a small vineyard in the Shenandoah Valley and were pushing the stuff like tin peddlers. In Jasmine's opinion the wine tasted like donkey piss, but for all these years she'd kept her counsel. Why start now?

'Olive?' She offered the bowl to JD. JD palmed a handful and ate them like peanuts.

'We had a whole bunch of olives in Mexico, didn't we, Lucky?'

'A whole bunch,' Sue Ellen agreed.

'They stuff 'em with any old thing. We had them with pimentos, with garlic, even chilies. Near took my mouth off.'

'Wouldn't sleep with him. I said no way.'

' 'Course, can't eat much else in the damn country.'

'It was soooo dirty.'

'I kept asking for some Tex-Mex. They looked at me like I was crazy.'

'They're not really too smart I think. Maybe all that sun . . .'

'We found a TGIF's, didn't we, Lucky?'

'Nearly fell to our knees and screamed, "Thank God!" '

'Had steak and potato. Some real food. Maybe that's why they're all so short. Shorter 'n dwarfs.'

'JD!'

'Well, they are!'

Sue Ellen giggled and swiped another olive.

'Oh, heavens,' she exclaimed, raising an eyebrow when Jasmine walked in holding high their first course of freshly pan-fried crab cakes. 'All that grease,' she murmured. Jasmine turned and surveyed her new mortal enemy.

'I could make you a small tossed salad.'

'Oh, no.'

'I insist. Won't take a sec.'

'But . . .' Sue Ellen's nostrils sniffed the delicious aroma coming off the lemon-dilled patties as Jasmine set one down in front of JD, practically taking off Sue Ellen's nose. Sue Ellen pouted at the perfect golden orbs, the delicious crunch JD made with his fork, the ecstatic smile on his lips as his mouth closed around the hot smooth mash. She picked her way dejectedly through her mixed baby greens.

Later, JD followed Daniel into the basement to help him fetch another bottle of wine.

JD looked around. 'The place is holding up.'

Daniel extracted an expensive bottle from the second refrigerator they kept in the basement. He had spent twenty dollars more on the wine than he had planned. But he always did that when JD came over. JD took the bottle and examined the label. He handed it back to Daniel without comment.

'We just put a pool back behind the Jacuzzi,' he said. 'You'll have to come over this summer and take advantage.'

'You're looking in good shape.'

JD smiled and patted his doughy belly. He glanced quickly over to the door, then leaned toward Daniel. 'I'm seeing someone,' he whispered.

'Seeing someone.'

'You know.' He pumped his fist quickly in the air.

'Ah,' said Daniel.

'Does a man good. Best exercise in the world, if you know what I mean.'

'Daniel,' Jasmine called from upstairs.

'Coming.'

'You wish,' JD cracked, and snorted heavily into his glass of wine.

The next day, Daniel hunched at his desk, working the phones.

'Oh, come on. Ten months is nothing. Studio Theater took three years to pay their electricity. Hello. Hello?'

Daniel slammed down the phone.

'Philistine.'

'Temper, temper, teacher.'

Daniel looked up to find Josh, a young former student who had left ten months previously to try his hand in L.A. Josh, in a sparkling white, pressed T-shirt under an equally new and shiny black leather jacket, settled into the broken armchair facing Daniel's desk and glanced around.

'Good to see things haven't changed.'

Daniel leaned back and contemplated this child-man whose only talent, as far as he could tell, was excellent taste in shoes and an electrifying smile. 'What are you doing back? Get fired wiping tables?'

'How about second lead in a White House thriller.'

A pit opened in Daniel's stomach. 'The one with Morgan Freeman?'

'No other. I respect him like a father. But, you know, I learned a lot from you.'

Daniel waved him away.

Josh leaned forward and fixed him with a serious stare. 'No, really. You were the man. Taught me everything I know.'

Daniel shrugged, embarrassed to be pleased. 'Well, glad to be of help.'

Josh leaned back and crossed his crocodile wingtips. ' 'Course, had to dump most of it when I hit L.A. All that crap about choices. Waste of time. Where do you come up with that shit? But, hey, some of it was real helpful.'

'Well, maybe you weren't doing it right. Why don't you stick around for class? Learn something.'

Josh pulled himself up to his six-foot-two height. He was so squeaky clean he made everything else look covered in dust.

'Love to, but gotta go,' said Josh. 'Lunch with Morgan.'

He paused at the door.

'You still haven't fixed the sign outside.'

Daniel looked up wearily.

'Trouble finding us?'

Josh grinned. 'Hell no. But I'll send you some bucks. Got to spruce this place up. People are gonna want to know where I began.'

'Hello there.'

Tina stood at the door to Daniel's office.

Daniel had not moved since Josh left. For a full hour he had stared up at the broken ceiling fan, his mouth dry, his eyes blank. Tina sauntered in and leaned forward, breathing softly in Daniel's space. 'That last thing you said about choices. I was wondering if you could explain it a little further.'

Daniel didn't move.

'Daniel?' She gently stroked his shoulder.

Daniel slowly lowered his eyes and took her in. The short brown suede skirt, the tall suede boots, the extra dab of lip gloss, the swaying mounds of . . .

'Choices. Yes, that's always a difficult one.'

'Do you have time?'

Daniel rotated his head violently around his neck to restart the blood flow. 'Got about a half hour. Need some coffee though, you want some?'

'Sure.'

'Come on then.'

He led her out the door onto Fourteenth Street. The café culture hadn't hit east of Dupont Circle yet, so he walked her across to the heavily barred 7-Eleven and handed her a Styrofoam cup.

'Regular or decaf?'

She was staring at the two drunks batting ineffectually at each other in the chips aisle.

'Hello?' he prompted.

'What?'

'Regular or decaf?'

'Oh, regular. Please.'

Daniel reached into his pants pocket for change.

'Here,' she said. 'Let me. You're helping me out.'

He waved her away and laid the coins out on the counter. Brad, the long-suffering cashier, grinned as he snapped them into the cashier drawer.

'Mr Man, Mr Man,' he chanted.

Daniel tapped the counter, then led Tina outside. He leaned against a lamppost and watched her cringe as litter skimmed over her feet.

'So what do you want to know?' He took a long hot sip and held it in his mouth like it was a bong hit.

'Well.' She kicked away a Big Mac wrapper from her shoe. 'I'm a little concerned about how far back the choices have to go. You mentioned the good actors go back about four. But doesn't that get confusing? I mean, say I make the choice my mother died when I was eleven which is why deep down I'm scared to have a relationship but then I make the choice that I had a great relationship with my dad so that's why I'm coming on to this guy but then I decide that this same dad left my mother on her hospital bed so all men are pigs . . .'

A stumbling drunk slurred by, leaving a trail of 'Gimme some of that. Huh, huh. Gimme some of that. Huh, huh.'

Tina stepped closer to Daniel. He could smell the sweet caffeine on her breath. He reached out and rubbed her arm affectionately.

'You were expecting the Ritz?'

'Why did you put the theater here?'

'Only place I could afford. You should have seen what it used to be like. In fact, housing price these days, they'll probably push me out soon.'

Daniel sipped his coffee and surveyed his domain at Fourteenth and S Streets. The neighborhood was flirting with gentrification, but nothing had really changed. There were a couple more theaters than when he started twelve years ago, but still you had to provide a parking lot with an attendant to soothe your patrons' fears. Even then, more than 50 per cent of possible patrons wouldn't dream of turning north from K Street to the quieter, darker eastern section of Northwest.

Tina pressed closer. 'But why are you here? In Washington. You're so good. Like New York good. L.A. good.'

Daniel paused, then gave his usual excuse. 'I couldn't leave my family.'

Tina looked up at him, her eyes brimming with tears. 'Wow, that's so beautiful.'

'What is?'

'Your sacrificing yourself for your family.'

Daniel shrugged and looked away stoically.

Tina took his hand.

'Does . . . does she understand what you've done?'

Of all the herbs, Jasmine thought, basil was her soul mate. She rubbed her fingers over a leaf and sniffed deeply at the pungent, almost licorice scent. Basil was sensuous, liking to stretch out green and silky under a hot sun with its feet covered in cool soil. Basil married so well with her favorite ingredients: rich ripe tomatoes, a rare roast lamb, a meaty mozzarella. Jasmine plucked three leaves from her basil plant and slivered them in quick, precise slashes, then tucked them into her salad along with a tablespoon of slivered orange rind. Her lunch today was to be full of surprises. She wanted to impress as well as amuse this particular guest. They would start with a tomato soup in which she would hide a broiled pesto-stuffed tomato that would reveal itself slowly with every sip. Next she would pull out chicken breasts stuffed with goat cheese and mint. Then finish with poached pears, napped heavily in eau-de-vie-spiked chocolate.

Jasmine gave a last swirl to the tomato soup, peeked under the double boiler cover where the chocolate kept warm, and turned down the oven; the chicken breasts were browning too quickly. It was time to get herself ready. But as she dashed up the stairs to dress, the doorbell rang. She swore, wiping the crusted sauces off her sweatshirt as she raced for the door.

Henry Nicholls stood leaning on his umbrella staring down at her peonies. He was to be her secret weapon. Henry, her agent, knew everyone. He was particularly good friends with Garrett, her former publisher. Henry was invited on those coveted fishing trips and to Garrett's impressive country estate in St Mary's County. Jasmine was hoping he might persuade Garrett to change his mind. Barring that, sell her idea to another publisher. Problem was, she'd never felt particularly comfortable with Henry. He always managed to make her feel as if she were the runt of his impressive, talented, and lucrative litter. That if she didn't shape up, write something, for God's sake, that would sell, he had half a mind to drown her in his back pond.

'Henry, come in.'

'I see your peonies are in the last throws of hydrolacadia.'

'Excuse me?'

'Excessive thirst.'

He sauntered in, handed her his umbrella. She took it respectfully like a maid and placed it carefully on the best chair in the hall.

'Come in, come in. I'm so glad you could come.'

'Don't have more than an hour.'

'Of course not. Working man like you.'

As she waved him through the kitchen to the wicker chairs in the conservatory, she briefly opened the oven door. His nostrils twitched.

'An aperitif?' she asked.

'Why not?'

'A glass of Pouilly-Fume? Or maybe a nice white wine spritzer? Or perhaps a sherry?'

'Scotch and water.'

'Good idea.'

He sat back in his chair and pulled out a pack of Luckys, unfiltered. As he puffed his thin face disappeared in a cloud of smoke. He reached wordlessly for his drink. Jasmine took a gulp of her sherry and sat down.

'You're probably wondering why I asked you . . .'

'Heard about your bright idea.'

'. . . yes.'

'Lotta competition in cookbooks. For the life of me I can't figure out why.'

'I think I could make a contribution . . .'

'Save it, I'm not the gatekeeper. But I might be able to tell you a thing or two about going about it the right way instead of writing desperation all over your forehead.'

Jasmine blushed down to her fuchsia-painted toenails. 'Shall we start on the soup?'

He heaved himself up and flopped back at the kitchen table she had cozily set up with colorful Italian place mats and napkins. He tucked his napkin in his shirt collar like a child and tossed back a mouthful of the exquisite Stag's Leap Napa Valley Chardonnay she'd bought for the occasion. He sucked his teeth and chased it with his last sip of scotch.

She spooned the broiled tomato in a deep bowl and poured the bright soup around it. She placed it in front of him and waited. He tasted it, reached for the salt shaker, and gave it a good dousing. He slurped away noncommittally while she sat down with her bowl.

'I think I could do a really good job.'

'Doesn't matter a damn. People get contracts they shouldn't get all the time. Nothing to do with actual merit. Everything to do with perceived merit. That's what you've got to work on. People's perception of you.'

Jasmine watched him scoop the pesto into his mouth. She waited for the orgasmic response. Instead he reached for the salt again.

'How do I work on that?'

'Attitude. PR. Phone calls. A lot of people won't do it because they say to themselves they shouldn't have to do that. They're artists, not flacks. And if there's a God — which there isn't — he'll make sure the world perceives their gifts and hands it over. So they sit there for years waiting like girls by the phone. Pitiful sad. Then there's others, no more ability than a garden snail but who convince the honchos that not only are they the right person for the job, they even toss in the fact that they really don't want the job and it's gonna really cost them.'

He let his spoon fall back with a clatter and wiped at his glistening chin. She presented him with a delightful plate of crispy chicken breast oozing a creamy goat cheese sauce surrounded by delicately simmered baby vegetables. He poked suspiciously at the sauce.

'What is this?'

'Goat cheese.'

'I see.'

'You don't like goat cheese?'

Henry shrugged. He started picking dejectedly at the vegetables.

'Would you like a sandwich?'

'Got any salami?'

'Yes. Salami, ham, I think some turkey. Swiss? Cheddar?'

'Sounds good.'

She whisked the offending plate away and dug into her refrigerator and returned with a mile-high mustard-and-mayo-laden extravaganza. Henry belched appreciatively. Jasmine made a mental note to forget the pears and to serve the chocolate sauce over vanilla ice cream instead.

'PR, huh?' she prompted.

Henry chewed steadily, mustard bubbles escaping from his lips. 'I'm saying don't beg. Act like you're above it, like you'd being doing them a favor for taking it.'

'But if they're not even considering me at this point, how do I do that?'

'Remember high school and the most popular boy? You didn't get him by being real sweet and asking really pretty if he'd ask you out.'

'No, that never did seem to work.'

'The girl that got the popular boy acted like he would do until she could catch herself a college boy.'

'You're saying I should go up to Garrett and say "I know you weren't considering me, but I'm not considering you either. What I really want to do is jump to Doubleday"?'

'You wouldn't be the first.'

'That's crazy.'

'Do it your way then. Whatcha gonna do? Send him home-baked cookies with little heart-shaped notes?'

Jasmine tossed back her wine. This whole idea was turning sour.

'I just thought there was an easier, more direct way.'

'This ain't kindergarten, dear, you won't get your turn if you wait patiently in line. What's for dessert?'

'Home-made vanilla bean ice cream with chocolate hazelnut sauce.'

'Geez, what are you trying to do, kill me?'

He handed her his plate and rubbed his hands in anticipation. 'If it makes you feel any better, I'd publish ya.' As she placed his ice cream before him, he added, as if an afterthought, 'But I'm no publisher. And from the talk I had with Garrett this morning, you're out. And if Garrett won't publish you, doesn't look likely that anyone else will. You're a little light with that sauce. How 'bout another spoonful?'

Daniel followed Tina through her door.

'Sit down, make yourself at home.' Tina disappeared into the small kitchen and rummaged around in the cupboards.

Daniel sank back into the worn couch. The coffee table, he noticed, was grimy, cluttered with *Cosmo* magazines, a pair of chopsticks, five teaspoons, and a dog-eared chart featuring starches, proteins, and carbohydrates. What must have been a five-year-old head shot took prominence in a group of photos above the couch.

As the afternoon sun streamed in, lighting up the dust in the air, Daniel wondered what the hell he was doing. Just as he had wondered driving the car over Key Bridge, up Wilson Boulevard, right at the gas station, five doors down on the left. Again wondering as he walked up the sidewalk, passing through her door, each step bringing him closer to what he wanted. And didn't. But did. Badly.

'Try this.'

She set down a large glass filled to the brim. 'Carrot, cranberry, and wheat grass. Freshly juiced. Drink one of these a day and you'll live to be a hundred and fifty.'

She tossed hers back in one gulp and collapsed back on the couch next to him, as if abandoning herself to what was to come. Daniel took a careful sip from his glass.

'Well?'

He nodded noncommitally, while inside his head continued his debate: 'After all, everyone does it, what's the statistic, seventy per cent of men, why do I have to be the wimpy thirty per cent. No one will know. All the great men have mistresses, it's only the dumb, middle-class beta dogs who don't. And isn't it biological anyway? Didn't society infringe on us? It's only nature.'

'You don't like it.'

'It's sweet,' he allowed, letting his eyes glance along her exposed knees. 'After all,' he continued in his head, 'men are made for several sexual partners. A person can't be everything to you. I'm saving my marriage. It's a pressure valve, otherwise, I might look more seriously. I'm really saving my marriage. Anyway, it'll just be once. In, out. Thank you, ma'am. I mean, what does she expect anyway? Just once. Really. Just once.'

Daniel set down his drink and leaned over Tina. He cupped her firm ass in his hands and felt the delicious stirring. He slid his hand up her curved waist to her heavy breasts, big and lovely and firm.

Careme peered into the Styrofoam cooler at the small gray mouse. She smiled and gave it a soft stroke of her finger before reaching in and lifting it by its tail. In her cage, Medea turned an interested eye toward its feeble squeaks. Careme placed the mouse on the sandy soil beside her. Medea's tail slithered forward and curled around the unfortunate rodent and began to squeeze. Even Careme had to look away.

In doing so, she caught sight of herself in the oval mirror across the room. She moved closer. She flared her nostrils wide, then threw all her hair in front of her face and stared through it like a curtain. She liked the look. Very *Vogue*. She opened her mouth wide as if she was silently screaming to get out of her hair-bound cage. She would make a good fashion designer, she thought. She had the ideas.

She suddenly threw back her hair and pouted her thin lips, pushing up at her breasts and poking out her flat buttocks.

'Hey, there,' she murmured. 'Hey, there. Like some of this?'

She pulled her shorts down low on her hips. 'Huh, want some of this?'

'Or this?' She stretched up her top to reveal her flat, scrawny chest. She frowned. She pulled down her shirt again.

'Ooooh, yeah. Ooooh, yeah.' She growled softly into the mirror, inching her shorts and panties down her thighs. She turned again to reveal a butt shot.

She kicked away her shorts and stretched down to touch her toes, flinging up her head to gaze into the mirror. A half turn and she hopped onto the bed, falling spread-eagle. She thrust up her pelvis, closed her eyes, and delved into her favorite fantasy, in which she lay doused in swirls of butterscotch and fudge sauce, an unidentified man rolling her in chopped almonds. In one hand he held high a bowl of whipped cream.

'You want it?' he grunted. 'You want it?'

'Careme?' Her mother stood on the other side of the door.

Careme squawked. She flipped over and slid off the bed, falling with a thunderous thump to the ground.

'Careme, can I come in?'

Careme grabbed the shorts that had fallen

over her teddy bear's eyes. She struggled into them as she ran toward the door but caught her shin on the corner of the bed.

'Ow!' Careme doubled over, her shorts still at her knees, pawing hopelessly at the gash in her leg.

'Careme! Are you OK?' Her mother rattled the locked doorknob.

Careme pulled up the shorts, catching her thumbnail and tearing it off, low at the base.

'Oh!'

'Careme!'

Shoving her bleeding thumb into her mouth, Careme hopped to the door and opened it a crack.

'What?'

'What are you doing in there?'

'Nothing.'

Her mother's eyes grazed her face, looking for clues. Careme's hot pink cheeks remained steady.

'I've made a doctor's appointment for you.'

'Oh, come on.'

'Thursday afternoon. You'll have to leave school early, but it was the best I could do.'

'I don't need . . .'

'He's a nutrition specialist. I'd like to hear what he says.'

'It's a man doctor?'

'Only one I could find. But you should like him. He's young. Sounds about twelve and foreign.'

'Fine.' Careme closed the door, fell back on the bed, and nursed her throbbing body.

Tina glanced at the clock as Daniel pulled up his socks. Nine-thirty P.M. God, where had the day gone? They had spent the entire afternoon and evening having sex, eating, drinking, and sleeping. Mostly sleeping, actually, passed out across her futon like two skid row drunks. Her head pounded, her mouth was drier than central heating, her hair . . . don't even go there. Tina stretched. Every muscle ached. 'I think I'm dying.'

Daniel grunted. He stood up and ran his hand through his hair. He let out a long puff of air. 'Hate to sleep and run,' he said.

Tina shrugged on a long T-shirt and followed him to the door. She tripped over one of the bottles of champagne they had consumed. Daniel caught her as she sank toward the floor. She giggled into his neck.

'So,' he said as he kissed her lightly on the lips.

'So,' she said as she kissed him back.

'I'll call you,' he said.

Her smile tightened on her lips. 'OK,' she answered.

And he was gone.

Tina surveyed her apartment. A broken wineglass in her sink. Crumpled fat-free chips embedded in her couch. A carton of low-salt Chinese tipped over. A puddle of sweet and sour had seeped over her sweater.

Shit. She grabbed the sweater and held it up, a bright orange stain splashed across the breast. Tina twisted it into a ball and tossed it in the corner. She glanced at her watch. When was the last time she'd consumed protein?

Outside, Daniel looked back at Tina's window a moment. Then, with a relieved grunt, he folded himself back into his car. Jesus, he had done it. He had really done it. He had gotten naked with another woman and stuck it in. And out and in and out and had come. The whole shebang. Jesus. What horrified him was how good he felt. He felt guilty, he was sure, somewhere. But the thrill hadn't burned off yet. The adrenaline still careened with excitable donkey kicks through his body. He was now part of the clan. He shoved his car in gear. His technique hadn't been bad. Too quick the first time. But, hey, that was to be expected. He hadn't been this excited since . . . Damn, how long ago was it? Luckily his flag time hadn't been too long. And Jesus, what a body she had. Hard, then soft, and hard. And the way she squirmed . . .

Daniel had to park five blocks from home. A good thing, he thought philosophically, since he had a renewed boner the size of a Budweiser pressing against his pants. The cool air would bring it back to its senses. As he stuck his key into the front door, he paused. He stopped to brush any offending hair from his clothes. He took a swift sniff for any perfume. Suddenly a knot of terror clutched at his throat. What if Jasmine was on the other side of the door? Waiting? Knowing? A bead of sweat broke from his forehead. His tryst suddenly seemed to take on a bad smell. He felt sick. He turned the key and slowly, breathlessly opened the door. Inside the hall was empty. He crept in. He held his breath to listen. Nothing. The top hall light was left on to welcome him home to bed. Daniel let out his breath and grinned. Forgetting his terror and patting his belly, he headed for the refrigerator.

In the kitchen, Daniel found his wife sitting at the dish-strewn table, staring glazed at the wall. That wouldn't have been strange in itself except for the fact that she had painted war slashes across her cheeks in chocolate sauce.

'Jasmine.'

No response.

He tapped her shoulder. She looked up as if just awakening. She made a swipe at the chocolate on her face and licked her finger.

'Is it me?' she asked. 'Or is everyone a yellow-bellied, insincere, weak-boned sapsucker?'

Daniel took a step back. The queasiness returned.

'I mean, look,' she said, 'just look at the state of the world today. Everyone searching for love and no one finding it.'

Daniel blinked rapidly. Maybe a quick confession would be best. No, he couldn't do that. She'd torture him. He glanced around the kitchen. She had the utensils and she knew how to use them.

'And the powers that be refusing to give it to them,' she continued. 'Who put them in charge? What do they know? After all, all people want is a little love, a little affection. They want a full-body sensual experience. They want satisfaction! Am I right?'

Plus he'd read somewhere that wives just didn't want to know. JD had said so too.

They don't want to know, they don't want to know, they don't want to . . .

Jasmine brought her fist down to the table with a bang. Daniel jumped. 'All this no fat, no salt, no this, no that. It's got to end. People have got to have what they need. Don't you think so, Daniel?'

Daniel's face flushed with relief. She was talking about food. Of course she was. Yes. Oh, yes. 'Oh, yes, I do. I do. I do,' he said and slipped quickly out of the kitchen.

Chapter Five

In the morning, Careme stretched long in her bed and thought about that night's party. Troy would be there. With his dark hair and dark, dark eyes. And his long legs and big arms. And he'd take her upstairs and they would lock the door to one of the bedrooms and he'd lay her down on the bed and he'd do it. And she'd be a woman. A full-fledged sexual woman. And she could go to parties and no one would ask her, 'Are you still a virgin?' 'Virgin, virgin. What are you, the Virgin Mary? What are you waiting for, God?' And it would be good and he'd be so good. And it would be over.

And then they would come down from the bedroom and everybody would, like, know and she'd be really cool and the guys, they would think she was cool and the girls, they'd be so jealous because she lost it with Troy. And they'd have a glass of wine or something to celebrate. And he'd drive her home and kiss her sweetly on the lips and watch her as she walked inside. And she'd come back to this room, to this bed. But she'd be different. She'd be a woman. A real live woman. She'd probably have to change the room. What did a real woman's room look like? Well, for one thing she'd have to ditch the posters. Real women had real art. She could go down to the flea market and buy a painting. A real one. With real paint. Oils. Could she ask to have a bidet in the bathroom? Isn't that what real women used? Her mother didn't. But of course that was her mother.

Careme stood up gingerly. Tonight she was going to be a woman. She fingered through her closet. What should she wear on her last day as a child?

When Jasmine woke, her soft body was alive under the covers, coiled and ready. She lay listening to the strong water of Daniel's shower hit the white porcelain tub and pretended it rained down on her body.

The shower cut off and she listened as Daniel climbed out and took a swig of mouthwash, swigging it around the inside of his cracked teeth to disinfect the aging musk of his mouth. Jasmine, no doubt, had the same decomposing smell in the morning. But Jasmine usually forgot to do anything about it, believing that a good shot of strong hot coffee should be enough to burn away the most offensive of smells. The door opened and Jasmine continued to lie with the sheets over her face like a shroud. She listened to Daniel pad about as he tugged back the curtains and inched himself into his new too-tight black jeans. She could hear the hangers swing back and forth as he grabbed a shirt, the top left-hand drawer of his dresser slide out as he rummaged for socks, the scrape against the floor as he picked up his shoes and walked out the door. Her mute body raged inside her. The flannel against her thigh felt like silk, the line of buttons caught beneath her right buttock probed like fingers, the rustle of sheet sounded like a deep-throated, urgent whisper. Jasmine closed her eyes and moaned in frustration.

It wasn't easy being a middle-aged wife. That asexual feeling you got when you spent hours on your hair and hundreds on your clothes only to arrive at a dinner party and be completely ignored in favor of a young woman in no makeup and a slipless Gap dress. That careful formality your husband's friends treated you with, as if you'd become a sacred eunuch. That often-unspoken, unacknowledged feeling that your sexuality had as much pizzazz and enticement as your washer-dryer.

Now Jasmine's most satisfying sexual experience came from her hairdresser, who once a month for Jasmine's wash and cut would massage the back of her head with such firmness and penetration that she'd find herself whimpering with pleasure. The other patrons would look up from their *Cosmo* and *Glamour* magazines, but she didn't care, she concentrated fully on his thick, insistent fingers, the ecstasy which released itself at his touch and poured over her head and body like hot liquid sunlight.

There was sweetness in marriage, of course. Smiles across the room. An occasional candlelit dinner out where you actually felt like a grown-up and stared with wonder at all the cosmopolitan couples chattering around you. The surprise birthday treats because your husband was the only one in your family you had trained to give to you. And, of course, who could give up the stability? The knowledge that if you did fart in bed the odds were your husband would return again the following night.

Jasmine followed Daniel downstairs to the kitchen. She opened her cupboards and began pulling down ingredients for bread. Bread. That's what she wanted this morning. Bread. Yeasty, warm, slathered in butter or dipped in olive oil. Salty, crunchy, nutty, or oniony. White, wheat, cornmeal. It is the staff of life. The stuff of life. Woah, girl, Jasmine thought, as she dumped the semolina flour into the warm yeast and began to stir, she was starting to sound like a Food-section lede.

Ah, but today was a new day and she had a new plan. She had renewed hope. She wasn't going to let Henry put her off. Henry who would eat shit off a spoon if it was covered in chocolate sauce. What the hell did he know anyway? No, this time she was going to take control. She was going to find her own publisher. She was going to go to the people directly. It was all about control. Control of product, of distribution, of capital. She, not the middleman, was going to be in charge.

In fact, she thought as she threw the bread dough viciously against her marble board, she was going to take control in everything. Her career, her relationship with her daughter, her bed. Especially her bed.

Jasmine glanced over with hooded eyes to where Daniel tucked into his Fiber One. Because, after all, wasn't it always a slippery slope, that combination of career and marriage? She was, she'd be the first to admit, a bit obsessive about her career. But that was to be expected. Food was a serious business.

And she had had to take it seriously. And now more than ever she had to fight her battle. Still, life was an assortment of battles. And her most enduring one had always been her marriage. Anyone who said different was just deluding themselves. Of course, sometimes you had to give more than you got. Often. Mostly. But giving in a committed relationship was joy. Thorned joy. Yes, that was the term. Thorned joy.

She made herself smile at the sodden crunches emitting from Daniel's mouth.

'You know I was so caught up in my own troubles last night that I forgot to ask about your day. Was it good?' She smiled.

Daniel stopped crunching. His eyes blinked rapidly. 'Just might turn these guys into actors yet,' he gurgled.

'What are they now?'

'Gorillas.'

'Even the girls?'

'Especially the girls.'

Jasmine laughed and brushed by him seductively, goosing him with a mischievous hand. Daniel jumped as if stung by a bee.

Jasmine stepped back. 'What's the matter?'

'Nothing, just . . . I didn't see you coming.'

She caught him by the lapels of his shirt. 'Well, you better watch your back,' she growled into his neck. She released him and merrily strode out of the kitchen. Yes, tonight, she said to herself, she was going to commit grand passion. Enough of this living like two polite roommates who climbed into bed each night as if sharing a bench at a bus stop. Tired, cranky, waiting for something to take them away. No, tonight she was going to extend her neck, jut out her teeth, and pounce. She was going to splay her prey beneath her, sink into his tender parts, and look up to the sky with juice on her lips. Ah, yes, and he would moan with thankfulness.

Tina sat on her couch and mulled over the previous night's coupling like a surgeon, dissecting segments into manageable bits. The invitation. She had thought long and hard about that invitation, wanting it to be coy but restrained. Entertaining but serious. She didn't want him to think she did this kind of thing casually. Occasionally, certainly. She was, after all, a new woman, free with her sexuality, competent in its care, adventurous in its expression. But at the same time, and this was extremely important, he needed to feel as if something special had occurred. A slight bondage, however light. So she had invited him over for a drink. When he had first demurred, she stressed how lost she'd been feeling since she had not gotten that coveted soap opera role and though he probably had better things to do she would so much appreciate a supporting hand. He bit. The rest was a breeze. Even quite pleasurable. She'd never done it on a television before. And frankly, because these things matter, his had been a fair size. On closer inspection she saw that it had a funny bend to it, curving to the left. She wondered what the long-term effects of that would be on one's vagina. But afterward, even though she realized, of course, he had to go, she couldn't quite get over the fact that she felt slightly like a fifty-dollar call girl. And he had promised her he'd call, which, by — she looked at her watch — ten A.M. he had not, and she wondered if he was trying to get a clear shot at the phone. Privacy in his house with that wife of his, she imagined, was nil. So she sat there, stroking her terrier, Sugarfree, and juicing her way through an extra-large bag of organic carrots which she reserved for extra-stress moments like these, and waiting. If he only knew how badly she hated to wait.

Daniel settled himself on top of his regular stool at Kramer Books.

He ordered his usual skim-milk caffe latte

and super bran muffin, and opened up the Weekend section of *The Washington Post* to the theater reviews. He took a long, satisfying slurp of his coffee. Only last week, he'd been a nobody, drinking his sorry latte, wincing at his bad reviews. He'd been about to pass over to the other side of forty, a sexless cog, a good boy, a mere citizen in the totalitarian state of marriage. But today, face it, he was a stud. He was one of the guys. He was a rebel. With a cause. What a cause. He smirked. A satisfied young woman lived over the bridge, probably still in bed, exhausted by the evening's gymnastics.

'Daniel.'

Daniel jumped.

Tina stood next to him, her hair still tousled but her lips berry fresh.

'I thought you might be here.' She hopped onto the stool beside him.

'Bagel, toasted,' she said to the waiter. 'Can you put this on it when it's done?' She handed him a small Tupperware container. The waiter opened it and sucked his teeth in disgust.

'It's just carrot tofu whip. High in beta-carotene.'

She rummaged in her bag, which Daniel noted was the size of a small laundry sack.

'You forgot your book.'

Daniel looked confused as she handed him his book.

'Look inside,' she urged. On the front page she had inscribed *Heavenly memories* and the date. 'I was going to write more but you never know who might see it.'

'Aren't I supposed to be the one to inscribe it?'

Tina shrugged and took a delicate bite of bagel. 'You didn't strike me as the conventional type.' She grinned, her teeth lightly smeared with carrot tofu whip, high in beta-carotene. 'Want another coffee?'

Daniel ordered another one, slightly annoyed that his triumphant breakfast was sullied by his triumph.

'How did you know I would be here?'

'I noticed you once here a couple of months ago and then saw you a couple times after that. Figured it must be a ritual.'

They sat in silence a moment, Daniel's mind whirring. He glanced down at Tina's jeans, which encased her small hips like a glove. The snug sweater left little to the imagination.

'Not working today?' he asked as casually as he could.

She caught the drift and smiled.

'Called in sick.'

'Are you?'

'No, just tired. Aren't you?'

'Was. Not anymore.'

She grinned again, looking at his lips.

'That's too bad, I was going to offer you a bed.'

Daniel's groin thumped.

'You done?' He paid for the breakfasts and hurried them out.

As Jasmine savored the sugar crust on her cappuccino, she remembered how Careme had skimmed through the kitchen that morning, late, Jasmine noticed, for school. Tall, lanky, bright hunks of shiny hair falling over her face, so effortlessly gorgeous it made Jasmine's heart ache.

'Home for dinner?' she'd called after the black-enrobed nymph.

'Fine,' came the reply, and Jasmine wondered as she surveyed her messy kitchen why all her innocent meal invitations ended up sounding like General Patton commands. She shrugged and breathed in the silence of her house. An omelet. A perfect classic omelet. That's what she needed. She reached for her omelet pan. And had anyone asked, she would have been ready to tell them that an omelet pan should be simply wiped out after use, never washed, and kept only for omelets or plain fried eggs.

And if asked she would have told them how to heat a large dollop of butter in a hot pan until foaming. How to add four beaten seasoned eggs and stir with a fork for eight to ten seconds until they start to thicken. How to pull back the egg that sets and tip the pan so that the uncooked egg pours to the sides of the pan. How to let the omelet cook until the bottom is slightly browned and the top lightly set, then sprinkle with Parmesan cheese and tilt the pan to one side. How to use a fork to roll up or fold the omelet, slide the omelet out of the pan onto a warm plate, and serve immediately. If asked, Jasmine would have mentioned that for this particular omelet, she folded in cooked pumpkin mashed with butter, sprinkled with grated Parmesan cheese and tucked in.

Her eyes fell on the cappuccino maker and she struggled with the thought of making herself just one more. She knew it would be a mistake. By two P.M. her pupils would be dilated past her eyebrows, but the thought of hot, sweet, warm milk and arabica beans proved too strong. She reached for her oversize Starbucks coffee mug.

Well, coffee turned into coffee and cake curled up around a new cookbook, which turned into a comforting hot pea and mint soup snack, which turned into the trying of a new recipe for raspberry brownies. After a double helping, Jasmine was free to disappear upstairs.

She stripped, letting her clothes fall to the floor, and examined herself as carefully as she would a plucked chicken carcass. Well. She nodded at herself. She bit her lip. Not exactly magazine material. Her once-rich breasts lay like wine sacks against her well-padded ribs. Her belly pouched out in a roll like a pale kielbasa. Still, her skin was smooth and unblemished, as if she had been cast in Italian pale-veined marble. Her thighs were heavy but solid, an inviting gateway to the deep mahogany bush that erupted below her belly. She turned halfway, peeking seductively at the mirror like an odalisque, and examined her bottom, which, though weighty, still held up like two melons.

She turned the water tap on to hot and went to work. She examined the package again. Brown henna. It promised her rich, thick, chestnut hair. It was an ancient beauty secret. Cleopatra herself used it and look at her sex life. Jasmine sniffed at the green powder. It smelled like a combination of old mowed grass and dung. Jasmine touched her locks, which were becoming thinner and spiked with a wiry gray. She read the side of the box like a recipe and used a measuring spoon to mix the water and henna. She swirled it together, pushing at the lumps with the back of the spoon. Then, closing her eyes, she clumped the mixture on the top of her head. It sat there like gritty oatmeal. Slowly she massaged it into her scalp, wiping away the clumps that plopped onto her nose. She then wrapped her head in a plastic bag and checked her watch. Twenty minutes. Plenty of time in which to mix and knead the rosemary and onion bread for dinner.

An hour later she remembered her hair and ran to the tub. She watched the dark chocolate color swirling down the drain and smiled, hopeful. She clicked on the dryer and teased her hair, pulling at the roots so that her tresses would rise and billow about her face in abundance. She clicked off the dryer, stepped back, and surveyed her work. Her hair, which erupted from her head like foam from a shaken beer bottle, was the color of a ripe eggplant.

Tina grabbed her professionally painted toe, stretched her leg out like a ballet dancer, and breathed. Daniel lay back against her many varied pillows and smiled, his member snoozing like a puppy in the curls of his groin.

One last leg pull and Tina hopped from the bed. A wrap of her terry cloth bathrobe and she padded out of the bedroom. She returned with a tray piled with dishes of chopped hard-boiled egg white, sliced turkey, wobbly bits of tofu, and a huge dish of chopped apples. She settled herself and the tray back among the sheets and nudged Daniel.

'Go on, dig in.'

'What the hell is that?'

'Just your passport to great health and vitality.'

'I don't think so.'

Tina plopped a wet piece of tofu in her mouth and followed with a handful of apples. She chewed and hummed with studied concentration.

'What are you doing?'

'I'm making space for the sacred act of food digestion.'

Daniel buried his head under his pillow.

'Mmm,' she murmured. 'You don't know what you're missing.'

Daniel unburied himself and swung himself out of bed. 'I've got to get back.'

Tina gave his body an appraising look.

'I bet you think detoxing is enough.'

Daniel's ego withered in front of her penetrating look.

'Oh,' she continued, scooping egg whites into her mouth, 'I know all about detoxing: psyllium powder, raw impact, skin brushing, linseeds, spirulina . . .'

'Spirulina?'

'You don't know about spirulina? A very potent cleanser and energizer.'

'Where do you get it?'

'I've got a special supplier.'

'Really?'

'And of course the rope.'

'You do the rope?'

'Any serious detoxer does.'

Daniel winced.

Tina observed him, chewing, bits of egg white clinging to her lips. 'You're not that committed, are you?'

'Well . . .'

'No, I can see. One big bowel movement and you call it a day.'

'Isn't it enough?'

'It's not about bowel movements, Daniel. It's about reenergizing yourself. Becoming another life force. Pooping ain't gonna do it. I mean detoxing is very important. We've got a lot of stuff to get rid of, mucus, heavy metals, serious waste particles which have accumulated over the years. Just clinging to the colon wall and clogging up our digestive tract. Preventing the absorption of vital nutrients.'

Tina stood up and let her robe fall to the ground. Daniel had to admit, whatever it was she was eliminating, it was doing great things.

'Don't get me wrong, detoxing is a great start. But it's a rethinking of your physical and nutritional needs I'm talking about . . .'

The phone rang, interrupting her. Only it didn't ring, it played a tinny Beethoven's Fifth. The answering machine clicked on before the second bar was finished.

'Listen, Tina, I can't make tonight,' a male voice began before Tina sprang to the machine and turned down the volume to mute. She gave Daniel a quick glance, walked quickly over, and drew him close.

'Where was I?' she murmured into his neck.

OK, Daniel had to admit, he was jealous. It hadn't occurred to him that she would know any other male.

'I gotta go,' he said, a bit peevishly.

'You sure?'

'Positive.'

'How about a little protein for the road?' Her hand slid down along his trousers and unzipped. With the other she reached over and grabbed a large slice of turkey. When she wrapped it around him, he almost laughed. But then she began nibbling.

'Can't leave the Zone. It will give you vitality like you wouldn't believe,' she stopped to murmur.

Daniel fell back onto the bed, teeth clenched.

Afterward, she snuggled close. 'Oh, Daniel, aren't you glad we found each other?'

'Oh, yes,' he breathed, his vitality fully restored.

Careme wore white. She thought it was appropriate. She felt like a maiden at the altar. She glanced over to her high priest, who was in the midst of shoving a large handful of mustard pretzels down his throat. Careme shifted to her other high heel. She and her friends had arrived early at Scott Meal's party. Too early. She checked her watch. Barely nine P.M. But she had been anxious to get started and had railroaded them through their preparty ritual of drinking a six-pack out in the car. No party could be entered before this tête-à-tête fueled by beer, usually procured by Alessandra, who snuck it from her parents' overflowing pantry. They would drive, park near the party, and then settle back to sip and plan the evening's maneuver.

Alessandra peered into the visor mirror, separating the lashes of her heavily mascaraed eyes. Lisa grimaced at her beer. 'Guinness? What is this? It tastes like beef stew.'

Alessandra shrugged. 'It's all I could find. The shopping is tomorrow.'

Careme stared out the window, dreaming of the looks she would get as she walked in. The sighs from the unchosen boys, the envy of the other girls. She pictured herself as she glided through the crowd, which parted as she made her way toward Troy, who stood like a knight, his hand out for her, his chosen one.

Alessandra snapped the visor shut. 'Well, look out, boys, here we come!'

'Whatever,' said Lisa.

But now they stood, wall weeds in Scott Meal's basement rec room. The house, on River Road, had stood in Lafayette's time. Scott's father, head of the largest construction company in town, had refurbished it and added tennis courts, a pool, and a professionally sized putt-putt course. It now reigned over the Rock Creek Parkway, three stories high with four long pretentious white columns.

Scott's friends were asked to use the side

entrance that led directly downstairs into a cavernous, almost monastic hall. Medieval high-backed chairs stood against walls the color of tarnished gold. Heavy brocade curtains covered the tall French windows and had to be wrestled back to gain entrance into the back courtyard. On this early October night, torches had been stabbed into the rhododendrons. But so far the teenagers had resisted the chilly air and remained sprawled in the oversize leather couches that marked the center of the room in a square. She looked over to where Scott, an overbearing host, was asking his latest guest whether she wanted a hard-to-find imported Bavarian beer or the 'house' wine, a Château Margaux.

'God, I can't stop eating these chips, they're sooo good.' Alessandra shoved another one into her mouth. 'What are they?'

'Blue corn, lots of salt.' Her mother's daughter, Careme knew the inside of Sutton Place Gourmet like her navel.

'Have you tried the dip, it's got something really good in it . . .'

'Anchovies, I can smell it from here.'

Alessandra's hand flew to her mouth.

'I brought some toothpaste,' said Lisa.

'I better go.' Alessandra scurried toward the bathroom.

'She can make such a pig of herself,' commented Lisa as she glanced over at Troy. 'Has he done anything?'

Careme shook her head.

'Don't worry, he'll make a move. He's just not drunk enough yet. Give him an hour and a couple more beers.'

Careme nodded.

'You ready?'

Careme nodded again and patted her small purse, which hung from a delicate cord around her neck.

'Where did you get them?'

'Family planning on Sixteenth Street.'

'Did anyone see you go in?'

'No.'

'What did you have to do?'

'Nothing. They couldn't give them away fast enough. I only wanted a couple. They wanted to give me a case.'

'My mother gave me some. She wanted me to be ready, just in case.'

'Why didn't you tell me?'

'I didn't want her to think I used them. I keep them on my dresser, all five of them, next to my baby picture.'

Alessandra came back with gleaming teeth. 'What's going on?'

'Nothing, the boys are getting drunk and we're waiting.'

Alessandra nodded, looked longingly at the dip, and took a sip of her beer.

Daniel paused outside his bedroom door and thought he heard the beautiful peaceful sound of his wife's deep sleeping. Smiling, he quietly inched the door open. In the darkness, he padded toward the bathroom. A click of the bedside lamp and Jasmine revealed herself stretched across the bed, her naked body teasingly covered in her raspberry kimono, her cleavage deep and willing, her hair teased and molded about her head like a cluster of grapes.

'Hello,' she said, her voice low.

Daniel stopped in his tracks.

She patted the mattress. 'I thought you'd never come home.'

Daniel's eyes gauged the distance to the bathroom. The path veered him dangerously close to the bed.

'Boy, am I beat,' he said, stretching his arms heavenward.

'Hard day?'

'Killer.' He rubbed the back of his head as if the weight of the world had perched itself on his neck.

'How 'bout a back rub?'

Jasmine reached out and grabbed him by the waist. Daniel's hands instinctually reached down to protect himself. Jasmine took the hint and lowered his zipper.

'Oh,' he said.

'Mmmm,' she managed.

'Oh, oh, oh.'

'Mmmm, mmmm, mmmm.'

It was quick. Jasmine lay back. It was her turn. Daniel leaned forward and sank down into her waiting breasts. He breathed in the familiar smell and smiled. Jasmine enveloped him with her arms and waited. He sank deeper and deeper. She waited and waited. Soon she was aware that Daniel's mouth had fallen open and his breath had evened, only periodically shaken by a strong twitch that jerked his whole body. Jasmine sighed. Weighted down by Daniel's prone body, she fumbled with one hand through the drawer of her side table. She pulled out a pack of Camel Lights and a lighter. She lit, then sucked the cigarette for all it was worth and let her head fall back as the nicotine flooded and soothed her brain. Daniel wrinkled his nose in his sleep.

Chapter Six

The next morning, Careme shoved her head under her pillow and wondered briefly how long it would take for her to suffocate. When she finally gave up and flopped over in bed, she saw the white outfit that she had ripped from her body the night before. It lay on the floor in a puddle of virginal frustration. She groaned, mortified. Her unwanted maidenhood. Her unwanted lips. Her unwanted flesh. For three hours she had sat perched on the edge of the couch like a mourning dove patiently waiting for Troy to make a move. She had nursed her one bottle of beer until the last swallow was so warm and full of saliva she'd almost gagged. She'd stayed clear of the toxic dip and the blue corn chips. Only when the clock struck midnight and Troy had stumbled out with his buddies without a backward glance had she admitted defeat.

Maybe it was her breath. She cupped her hands over her mouth and puffed and sniffed. No. Maybe it was that chunk of cellulite which stubbornly clung to the back of each of her thighs. But he couldn't see that. She had carefully covered that with the A-line of the dress. He must have guessed, because he had stayed with his friends all night, drinking and burping and playing pool and swaggering and not once looking over at her. She'd always heard of girls being dumped after the fact, never before.

Tears clung to Careme's eyes. It had never occurred to her that she would be rejected. She thought the whole world wanted to sleep with her. And now she wasn't so sure anymore. The one guy she wanted to, didn't. She sniffled as she shuffled from her bed. She knew one guy loved her. And she was going to find him and he would make her feel better. She padded down to the kitchen to where she was certain he'd be eating his cereal.

Downstairs, alone, Jasmine sat buried in the Style section, rereading the first paragraph of the main story for the tenth time. She'd been at it for a half an hour, reading, realizing she hadn't understood a word, taking another sip of coffee and starting again. When her daughter came in, too skinny and obviously in a mood, Jasmine pushed a bowl of fruit in her direction. Careme eyed the selection and chose pear over banana because it had fewer calories. She cut wafer-thin slices and nibbled like a rabbit. She examined her mother.

'What did you do to your hair? It looks purple.'

Jasmine looked up at her daughter, her eyes as sharp as cut glass. Careme's eyes widened and finally blinked away. Jasmine returned to her newspaper and her bowl of praline fudge ripple ice cream. She was acutely aware of what she must look like. She'd spilled coffee on her kimono and her hair, greasy from all the gels she'd used, stuck to the back of her head. All night she had lain next to Daniel, staring up at the ceiling and counting the mildewed spots. Her buffed and clipped and perfumed body had slowly grown cold until by morning it had lain, a gelatinous bag of waste.

As she methodically scooped the ice cream into a face she knew was knobby with old makeup, she glanced over to her daughter. She took in the smooth skin, the strong bones, the chest that rose up and down with a powerful breathing. The pointy teeth that nibbled at a sliver of pear, the blood that tapped delicately at her temple, this beast, this beast that she had created, had sucked the life out of her.

'What?' said Careme.

Jasmine shook her head and looked away.

Careme snorted. 'Well, at least I'm not a tub.'

Jasmine dropped her spoon with a clatter. 'I'd like to remind you that when you were born I shed my blood for you. The blood that runs through those skinny little temples of yours is mine. That cold little heart came from my flesh. Those limbs leached every ounce of calcium from my bones. And those eyes and that hair were formed right here in this very belly. So if you have a problem with the way I look, too bad. You are me.'

'Never!'

Jasmine gave her a knowing smile. Careme glared back.

'Where's my daddy?'

Jasmine returned to her newspaper. 'He's dead. I sat on him.'

After Careme had rushed out, Jasmine leaned back against her seat and surveyed her domain. Ten years ago, she and Daniel had bought their house in Georgetown. West Georgetown, as one Georgetowner had sniffed to her one night at the association meeting, implying that even in an area as small as this they had managed to divide themselves. And it was true, the small wooden houses on her street resembled servant quarters compared to the imposing brick mansions on some blocks. Still, they all cost an arm and a leg and the only reason Daniel and Jasmine were able to afford their house was because someone had been murdered in it. In fact, Jasmine was convinced she could still see bloodstains on the wooden floorboards in the bedroom. It hadn't been a murder that made headlines, mainly because it was a poor old man who lived alone who had been shot once in the heart by a burglar. Not very sexy for the six o'clock news. His son drove up from North Carolina and immediately put the house on the market. The sale was concluded in two days. Jasmine stood stunned on the steps with the contract in her hand, the yellow DO NOT CROSS POLICE tape still across the door.

Her first bit of business had been to install bolt locks. The second was to cut down the hedge behind which the cops had told her the burglar must have watched his prey enter his house. The house was the size of a doll's house. A tiny dungeon of a basement, a small nugget of a living room, a bite-size kitchen and utility room on the first floor, and a narrow staircase leading up to two bedrooms and a small bathroom.

Working almost entirely on her own, she tore down the back wall of the living room and added a small conservatory. She whitewashed the basement and stocked it with her indispensable second refrigerator. She then turned her sights to her dream room.

She combined the small kitchen and the mildewed and dark utility room into a metallic kitchen wonderland of recessed lighting and appliances. Back where the old stained stove used to sit rusting she placed a large marble dining-room slash worktable. Where old oil drums once sat leaking she placed a bright turquoise hutch. And where she had found the skeletal remains of a long-limbed cat, she stationed a six-by-ten-foot-high bookcase, completely jammed with cookbooks.

It was entirely of her own design. A cook's kitchen. The cooking burners were not set up two by two but in one long row of four at the back of the maple counter. This way she didn't have to lean over the fire when she cooked on several burners. It also made for additional work space in front. Her forty-odd herbs and spices were displayed neatly in a gigantic spice rack made for her by Daniel. She had all the extras: the brick pizza oven, the built-in pressure cooker/steamer, the multiple kebab skewer fitting for her oven. But her drop-down cutting block was her prize invention, a huge block of hard maple that swung down to reveal her collection of knives.

Every day it was in this room that she sat down and concocted recipes from the visions in her head. She tested and retested, searching for the perfect recipe, the simplest, most delicious mouthful. She then gathered those recipes and tried to weave them like strands of garlic into a satisfying work of art.

Jasmine placed herself in a long line of visionaries: François Pierre de la Varenne, Auguste Escoffier, Marie-Antonin Carême. She adhered to the classical French line, treating their teachings like a religion. She completely agreed with Brillat-Savarin's remark that the discovery of a new dish did more for the happiness of mankind than the discovery of a star. She revered La Varenne, that genius who developed roux, the first fish fumet, and the exquisite duxelles, which he named after his boss. Ah, those were the days when men were gluttons and proud of it. The days when food was prized, not shunned like some leprous disease. Deep in her gut Jasmine was convinced she had been born in the wrong era. When things got too awful she closed her eyes and thought of

Louis XIV eating his way through his usual dinner of three soups, five entreés, three fowl, two fish, a variety of vegetables, a roast, shellfish, and dessert. He'd finish it all off by popping a few hard-boiled eggs into his mouth. What a man. What a pleasure he must have been to cook for. Of course it wasn't all easy business. In 1671, the chef who worked for Princesse de Conde threw himself on his sword when a fish course failed to arrive on time. But that was life. It was a tough business.

She kept exact notes, she retested each recipe at least five times, she answered each and every one of the numerous letters she received from her fans. Lone wolves calling out in the wild for culinary companionship, that's what she called them. Kindred spirits, men and women who did not blink at a recipe for offal or shudder at the addition of blood to a finishing sauce. Foodies who were not bound by the current guilt that seemed to plague eaters these days. Mostly they were older, some held hostage and hungry in the homes of their vegetarian children. Occasionally she received a note from a young teenager tired of the carob treats his hippie mother brought back from the health food store and longing for the decadent, forbidden treat of real chocolate. Sometimes it was just your average Joe yearning for the OK to sauté his onions in butter rather than the now ubiquitous lite margarine.

Jasmine hugged herself as she looked about. This was her room, her domain, her salon, her retreat. And when the world became too large for her, too messy and impolite and unfeeling, she lumbered into her kitchen, sat in a tall-backed chair, and soaked up the presence of the metal pans colluding with her. They were her army, she their general, and any battlefield, theirs for the taking. Life, she thought, was never so simple as when she started to cook.

Tina sat in her apartment and fretted about what to do next. She'd been reading affirmation books lately, listening to tapes at night as she slipped into sleep, and they all told her she could be anybody she wanted to be as long as she chanted affirmations ten times a day for the next thirty days. And if she didn't see a marked improvement in her situation she'd get her money back, guaranteed. So she'd sat down and doodled a bit. After all, figuring out what you want to be is a tall order. It means deciding what you no longer want to be. Because you can't be a prima ballerina and the president of the

United States. You just won't have the time. Besides, who would comprise your core constituency to propel you into the White House? Sugarplum fairies? Please. You can't be a wife and mother and the next Mata Hari. In fact you have to decide between being the wife or mistress, but that's another story. You can't even be a poet laureate and a movie star. They'd never take your writing at face value again. So direction starts with choices. Hard ones — irreversible ones. Tina sat at her glass coffee table and thought hard. Then she began. She limited her affirmations to four, as the book suggested. They were:

I am a famous actress.

I am a wealthy woman.

I am the wife of a rich man.

I am a regular on *Good Morning America.*

She stared at the last one a long while. It was, if she were to admit it to herself, her most fervent wish. *GMA.* That would be the ultimate. She practiced often. Often at night before she drifted into sleep she gave imaginary interviews to Joan Lunden, smiling self-deprecatingly while Joan gushed over her latest role and tried to get her to reveal her latest love affair (which is why it was hard to reconcile with #3 on the list, but she'd have to make sure she married someone who understood, who had a flexible job, who could stay home with the children while she traveled on location). And well, on location, with your leading man, what do you expect? It's almost mandatory behavior, favored to get the creative juices flowing, so to speak. But of course she'd be exceptionally discreet. She imagined the designer clothes she'd be wearing, the makeup girl who would rush up between takes with the puffball, the fruit basket and cappuccino waiting for her in the greenroom. The perfect tone she'd set between being a young, talented genius and a sultry woman of the world.

Tina stood up and stared at the mirror and solemnly repeated her affirmations ten times, peering closely to see if there was any instantaneous change.

Jasmine sat in Missy Cooperman's office with a box of her very popular coffee and caramel cream puffs on her lap and watched the workings of the newspaper's small Food section through Missy's glass office window. She had come to pitch an article idea. Missy, showing off how terribly busy she was, kept her waiting. Finally Missy looked over her eyeglasses at Jasmine.

'I'll be with you in a minute,' she said, and hit her buzzer.

'Tim, set me up at Chez Gerard's, four for one-thirty.'

Her assistant, Tim, who sat right outside her door, nodded his head, his mouth full of cream puff. Jasmine tried not to think of the glorious meal Missy and her chosen few were going to have on Missy's vast expense account.

'Well, what have we here?' said Missy unenthusiastically as Jasmine placed the open box on Missy's desk.

'A little something to get you through the day.'

'How nice.' Missy made no move for the box. Instead, she took off her glasses, brushed invisible crumbs off her jacket, and clasped her hands.

'I'm ready,' she said.

Jasmine took in the arty black-and-white photos of fruit above the desk, the pictures of Missy shaking hands with famous French chefs, the coffee-table-size cookbooks stacked where her in-tray should be. She knew it was going to be a hard sell, but she had come prepared. She leaned forward and began.

'I'd like to do an article about fat.'

Missy frowned, as if the smell of rancid butter had filtered through the long tendrils of her patrician nose. 'Fat,' she murmured.

'And its glory.'

'I fail to see the connection.'

'I'd like to do an article telling the truth. Telling the world that fat is not so bad. That it could do the world a whole lot of good. I mean, we're all going to die anyway, might as well die happy, right?'

'The idea is not to die.'

'Ever?'

'Preferably.'

Missy smoothed a stray hair back into the confines of her blond do. Jasmine didn't know how to proceed.

Missy clicked her pen on her desk impatiently. 'My public is interested in food as medicine. Food as intervention. The food we eat will determine the state of our life for years to come.'

Jasmine was stumped. She tried another tactic. She shifted in her seat and dropped her voice. 'But hasn't the world conspired against your readers long enough? Offering them lite, offering them diet pills and diet books. When they are crying out for that warm hug that only fat provides. And until they have it, just a little bit, they'll never be satisfied. Ever. So I say give them a little hug. Give them fat with a capital F to help your readers get through the day and be happy.

'Take this cream puff, for example.' Jasmine leaned forward and helped herself to a cream puff. 'You might call it fattening. But in reality, it's heaven on earth. The fact that I was able to take separate ingredients like butter, sugar, flour, coffee grounds and mix them together to create this, this . . .'

She took a huge bite and closed her eyes as she savored its gooey coffee-creamy filling. Missy recoiled. The office was silent except for the sound of sticky chewing. Jasmine popped her eyes back open and continued. 'It's like religion in a way. Fat as God. If we turn our backs on it, people will search for it in strange ways. Like in rampant materialism or in satanic cults or in oversize bags of nonfat potato chips that they eat and they eat and they can't stop because what they're really looking for is fat.' Jasmine paused for a response, but Missy's eyes didn't blink. Jasmine leaned forward for the kill. 'When you come right down to it, isn't fat love? I mean, isn't fat a form of self-love? Allowing yourself to eat fat. To revel in it. What bigger love is there?'

Missy's face had taken on a peculiar look. It looked piqued, pained. Her rarely seen teeth, fanged like a wolf's, glimmered in the office light. Jasmine suddenly realized that Missy was laughing. She laughed as if she had a pain in her black heart and clutched at it, weak with mirth. Jasmine tucked her idea back into her mind as into a satchel.

Missy wiped the corner of one eye with a balled Kleenex and looked at her watch.

'Any other ideas?' she demanded.

'That is my idea.'

Missy leaned on her buzzer. Tim stuck his head through the opened door, his nose still dotted with caramel sauce. 'Yes?'

'Get me the files on diet spreads.'

Jasmine left Missy's office without a word.

Betty sat rigidly on her living-room sofa, her willpower draining from her like an oil leak. Horrible man. Sadistic, cruel man. How could he? Flowers. Give her flowers. Or perfume. Or a bright, silky scarf. But no, the man arrives home, guilty about something obviously, too many late nights at work, boss driving him too hard, and what does he show up with? A box of chocolates. A two-pound box of Godiva chocolates. Creamy milk chocolate wrapped around perfect whole hazelnuts, bitter dark and orange, white and raspberry swirls. She had politely eaten two under his indulgent eyes, her taste buds practically seizing up at the forbidden treat. And then she had firmly closed the lid and wrapped the box in Saran wrap, then covered it in a plastic bag and then put it in the freezer. To save. For a time.

When she didn't want them so much.

And now she sat in the living room, fifteen paces away from the freezer. And they called to her like children and she closed her eyes tearfully, trying not to listen to their screams.

Betty stood up and held her chest. Deep breaths. That's it. Deep breaths. Perhaps a nap would help. It usually did. Yes, sleep would be good. Comforting. Soothing.

She padded through her immaculate white living room with its matching white curtains and sofa covers to the base of her stairs. She rubbed at the polished wood of the banister. And she wondered as she began her slow ascent whether her husband would be home late again that night.

Careme was confused. Now, it seemed Troy wouldn't leave her alone. He eyed her that morning in class as if they had done something, smirking at her as if the two shared an erotic secret. Lisa nudged her, her eyebrows raised.

Then he passed her in the hall, close, clamping his solid hand around her neck and whispering in her ear, 'You looked sooo good last night.' And then traveling on, leaving Careme speechless and late for class.

After the three o'clock bell, he was waiting for her in the parking lot. Alone. He held a calculus book and his brown leather jacket. She glanced down at his untied high-tops, up along his thin black corduroys, up past the white shirt, up past his Adam's apple, to his lips.

She stopped in front of him.

'Well,' he said.

She sucked in her tummy. Maybe it wasn't too late. Maybe this afternoon. Wouldn't Lisa be surprised?

Troy cocked his head. 'You got someplace to go?'

'We could go to my place.'

He smiled, reaching out to draw his finger down the side of her hips.

'What I meant was, do you have time for a little chat?'

Careme died a quiet, quick, horrifying death. She held her breath.

'We could go to my place,' he mimicked, then laughed, his teeth white, clean, large. Careme could feel the whole parking lot vibrate with his laughter. She stared at his high-tops. He leaned down to smile into her eyes.

'Got to pace yourself.'

Still, Careme couldn't move. He nudged her playfully, then wrapped his hand, strong and warm, around her shoulder. 'Come on, I'll drive you home.'

★ ★ ★

Jasmine was surprised by Troy's eyes. They bored into her. It wasn't usual. Usually boys of that age looked right through her as if she didn't exist. She was a wall, the pavement, the dull gray sky. But Troy stopped and peered directly into her eyes as if he were rummaging in a closet.

'This is Troy,' Careme announced, revealing a tall, gangly high school boy behind her. His worn white Oxford shirt was rolled up to reveal strong hairless forearms. Careme then waved in the direction of her mother. 'My mother.'

Troy smiled, stuck out his hand. 'You write cookbooks.'

'Yes,' Jasmine answered, surprised.

'I've read a bunch of them.'

'Really?'

'Yeah, my dad's girlfriend gave me one. Trying to fatten me up. I really got into it. Started buying my own.'

Careme pulled at Troy's hand. 'We just want a drink and then we're going upstairs.'

Troy didn't budge. 'I loved your *Use It or Lose It*.'

Jasmine grinned. 'You did?'

'Mom, please. Troy, what do ya want to drink? Pepsi, orange juice?'

'Would you like a glass of wine?'

143

Careme stared at her mother, but her mother was staring at Troy.

'Love one,' he said.

Jasmine led the way into the kitchen. She reached into the cabinet and pulled out an excellent St Emilion. Troy clambered onto one of the high stools at the center counter.

'Careme, why don't you get down the glasses, honey?'

'We're gonna bring our glasses into my room.'

'If that's what you want.' Jasmine popped the cork easily and wiped the edge clean.

Troy looked around as if it was a studio. 'Oh, no, let's drink it here. So this is where you work?'

'Well, I do most of my writing in the bedroom.'

'But this is where the creations are made.'

Careme snorted. Jasmine laughed and poured three full-size glasses. She pulled out cheese quiches from her refrigerator and set them in the oven.

'Mom, we're not hungry.'

'Oh, I am,' said Troy, swirling the wine in his glass. He sniffed at his wine, then drank thoughtfully. His full lips puckered into a pout as he savored the aftertaste. He cocked his head. 'Cherry and vanilla?'

'Good. A bit of blackberry too, I think.'

'Nice finish. Sweet and ripe yet firm.'

'Why yes, I thought so too.'

Careme took a sip and made a face. She pushed away her glass and sidled over to the refrigerator for a glass of ice water. Her thin hands picked at the cluster of grapes on the counter. Troy settled himself comfortably.

'I've been doing a lot of cooking myself,' he said.

'Any specialties?'

'I like sauces. You know, béchamel, hollandaise. I'm working this week on a good soubise.'

'Ah, a sauce man.'

'Makes or breaks the cook, so they say.'

'They're right. I find the secret to soubise is the quality of onion. I bet if you use Vidalia, you'll knock 'em dead.'

'You think?'

'Positive.'

'All right! My first tip from the great cookbook author.' He turned to grin at Careme, but Careme was gnawing on a grape, glaring at her mother. Troy turned back to Jasmine.

'I'm surprised Careme doesn't like to cook.'

'There's no room,' Careme said.

Jasmine laughed. 'You know, she's right.'

'I think she's jealous.' Troy winked at Jasmine while at the same time leaning over to pat Careme on the head. Careme stared up at his hand. Jasmine was suddenly aware that she and her daughter's would-be boyfriend were talking about her daughter as if she were a pesky three-year-old sitting on the floor sucking on lemons.

Jasmine lifted the tiny quiches from the oven. She carefully placed the six bubbling tarts on her favorite plate. Troy looked over at the huge bookcase near the window.

'Wow, that's a lot of books.'

'There's more upstairs. I've run out of room.'

'I love cookbooks.'

'Would you like some?'

'Really?'

'I've got extra copies.'

'You sure?'

'Honey, why don't you go get Marcella's latest two books. I've got two copies each. At the bottom of the stairs.'

Careme tilted her head to the side. Troy placed his hand on her knee.

'For me?' he beseeched.

Careme shuffled off. Jasmine placed the plate of quiches in front of Troy.

'Eat,' she commanded.

Troy bit into the quiche with such a succulent mixture of delicacy and ardor it made Jasmine blink.

'Oh, man, oh, man. Oh, man,' he chanted.

She reached for one herself and tasted it professionally, dissecting each bite into its separate flavors.

'What do you think? A little more nutmeg?' she queried.

'They're unfuck . . . I mean, they taste just perfect to me.'

'Hmmm.' Jasmine took another bite. They stared at each other, chewing.

'Ever do any teaching?' Troy finally asked.

'Don't have time.'

'That's too bad. I bet you'd be great. I could use a good teacher.' He stared directly at her lips.

Careme returned, plopping the two books in front of Troy.

'Wow, Marcella Hazan. I love her.' He glanced up at Jasmine and grinned. 'After you, of course. Man, are these her latest?'

'Hot off the press.'

'Man, thanks a lot. Look at this, Careme, Duck with Salt Pork and Olives.'

'Yuck.'

He nodded at the book. 'You made any of these?'

'The quiches you're eating, as a matter

of fact. Page thirteen. I'm reviewing the book.'

'You mean I'm part of an article? Wow, check it out. You mean I'm participating in your writing? That's pretty cool. Don't you think, Careme?'

'I have to go to the bathroom,' Careme answered.

Careme walked out with a backward, hateful glance at her mother. Jasmine threw back her last swallow of wine. 'Well, I better get back to work.'

'Yeah, I better go too.'

Jasmine quickly wrapped the quiches into foil.

'Here. Take them. We've got too much food around here.'

'Thanks, Mrs . . .'

'Jasmine.'

'Jasmine.'

He stood staring at her again. Jasmine looked down at her hands.

'So, um,' he started, then stopped. 'Thanks again,' he finished, then disappeared out toward the faint noise of the toilet flush.

Jasmine reached for her daughter's full glass and drank a huge gulp, trying to drown every flame which seemed to have combusted spontaneously in all the erogenous parts of her body.

★ ★ ★

Careme stood by the front door as Troy walked out of the kitchen with his quiches. She opened the door wide, waving him through with her hand like a bullfighter.

'Oh, come on, Careme.'

'See ya.'

He reached out and traced a line down between her bony collar-bones to the edge of her tank top.

'You mad at me?'

'Why don't you go home and eat.'

'I was just being nice.'

'Uh-huh.'

He traced around her small tangerine breasts.

'I promise not to be nice any more.'

Careme grinned. 'Promise?'

His finger continued down the steep slope toward her concave belly.

'Why don't we go to your room?'

'Can't. She's here.'

'We could drive somewhere.'

Careme rolled her eyes. 'That's so high school.'

Troy laughed. 'Heaven forbid we act our age.'

'You know what I mean.'

Troy took in her pout, her leaden eyes, her crossed arms. He weighed the quiches in his hand and made his decision.

'You're right.' He shoved his hand into his pants for his keys and stepped out the door. Careme's eyes widened with a jolt.

'Where you going?'

'Home.'

'Why?'

'Still have a lot of reading to do.'

Careme trotted after him. 'But . . .' She stared at him as he carefully placed the quiches in the backseat of his old blue Subaru. He smiled at her over the car. 'I'll call you.' He slid in. Careme banged on the window. He opened it.

'Maybe we could study together,' she offered.

'Hmmmm, better not. We'd get nothing done.'

'But . . .'

'Hmmm?'

'I thought that was the whole idea.'

'You keep that thought.'

Troy shifted his car into gear and, winking at her, screeched off. Careme stared after him in a panic, convinced again that her mother had just ruined her life.

'Careme?' Jasmine called when she heard the front door slam. No answer. 'Careme, honey, come here a sec.' Careme came in to find her mother nursing her wineglass and staring glassily into the darkening garden. Jasmine turned her face to Careme and smiled her motherly smile, which just about sent Careme scratching up the walls.

'Isn't Troy nice? You haven't mentioned him before.'

'So?'

'Well, he just seemed nice, that's all.'

'Fine.'

'Are you guys . . . ?' She stopped.

'What?'

'Well, are you guys seeing each other?'

'We see each other all the time.'

'You know what I mean.'

'Whatever. I've got to do homework.'

'Why don't you eat something. What have you eaten today?'

'Plenty.'

'Like what? I didn't see you have any breakfast.'

'Not everybody eats breakfast.'

'It's a good idea.'

Careme shrugged.

'Well, have a pear or something.'

'I'm not hungry.'

'You think it looks attractive but it's not.'

'Tell that to the magazines.'

'Oh, so that's the game. You want to be a model.'

'I didn't say that.'

'Then eat.'

Careme turned to leave.

'Careme?'

'What?'

'You can talk to me, you know, about anything. About what you might need to know.'

Careme stared impassively at her mother. Jasmine turned red but kept on.

'About men and relationships. When you're ready. I think it would be a good idea if you talked to me.'

'Oh, Mom.'

Careme rolled her eyes and walked out and Jasmine sat back with her wine and remembered how it was yesterday that she had been the world to Careme. How three-year-old Careme used to chant in the bathtub about how much she loved her mommy. A daughter. She had been so thrilled. Here was her chance to give her everything she felt she hadn't received, physically but especially emotionally. She had praised her, told her she could be anyone she wanted to be. She had told her repeatedly how beautiful she was, how smart. How special. She knew it was supposed to be a phase. Teenagers. But she thought it would have been different with her daughter. She thought they would have overcome that. Her baby, Careme. With no teeth and no hair. With her fat red bottom which glowed angrily no matter how much care she took. With her three-times-a-night screaming and poos that would have made a baboon swoon. Her baby, Careme.

Jasmine pushed herself up from her chair. Truth be told, she was thoroughly sick of Marcella's cooking and Marcella's happy talk. Even though Jasmine was supposed to try Marcella's Stone Plum Soup tonight, she pulled at her baking cupboard. She wanted chocolate. She wanted oozing, rich, creamy, comforting chocolate. She would throw chops on the grill and toss a salad for dinner. Tonight, she was going to concentrate her efforts on dessert. She pulled out her big bowl and mixer. She took down blocks of chocolate, vanilla, sugar. Poked her head into the refrigerator to count the eggs. Ten. Just enough. Her mouth watered, her tongue repeatedly swallowing the swamp that had become her mouth. Cream? A pint poked from behind the mayonnaise. She smelled it. One day to spare. She padded to the liquor cabinet and examined her choices. Brandy, amaretto, Grand Marnier. Mmm, yes, Grand Marnier, a subtle orange swirl. The chocolate and butter wobbled over the heat of the double boiler. Unctuous and smooth. Jasmine beat the eggs and sugar until lemony light. She poured in the chocolate in a long professional sweep. A few deft turns of the spatula turned the mixture into what she really craved. She stood over the bowl tasting slabs of it from the spatula. A good dash of Grand Marnier. Another taste. And another. She had to discard a number of egg whites to fit with the reduced mixture. She finally tipped the glossy beaten whites into the chocolate. Expertly folding the whites, she sobbed. She smoothed the top while wiping her nose on her sleeve and slid the mousse into the refrigerator, blind for her tears. She leaned against the closed refrigerator door and, holding her sickened stomach, really let loose.

When Daniel came home he found his wife sitting at the dish-strewn table, staring glazed at the wall, her eyes red and puffed, a half bowl of mousse cradled in her arms. No chocolate slashes this time, but puffs of whipped egg whites dotted about her head like cotton balls. Daniel opened the refrigerator and reached for a beer.

'Fight with Careme?'

Her eyes lifted themselves with difficulty to his face.

'Is that her name?'

Daniel smiled. He took out a spoon and made a swipe at the mousse.

'Mmmm.' He clamped onto the spoon like a babe at a nipple. When he had finally sucked it clean he cocked his head to the side. 'What do you think? A touch too much Grand Marnier? Not that I'm complaining. But if this is a recipe or something.'

Jasmine sat there dully while he rooted around in the bowl on her lap. He shook his head.

'How many times have I told you. She's playing you like a violin.'

Jasmine closed her eyes.

He reached down into the mousse again. 'What's for dinner?'

'You're eating it.'

'And scrumptious it is too.'

Jasmine laughed. She threw back her head and let out a loud cackle. Daniel grinned. He loved the way she laughed. It was what had drawn him to her. Her complete abandonment to any humor. Especially his. Jasmine handed him the bowl and made her unsteady way to the sink, where she splashed cold water on her face. She pressed the cold droplets against her burning eyes.

Daniel knocked on Careme's door.
'What?'
'It's me.'
No response.

'If you ever have plans to drive my car, I suggest you let me in.'

The door swung open, Careme pushing it open from the bed with her foot, barely missing a beat to her headphones. Daniel surveyed the chaos and found a small patch of bed to sit on. Careme stared at him, bopping her head back and forth to the tinny clang clang that emitted from the headphones. He reached over and pulled one away from her ear.

'Have you noticed anything strange about your mother?'

Careme laughed.

'Jeez, Dad, you've been married how many years and you're just now noticing it?' She flopped back on the bed. Daniel held out his hand. She reluctantly took off the headphones and handed them over.

'You guys in a fight?'

She shrugged. 'I don't know.'

'She does nothing but worry about you. Give her a break, OK?'

'Fine.'

'Why the attitude?'

'It's just . . . oh, nothing.'

'Come on, what?'

'I'm not going to be like her when I'm her age.'

'Yeah, that's what we all said.'

'Not in a million years.'

Daniel smiled ruefully. He remembered how sixteen years ago, when Careme wrenched herself from Jasmine's body, he thought he was going to faint. The blood, the pail of vomit by Jasmine's head, the screams. It had been war. But who had won? Careme, slick with blood, squirmed under the lights, looking more like a subterranean rodent than human. The nurse handed her to him and in a daze he stared down at her, racking his brains for the merest sense of connection. He laid her on Jasmine's breast and watched as the creature rooted for it, one eye gummed shut, the other staring blindly up at him. It wasn't until the third day that love stirred within him. This sucking, screaming, burping, shitting miracle was his. 'I love you so much,' he'd chant to her as he bathed her, 'I hope you love me too.'

Now as Daniel looked at his daughter's clear eyes and skin, her beautiful unlined mouth, her empty forehead, he felt great love for his wife. He was uncomfortably conscious that this love suddenly lacked any physical aspect. But it was deep, uncontrollable, non-negotiable, something akin, he had to admit, to what he had felt for his old dog, Ralph.

He heaved himself up from the bed, tapping her shoulder as he left. 'Be nice,' he said.

Downstairs, the phone rang. Daniel heard Jasmine's voice.

'Yes, he's right here.' Then a pause. 'Can I ask who's calling?'

Another pause.

'Daniel! Telephone!'

'I got it up here.'

He picked up the bedroom phone.

'Hello?'

'Your wife screen all your phone calls?'

'How did you get my number?'

'You're in the phone book. Why? You prefer to be unlisted?'

'No.'

'So. Hello.' Tina waited.

His head was whirring.

'Did you want something?' he finally managed.

'Oh, yes,' she breathed. Every loosely attached body part of Daniel's stood at attention. He smoothed back his hair. He glanced down the hall, wondering if Careme would sneak onto the line. He sat back on the bed and crossed his legs. He uncrossed them.

'I don't understand . . .'

She laughed. 'You don't? Would you like me to spell it out for you?'

Daniel grinned, sweat pouring down his back, wondering if Jasmine came on the line now would he get away with saying it was a prank call?

'I'm ready if you are,' he murmured, but suddenly squawked when Jasmine walked into the room holding an armload of laundry.

He stuttered into the phone: 'Uh, yeah, so I think if you read Meisner's book on the subject, he's good with choices. If you don't have a copy we can probably find one for you. OK?'

Tina giggled. 'She's there, isn't she?'

'Yeah, so just keep at it and I'll see you to-morrow. OK?'

'Awwwww.'

'OK? Gotta go. 'Night.'

He slammed down the phone. Jasmine jumped.

'Who was that?' she asked.

'Student. Bit of a psychopath. I've told them the home phone is off limits.'

Jasmine folded Daniel's underpants and watched him from the corner of her eye.

'Tina. Is she new?'

'Yes. No. I don't know.'

'You don't know?'

'Well, yes. I guess.'

'Is she any good?'

Daniel gulped. 'Good?'

'Is she a good actor?'

'Oh. Ha. No. Better keep her day job.'

Daniel disappeared into the bathroom to catch his breath. He stared into the mirror at his cheating face. He licked his dry, lying lips. He turned his face from side to side to examine his deceitful profile. He then smiled. After all, excess supply was the real culprit. Too many women. Not enough men. He was just helping out. Relieving the overflow. In France, where man was not so hypocritical, this taking of mistresses was considered part of marriage. Like a second home or life insurance, something that, if you could afford it, was considered a wise, almost mature thing to do. In fact, if Jasmine knew she might approve. She liked most things French. She'd probably think it was very continental. Very cultured. Very je ne sais quoi of him. Daniel reached into the medicine cabinet and gave his cheeks a slap of his favorite citrus aftershave. Ah, Jasmine. If Jasmine knew she'd sauté his balls in garlic butter and serve them up with a nice Médoc. He laughed deliciously. Proudly. Daniel stopped suddenly and covered his groin with his hands. If Jasmine knew.

Chapter Seven

Careme sat in the middle of her bed, legs crossed, breathing slowly, very slowly. The better to fully leach the nutrients from the air. A pamphlet lay on her lap. Her guide to pure living and exquisite weight loss. Air, it read, was the answer. Why hadn't she thought of it before? Who needs food? Air was chock-full of vitamins and clean oxygen. According to the Society of Edible Air, a human body didn't need anything else. This Western society's obsession with people stuffing themselves had to stop. A needless, time-consuming, and profit-making addiction. Careme wondered vaguely whether all the starving people in Africa had blocked noses or something. But it was enough to know that Careme would not be caught up with that dangerous westernized obsession with orally consumed digestants. Her innards and spirit would be lean. Breathe, it said, that's all you need to do. Careme had become a breatharian. She ate by breathing.

It was a bit drastic, Careme might admit to herself, only to herself, but it was necessary. She was obese. Obviously that was what had turned Troy off. He had taken one look at her and wondered how a heifer had wandered into the party. But she would shock his pants off. If she continued like this, by next week she would probably have lost ten pounds and Troy would be begging for her. And she would sashay right by him as if he didn't exist. She would stand tall and slinky and he'd be mesmerized by her long, lean line and he'd probably fall to his knees. That's right. On his knees. Careme screwed her eyes shut. Breathe, the pamphlet said. Breathe.

Jasmine stopped at the entrance of Sutton Place Gourmet and sniffed. Pumpkin. She could smell the gourds from where she stood. A good start. Let's see. She sniffed again. A bit of thyme. Not sage. Thyme. Her brain stretched and shook the cobwebs away. Ummm, pumpkin braised until meltingly soft, mashed with mascarpone and spread between thin layers of fresh pasta . . . a delicate cream sauce infused with thyme. Would it work? A touch of very, very slowly cooked and mellow garlic. That would be the trick. Dash of nutmeg. Yes. Jasmine was salivating as she pushed her cart toward the vegetable section.

Freshly spritzed vegetables lay glistening in brightly colored rows. Cabbages of cobalt blue, fern-green fresh dill, and cut pumpkin the color of riotous caramel. Jasmine rubbed her hands together. Autumn was a favorite season for her. Most cooks preferred spring and summer, yearning for fresh bites of flavor after a dark, heavy winter. The fragrant tomatoes, the bright bursting berries, the new spring vegetables as lively and adorable as new lambs. But Jasmine yearned for the rich tastes of the earth. She was a glutton for root vegetables, simmered in stocks, enriched with butter and dark leafy herbs. She imagined them creamy, melting on her tongue, the nutrients of the rich soil infusing her blood.

She palmed a whole garlic head in her hand and pressed lightly, looking for resistance. She rubbed the paper shell and sniffed. Too old. She was reaching for another one when the sign caught her eye. 'Why don't you nuke a baked potato tonight?' it asked. Jasmine looked around before ripping it from its slate.

Microwaves. Satanic boxes of hell. They had ruined cooking. Not only did they destroy any sense of culinary achievement, but now everyone thought you could get a decent meal out on the table in a half hour.

163

That was crazy. It took Jasmine a half hour just to decide what oil and vinegar she wanted to make a vinaigrette with. And it was a wonderful half hour. A glorious half hour where all that was important was her oil, her vinegar, and the infinite combinations that danced in her head.

No one wanted to put in the time. That was the crux of it. But they had to face facts; you can't nuke a potato in the microwave oven. You only get that really crusty skin and smooth soft center from a conventional oven. You had to drive a skewer through the center of each potato to avoid bursting before smearing the potatoes all over with butter, sprinkling them with crushed sea salt, and laying them on a baking sheet in the center of a preheated four-hundred-degree oven. Nuking. Don't be ridiculous.

Jasmine found it funny the tribulations people had with potatoes. Home cooks just never seemed to understand them. She'd eaten more soggy, hard roast potatoes than she cared to admit. And she'd always tried to slide the secret into the conversation with the hostess, that what a potato really needed was parboiling and hot fat. And she'd go on, as politely, as nonargumentatively as she could, about how to peel the potatoes, cut into one- to two-inch pieces, and boil in salted water for fifteen minutes. How to add them to the oil, how if you're really living it up it should be goose fat, how the oil should come to at least half an inch up the sides of a roasting pan. How to roast them in a 450-degree oven for twenty to thirty minutes, then turn them and turn down the oven to 350 and keep on for forty-five to seventy-five minutes until very crisp and golden brown. And the hostess would nod and then ignore her for the rest of the evening. She was just trying to help.

Jasmine glanced over and saw Miranda Lane in the next aisle. She was leaning over, grabbing parsley bunches, ruffling their leaves, and then putting them back, unimpressed. Jasmine wondered what she had planned. A recipe for her new book, perhaps? A terror seized her. What if Miranda had discovered fat? No, she couldn't. Fat belonged to Jasmine. She would guard it like a junkyard dog. She perched on her tiptoes to peer into Miranda's basket: onions, carrots, tomatoes, tomato paste, fresh oregano. Obviously some type of ragout. Miranda thumped a plump eggplant with the tip of her finger. Of course, moussaka. Hmm, but what was the catch?

Jasmine followed at a discreet distance as Miranda made her way toward the dairy section. Jasmine pretended to read the labels on the eighteen types of gooseberry jams with extraordinary interest while watching Miranda stand as if transfixed in front of the butters. Jasmine held her breath. But then relaxed. In went 1 percent milk and a no-fat butter substitute. She shuddered. Imagine making a cream sauce with industrial by-product. Really, she thought, that was taking it too far. She felt pity for Miranda's audience and tiptoed away.

As she patrolled the aisles searching for ingredients she thought about competition. She tried to take a good, healthy, sporting approach. Especially with young women. She liked the idea of an old girls' network. She'd helped one young Chinese woman get her first cookbook published, *These Boots Were Made for Wokking*. She felt it was only right. Gone were the days of the slave mentality where there was only room for one woman at the top. Gone were the days of scratching out each other's eyes, whispering innuendoes to the powers that be. Now was the time for women to deal with the world and each other as equals. Of course, this meant you had to be prepared for some real competition. You had to be tough, watch your back, deal with interlopers quickly, effectively. Nothing personal. It was just business. She smiled. She then suddenly frowned, frustration sitting its fat buttocks plunk down onto her happiness. That reminded her. What on earth was she going to do about her book?

'Mrs March? . . . Jasmine?'

Troy peered down at her, his hands full of small, fragrant, perfectly formed figs. Jasmine's mouth spontaneously watered. 'Troy, what are you doing here?'

'I'm trying one of the recipes in the book you gave me. Figs in red wine.'

'Sounds delicious.'

'Hope so.'

Jasmine took in his clear brown eyes, so open, so confident. So appealing. She sighed. 'Your parents must love this. You cooking all the time.'

'My mom thinks it's weird.'

Jasmine laughed. 'Well, if it makes you feel any better so did mine.'

Troy smiled. An understanding, fully adult, friendly smile. Jasmine turned and began tossing items into her cart to look busy. Troy's eyes ran up and down her body. He finally returned to her eyes.

'You want to come over and try it?'

'No, I don't think so.' She grabbed the handle of her shopping cart and pushed.

Troy followed her. 'I won't bite.'

Jasmine blushed. Was he making fun of her obvious wanton desire? She was trying to be so nonchalant, and yet she had a sneaky suspicion she had the words 'I want you bad' flashing in neon red across her bosom.

'Jasmine!' Miranda had come round the corner and plowed right into Jasmine's cart. When Miranda spotted Troy, her mouth fell open.

'I didn't know you had a son.'

'This is a . . . friend.'

Miranda peered at her in disbelief.

'Of my daughter's.'

'Ah.'

'He's really into cooking.'

Miranda gave Troy the once over and smiled seductively. 'Well, hello, I'm Miranda Lane.' She waited for an ecstatic response.

Troy nodded. No recognition. He returned to staring at Jasmine.

Miranda tried again. 'You must have heard of my cookbook, *Jamaica Going Japanesa*?'

He wrinkled his nose and shook his head. He presented Jasmine with a fig. 'For you,' he said. Jasmine held the fig to her chest. Both women stared at the young man's buttocks caressed by thin tan corduroy as he walked away.

Miranda's lips pouted. She glanced into

168

Jasmine's cart, trying, Jasmine could tell, to figure out what recipe could be made with triple-crème Brie and Nutella. She gave up.

'So sorry to hear about Garrett,' she said.

'Hmmm.'

'What are you going to do?'

'Do?'

'For money. I mean, you're completely screwed now, aren't you?'

'Well, I . . .'

'I hear there's an opening at Safeway. They're looking for someone to come up with recipes using their frozen food section. They first called me. Can you imagine?' Miranda's laugh soared like a buzzard above the store aisles. 'I told them I was a little busy. But you . . .'

She stopped. Jasmine added a second jar of Nutella to her trolley. 'Gee, thanks, Miranda.'

'Hey, what are colleagues for?'

As Miranda clicked away, pushing her cart of low-fat horror in front of her, Jasmine pulled out her notebook. She did have a couple of ideas on what to do with her book. She wrote them down now: *Get it printed. Find a good cover. Create controversy. And destroy the competition.* The last, she underlined three times.

Dr Vijay was indeed young and gorgeous. Careme sat on his examining table clothed in just a light robe as his hands disappeared under its folds to prod and poke. He grabbed at her flesh and held it captive between the clutches of his small measuring instrument. Careme's cheeks were bright pink, her grinning lips screwed into a serious look.

Careme caught her breath. He turned his ebony eyes down to her.

'I hope I am not hurting you,' he said in a voice rich with Indian spice.

Careme shook her head as if in a trance. Jasmine rolled her eyes.

'Hmmm,' he said as he noted another calculation. Careme watched his lips. Jasmine tried to watch his hands. A few more calculations on his notepad and finally he stepped back. 'You may get dressed,' he said, and skirted the curtain closed.

He brushed past Jasmine without a word, leaving a scent trail of cardamom intermingled with antiseptic soap. He sat down at his desk and made scratchy notes with his pen, not looking up. Jasmine stared at his wall trying to read the dates on his diplomas. Careme finally emerged from behind the curtain as shyly as a new bride.

'You are fine, Miss March.' He finished his notes with a flourish. 'I'm writing you a prescription for Prozac. It will help you relax and help you eat. Will you do that for me?'

He glanced up to peer into her eyes. Careme dipped her head in submission and grinned OK.

'Now maybe you would like to step outside and I talk with your mother.'

Careme gave Jasmine a quick glance, an 'if you tell him anything about anything I'll kill you' look. She closed the door behind her reluctantly. Dr Vijay approached and held out his hand. Jasmine shook it, but he had a more comforting hold in mind. He caressed her fingers and looked deep into Jasmine's eyes.

'This is very difficult for you I know. But I wouldn't be too worried. Her fat deposits are still within normal range. And from my talk with her I have ascertained that she is not acutely psychologically damaged. Yet.'

Jasmine wondered if she was supposed to say thank you. Instead she said, 'But why is she doing this?'

Dr Vijay leaned forward conspiratorially. 'You know what I like to say? I think Freud was wrong. It is not sex but food that is the root of all neurosis.'

Jasmine blinked, surprised. 'Why yes,' she said. 'I think so too.'

Dr Vijay gripped her hands harder; his eyes shone with zealousness. 'Food is destroying young minds. It has become addictive, forbidden, filled with guilt.'

'Yes!'

'The powers that be, they should be ashamed of themselves, telling these young things to starve themselves.'

'That's right. That is it!' Jasmine wanted to bow down before the young man. Finally the truth. Finally someone with some sense. She had misread him. He was smarter than anyone that age had a right to be. 'You don't know how pleased I am to hear you say that.'

He nodded and smiled and gave her body a sweep of his amused eyes. 'Of course, some teenagers, it's much simpler. They just don't want to look anything like their mothers.'

Ray Chanders sat across the desk behind a microphone. His nose was the size of a potpie, which is probably why he's in radio, thought Jasmine as she settled herself in her seat. Her fellow foodie, Sally Snow, sat down beside her and gave her a long sly smile which Jasmine ignored. Jasmine was focused. Henry was right. Success is not for the wimps of this world. She had to prove that she was as ruthless as the next author. No one said you couldn't promote an unpublished book. She did not mention to Ray the fact that she had been dumped, that her book was not coming out this winter as she had hinted. He had assumed Garrett was publishing her again and she had let that assumption rest. Hopefully Sally would keep her mouth shut, at least until after the show was over.

'My favorite cookbook authors. So good to see you two back,' Ray crooned in a buttery voice.

'Can you not interrupt so much this time, Ray?' said Sally, popping a breath mint into her mouth. 'I get on a roll and you keep cutting me off.'

'I just get caught up in the moment . . .'

'It's annoying as hell.'

Ray blinked and looked back down at his notes. 'Right. OK. Well. Don't forget, speak clearly and not too close to the microphone. Any questions?'

'Nope,' Sally said, taking a delicate sip of her sparkling water, 'that's your job.'

'So it is. OK, ready? Here we go. Good afternoon, ladies and gentlemen, and welcome to "Chat Line." Today I have here with me two renowned cookbook authors who are going to talk about their latest works. Sally Snow, writer of such favorites as *No Cal, Sal, Don't Break My Heart*, of course who could forget her *Spiritual Guide to Party Snacks*, is now penning *Fresh Ideas for Fresh Families*. Jasmine March, author of many cookbooks including her latest, *Good Food* and *Better Food*, is now about to come out with *Really Good Food*. Welcome. Sally, let's start with you. As it's coming up to Thanksgiving, I wondered whether you had any special ideas for Turkey Day.'

'Well, Ray, in this time of Thanksgiving it's a good idea to think fresh. Fresh, fresh, fresh. Fresh cranberries . . . fresh turkey . . . a fresh apple pie straight from the oven . . .'

Ray chuckled his radio chuckle. 'Sounds fresh to me.'

'It's the key, I think, to cooking today.'

'Jasmine?'

Jasmine leaned cautiously towards the mike. 'I've been cooking the same Thanksgiving meal for twenty years, Ray. And its key is butter. Because butter is flavor. I'm talking about butter-basted turkey, buttered mashed potatoes, buttered corn . . .'

'You see, that's what I'm talking about,' Sally cut in. 'We have to get away from that. That whole butter-laden industrial-complex way of thinking. Fresh. Fresh ideas is what we need. How about a pineapple pizza. Or . . .'

Jasmine jumped back in. 'Isn't the whole point about Thanksgiving that it is traditional?'

'Make new traditions. Make new ideas. Fresh ideas. For fresh families . . .'

'I always prepare a double helping of stuffing because I eat half before it gets into the turkey,' Jasmine confided.

'That's about as fresh as yesterday's coffee grinds.' Sally flashed a beautiful smile.

'Fresher than what you call those sophomoric ideas of yours.'

'What did you call them?'

'Fresh. Fresh, fresh. You sound like a gagging parrot.'

Ray leaned forward. 'Ladies . . .'

'You wouldn't know a fresh idea if it bit you in the head,' Sally said.

'At least I don't need a sledgehammer to communicate to my readers.'

'What readers, you don't have any. Honey, your books are shredded and used to bind dog food.'

'Because a dog would choke on yours.'

Ray put up his hand. 'Well, that's about all the time we have . . .'

'Don't you wave that cleaver at me, Jasmine March,' Sally screeched.

Ray's mouth dropped open.

Jasmine had pulled a butcher's cleaver from her purse and was holding it up like it was show and tell. 'I am sick and tired of you writing lies,' she said. 'I'm sick and tired of everyone writing lies. The world is sick of fresh, the world needs flavor.'

'Jasmine, put the knife down,' Sally wheedled.

'America is starving. Starving for a real apple pie made with real butter, served with a gallon of real ice cream. Not frozen low-fat yogurt, not ice milk, not fat-free dairy topping. I'm talking about full-fat, creamy, buttery ice cream . . .'

Ray groped desperately for a button on his console which had lit up like a Christmas tree.

'We've got Gertrude Green from Gaithersburg on line three. Hello, Gertrude.'

'Hello, Ray, I just wanted to say, this is the first thing I've heard that's worth listening to on your ridiculous show . . . you go on and on about the stupidest things, but this, this is . . . the truth.'

'Thanks for your call. How 'bout John Dean from . . .'

'Ray, what she trying to do, kill us? I think these shows should come with some kind of warning . . .'

'Oh, please, this is Gertrude again, that's where your other caller is a complete moron . . .'

'Listen, fat lady . . .'

'Who you calling fat?'

'I can hear your fat butt wobbling from here . . .'

Ray reached for the off button to his whole console.

Sally leaned toward her mike. 'Fresh ideas for fresh families.'

'Fat is not a four-letter word!' yelled Jasmine.

Beep.

Ray clicked off the machine and stared balefully at the two women. Jasmine slid the cleaver back into her purse, crossed off the *Create controversy* item from her list, and drained her coffee.

Sally checked her lipstick in her compact mirror. 'Great idea, Jasmine,' she said.

'Thanks.'

'You going to Sue's?'

'Hope to.'

'Need a lift?'

Sally hooked her arm through Jasmine's and they traipsed out. Ray stared after them.

Chapter Eight

Jasmine opened her light-resistant spice rack and perused her spices. She ran her finger across the names, greeting them like old friends: nutmeg, cloves, coriander, fennel, cumin, caraway. All whole. She roasted and crushed her own spices. When the spices snapped and popped on the high-heat pan, the house would fill with an exquisite aroma. Sunshine would flood from the ceiling. Moorish wails would float through the windows. And just when they were well toasted, on the edge of ruin, she would whisk them from the fire and dump them into her age-old mortar and bear down on them with her pestle, crushing and releasing an even headier perfume, filling her nose and body with indescribable longing.

She longed for places she'd never been, foods she'd never eaten. And recently she'd realized she was longing for places she would never be and foods she would never eat. A subtle shift, a closing of doors. Her life was becoming less voluminous but more intense, like a reduction. It seemed unlikely now that she would ever visit Goa in India, as she had once wished. Oh, the food in Goa. She'd seen a travel show once on TV and had stared at the television with a wet and dripping mouth. The smackingly fresh fish, the bizarre vegetables which looked like claws, the riotous colors of ground spices.

Oh, the things she'd eaten in her youth. Fish still beating with life, bull testicles sautéed in butter till succulent and crispy, ortolans, those unfortunate birds drowned in brandy. She had draped her face with a white cloth and popped the bird whole into her mouth. The crunch was delicate, bursting with brittle juices.

Of course eating could be cruel. Veal, lamb. The eating of babies. The eating of another beast's flesh. Did fish have nerves? Did the hooks hurt? Her daughter thought so. And never missed a moment to tell her the agony in which the lump of meat on her kitchen counter had died. Birds shot from the sky. Life extinguished for another. Cows chopped and packaged while still breathing their last breath. In some parts of Southeast Asia they still captured small monkeys from the wild and tied them to tables, then sliced of the tops of their heads and dipped in their spoons. Jasmine grimaced. Where did the line pass between gourmet and grotesque?

Jasmine tried to concentrate on the recipe she was preparing, but where she should have had visions of tablespoons of caraway and cups of lamb stock, she had Troy's lips. And his teeth. Actually his tongue too, the little wisps of it that she had seen as it skittered in and out of his mouth when he talked. And something about his neck, the long line. Or maybe it was his jaw. Who knows? It worked. It all worked superbly. And she traveled in her head from his neck to his shoulder down his arm to his fingers. And wondered. And as she wondered everything in her body whirred and stirred like a blender. And she played with the sensations as if she had her hand on the pulse button and pulsed and pulsed and pulsed.

But she had to stop. This was her daughter's friend she was fantasizing about. Someone her daughter was trying to open her rigid little heart to. She was pleased to see her daughter had good taste. And how. Mmmm. She shook herself. Really, Jasmine. He was half her age and then some. She slapped her own hand. Off limits. No. No. Jasmine sighed. She had to pull herself together. Today she had to go visit her mother.

★ ★ ★

Alone in the kitchen, Daniel opened the box and pulled out his new Magimixer juicer. It had cost a fortune, but what price health. He set it on the counter and stood back contemplating the gleaming chrome. It was the color of revitalization. He let his hand roam its clean curves and shivered with anticipation. He then dragged over his sack of organic grapefruits and dug in, slicing each one expertly in half and feeding it through the juicy jaws of his new machine. When he finally stopped he had a pitcher of freshly squeezed elixir. He stood at the counter and drank it down, the juice spilling over the rim onto his working neck, down his shirt. He returned the glass to the counter with a bang and let out a huge burp. Ahhhh. He could feel his insides lifting up their hands in high fives.

The next shopping bag was crammed with an assortment of pure protein: pounds of nuts — almonds, walnuts, hazelnuts — and a carton of eggs which he immediately set to boil for a quick pick-me-up. He pulled out a block of tofu wobbling in its vacuum pack and regarded it queasily. But he was dead set on changing his life. Out next came the vitamins, the digestive enzymes, the free-form amino acids, the golden linseeds, the seaweed. And a rope. He dangled it in front of his face, then tucked it back into the bag. That could definitely wait.

He set the alarm on his watch to nudge him every three hours so he could top up his protein intake.

But first he had to endure a two-day cleanse. He had to purge his body of decades of unhealthy living so that his new diet could fully take effect. He looked at his notes written out in Tina's wide loopy script:

First thing in the morning: psyllium powder mixed with eight fluid ounces of springwater. Then herb tea, exercise, and skin brushing.

Breakfast: fruit, but no bananas.

Midmorning snack: the spirulina she had given him, the darling, a full half of her stash, mixed with ten fluid ounces of boiling water.

Lunch: sprout salad and three capsules of sea plant supplement.

Dinner: same as lunch.

Before bed: a fiber pack and herb tea and an abdominal massage.

Daniel tucked the notes into his shirt pocket, close to his heart. He smiled, pounded his chest, and popped open a beer.

Jasmine drove up to the little cardboard house on the edge of Falls Church. As she maneuvered her girth from behind the wheel, her mother opened the door and spryly hopped down the steps, her gray-streaked blond hair loose and flowing like a crone's. She wore jeans and a T-shirt sporting the muzzle of an endangered Siberian wolf. She gave her daughter a good, strong hug.

Inside, framed pictures of different kinds of wolves stared down from the walls like ancestors. Incense ashes covered the mantelpiece. Beeswax candles dotted the room atop tall, curved wrought-iron candlesticks. A dozen chairs still curved around the fireplace from the previous evening's channel session. Her mother batted away an imagined cobweb from her face.

'Coffee?'

'Mmm.'

Linda, as her mother liked Jasmine to call her, didn't discover food until after Jasmine had moved out of the house. Meals had always been for her a necessary but lackluster ritual. Jasmine couldn't remember a time when her mother had actually mixed together more than two ingredients for dinner: can of beans and a package of franks, can of mushroom soup and diced chicken, can of minced clams and spaghetti. Her particular crutch had been boxes of dried mixes: main dishes, cakes, dips, soups, orange juice, even milk. 'So much easier that way,' she'd explain to her horrified daughter. 'Lasts forever.' Not a fresh item had graced Linda's refrigerator except for eggs. After all, all you needed to add was water and the occasional egg. Her particular favorite had been Hamburger Helper. When the brand first came out Linda served one every night of the week. Look, she'd say proudly as she dumped the contents of the box into gray cooked beef, they come in so many flavors: classic cheese, spicy Mexican, zesty Italian. 'It's like going to a different restaurant every night!' The amount of preservatives that resided in her mother's gut must have been staggering. Still, Jasmine had to admit, Linda always did look exceptionally young for her age.

These days it was different. Linda had discovered food, or, more specifically, all the things she was allergic to in food. She had been through all the culprits: dairy, 'just loads you with phlegm, dear'; wheat, 'source of half the world's crime'; yeast, 'itch city'. Food had become the enemy. A right-wing conspiracy. Pushed by large corporations who were poisoning the earth with manmade allergens and dumping big-bucks agriculture onto a population that was biologically more suited to eating nuts, twigs, and dinosaur meat. So she haunted local health-food stores and cooperatives where you scooped pellets out of barrels and stocked up on gelatin-free multivitamins. She ran a Web site for equally food-nervous individuals called Food for Thugs, about how behind every benign food particle heartless additives lurked like hooligans.

But Linda did make the best coffee of anyone Jasmine knew. Hazelnut or vanilla mixes with just the perfect amount of hot soy milk in large pottery mugs she had picked up in the Shenandoah Valley. Jasmine could hear her rummaging around in her freezer among her various packets of coffee beans, thinking of the morning's blend.

'Careme came yesterday,' Linda called out.

'She did?'

'Yes, we had a lovely time. We had a little tea party with rice-flour scones.'

'She ate them?'

'Two.'

'Did she say anything?'

'Say anything?'

'Interesting.'

185

There was a silence in the kitchen.

'No.'

Then the whiz of the coffee grinder. Jasmine sat back on the couch and closed her eyes. She was intensely weary. She had half a mind to decline the coffee and climb into her mother's bed for a good two-hour sleep. Before she could make up her mind, Linda came in with two mugs of steaming coffee and a plate of toasted scones. She patted Jasmine on the shoulder.

'Relax, it will all work out. Remember how you were a terror.'

'I was never like this.'

'No, you were fat.'

Jasmine digested this along with her dry, no-dairy, no-wheat, no-taste scone.

Daniel rubbed the back of his neck. His 'once' had turned into thirteen times. Thirteen times in one week. He raised an eyebrow at himself. He didn't think he still had it in him. But God he was tired. His body was tired. His head was tired. His lying was tired. He was lying to everyone, to Jasmine, to his students when he came in late, murmuring about the bad traffic, after having screwed Tina in his office. He could see that some of his students knew better, especially after Tina, hair slightly askew, would slide into class after him. He lied to Careme, he lied to his friends, Jesus, he'd even lied to Tina when he missed one rendezvous not because of his car breaking down, as he had said, but because Jasmine needed him to pick up twelve lamb carcasses from the butcher's. Every moment had to be accounted for, to someone. And Tina had a strange way of acting very relaxed about the whole thing, no pressure, just fun, but then eyeing him as if she had a saber to his Adam's apple and was daring him to squirm away. Then she'd laugh, and jump back, raising her arms to show they were empty and it was all a game and what fun. Wasn't it?

Daniel closed his eyes. It was the weekend. Friday afternoon, five P.M. He'd go home, have a nice meal. He'd smelled rosemary that morning, simmering. Jasmine was working on a roast lamb instead of the usual fowl story for the holiday section. They'd open a nice St Emilion, maybe rent a video. And all weekend he'd take it easy. Maybe take Careme to a movie. It was a weekend thing they liked to do. Leave Jasmine to soak in a nice hot tub and then come back and settle down to another good meal. Daniel smiled. That was it, that was exactly what he was going to do. He stood up, fished around for his keys, his papers. But there she was, again. The scratch. At the door. Like a cat's. Daniel held his breath. The scratch came again, strong this time, like a tiger's. A tiger that had smelled blood and wanted in.

Daniel stood behind his desk. Well, he thought, maybe one more. In fact, definitely one more.

'Come in.'

A brown paper bag appeared first, then an arm, and then her body, wrapped in a clingy brown jersey dress. Tina pulled the bottle of champagne from the bag like a magician's assistant, her mouth wide, exuding an inviting 'ahhhhh!'

Daniel dropped his keys.

Within what seemed two seconds, he had her on the desk, her dress hiked up, her legs curled around his waist, her mouth doing funny things with his lips, driving him on.

Within another two seconds he was grimacing into her cleavage and finally feeling the pain where he had caught his knee on the side of the sharp desk. He straightened his back with effort.

'I've got to go.'

Tina closed her knees and hopped lightly from the desk.

'Wait a minute,' she said. She tiptoed quickly to the door and disappeared to the bathroom. When she returned, Daniel was zipped, packed, and dangling keys in hand. Her eyes narrowed.

'What about the champagne?'

'I've got to go.'

'Why?'

'Well . . .'

'She's waiting?'

'Well, I don't know . . .'

'Of course she is.'

She looked away, scratching at her neck, then crossing her arms.

'Maybe we should talk about this,' she said.

'OK,' he murmured, but stood there saying nothing. Waiting.

She uncrossed her arms and stared down at her nails.

'I mean, it's not like I think . . .' Again she stopped.

Daniel stared at the top of her head, his sweaty hand feeling the cold of his car keys. He'd screwed up, he thought. Screwed and screwed up, he thought, trying not to smile at the pun.

'This is just not my day, is it?' Tina reached over and grabbed the bottle of champagne. 'Married men,' she spat under her breath. She tucked the bottle under her arm and let herself out. Daniel stood in the middle of the room, guilty, relieved, and hungry as hell.

Jasmine had butchered the lamb herself, severing the head with her own electric saw and dismembering the carcass into joints. The cuts were endless; leg, shoulder, loin, saddle, breast, noisettes, and scrag, to name just a few. Her favorite was the neck, which she turned into a luscious rack of lamb by sawing down between the loin and middle neck and pulling away the elegant rib bones. The offal she saved for use in stuffings. Jasmine loved nothing better than lamb liver and kidneys sautéed briefly in a slightly spicy sauce but had yet to convince Daniel or Careme of their delicacy. The heart she saved for an evening when she had her home to herself and she could open a good burgundy and sit down to it, nicely braised and stuffed with fresh bread crumbs, sage, and onions. Sublime.

On this night, as she scraped the plates into the garbage, Jasmine worried that the bean casserole she'd made to accompany the roast lamb had been too salty. She had cooked the lentils slowly with vegetables and fresh rosemary, then tossed in duck, smoked sausages, chunks of bacon, cooking long and gently enough so that the lentils became meltingly soft, absorbing the flavors of all those around them and forming creamy, thickened juice.

It was all about absorption, Jasmine thought. In cooking as in life, the more you absorbed of life and the world and flavors around you, the richer you would be. The better tasting you would be philosophically. But Jasmine had been careless. At the last minute, unsure of herself, she had sprinkled in too much salt. Maybe in life she had been careless too. Maybe she had not absorbed enough of what was going on in her own household. Maybe someone close to her was simmering with troubles and she had tossed in too much salt. Instead of testing and tasting and finding out what was really going on. She turned her eyes on Daniel, who sat at the table, satiated. He had been so distant lately, so unavailable, so not interested in her. Those students of his worked him too much. They wanted so much of his time, so much of his energy. They were leeches. And he never said no. He was that kind of teacher: dedicated, innovative, tireless.

Careme had disappeared upstairs to ready herself for another party. Her untouched bowl sat congealing on the table. Jasmine whisked it away and set a tray of condiments in its place. It was just Jasmine and Daniel now.

'What would you like to do?' she asked.

Daniel yawned ferociously.

'We could get a video,' he said.

'We could talk.'

'We could talk.' He looked as if she'd just suggested stewed rat's gut for dessert. He rubbed his eyes.

'Jasmine . . .'

'I'm serious, when was the last time we had a nice chat?'

Daniel examined her face.

'OK, shoot.'

'I'm going.'

Careme stood at the kitchen doorway, dressed like a heroin addict: ripped jeans, mismatching shirt, charcoal eye shadow smudged around her eyes.

'Who's driving?' asked Jasmine.

'Lisa.'

'Have a nice time and remember to lock the front door when you come in. You've left it open twice in a row now,' said Jasmine. Careme turned without a word and let herself out the front door. Daniel stared after her, speechless.

'Who was that?'

'Our extremely too-cool-for-words offspring. Jesus, the way she acts you'd think we never had sex.'

Daniel stretched out his legs and extended his belly. But he didn't bite. Jasmine pressed on.

'You know, the way teenagers act. I think they'd prefer to believe they were conceived in test tubes.'

Daniel let out another roar of a yawn and scratched his groin. Jasmine placed her hands on his shoulders and tried a different tactic.

'You know you can talk to me about anything, don't you?'

Daniel's shoulders stiffened slightly. 'Sure.'

She smoothed his hair. 'Because I know it's been difficult for you. But you shouldn't let your students dictate to you . . .'

He pulled away. 'What are you talking about?'

She kissed him lightly on the top of his head. 'A woman knows these things.'

'What? What do you know?'

Jasmine sat down in front of him. A smidgen of sauce still clung to the side of his lips. She leaned forward and kissed it. He sat stock still. She unbuttoned his shirt and opened the jar of red pepper paste from the condiment tray. With a delicate finger she smeared the paste over his nipples. His eyes grew wide. She folded a clean cloth napkin and wrapped it around those eyes. She clasped his hand and dipped his fingers in a pot of honey and licked them. He was her very own lollipop. Daniel squirmed but still he said nothing. She drizzled olive oil over his shoulders and rubbed hard, insistently, as she would an expensive side of beef. A sprinkle of salt, a crack of pepper. She breathed in his scent and nibbled at his neck.

Daniel pushed away his chair and with a swoop had lifted her to the table. He began by dining on her ears, his favorite part of her, gnawing and chewing until he'd nibbled his way into a red-hot frenzy. Jasmine smiled. She felt better. She squeezed him close, nuzzling her lips to his neck, her choice animal part. Communication was the answer.

Chapter Nine

Daniel lay back on the couch in his office and groaned. A couple of weeks into Tina's dietary regime and he felt like hell. The week of colon cleansing had done him in. He felt brittle. He ached and pained. He had no energy. His mouth was a minefield of canker sores. His insides bubbled like an active volcano. His hair, he was convinced, was thinner. He flopped over on his side to relieve his bloated stomach and fumbled with one hand for the phone.

'Tina.'

'Daniel, you've got to stop being such a baby.'

'I'm dying here.'

'I keep telling you, it's just the toxins breaking up and being released into your bloodstream.'

'Where have they been?'

'They have been in the depths of your bowel. They've been stuck there for years festering, breeding bacteria, sapping your energy.'

'Oh, yes.'

'They've been giving you low-grade infections, low potency . . .'

'Never.'

'Eventually. And eventually disease. Big time. Like cancer. It's great that you're feeling this way. It means it's working. You should be so happy. Sometimes it takes much longer to feel this bad.'

'Oh, goody.'

'I've got to go.'

'Don't you want to visit a sick man?'

'Busy, Daniel, very busy. But don't worry. After tomorrow you'll be free and light. A new man.'

'What are you busy doing?'

'Good-bye, Daniel.'

Daniel belched hugely as he hung up the phone. He felt slightly encouraged and proud of his misery. Obviously, his toxins were not so deeply rooted as some. Obviously, he had kept himself in better shape and better internal form than most. Obviously, they had not yet attacked his manhood. Ah, he grinned, thinking of what his stamina would be when they were released. He shifted his weight and lifted his knees to better let the toxins escape from his bloated, putrefying body.

Jasmine maneuvered her tray to a table

next to the floor-to-ceiling window. On the other side of the glass, fall leaves swirled past her feet along F Street. A man walking by did a double take at her laden tray. She carefully removed her appetizer, her sandwich, her two side salads, her dessert, and her drink from the tray and placed the tray against the window. She mentally rubbed her hands and dug in. Croissant flakes clung to her lips as she chewed and scanned the other diners around her. Three men slurped at their iced teas, their cell phones placed like cutlery beside their meals. At a table for two, an old woman with a small pointy mouth like a tabby cat's methodically spooned her way through a dish of ice cream. Jasmine felt a chill of loneliness. The woman balled her napkin into her dish and with shaky hands dutifully carried her tray to the bin. But as she tried to dump the tray, futilely clanging it against the wide mouth of the bin, a couple pushed by her and upset her balance. She tumbled back but was mercifully stopped by the wall. Jasmine rose to help, but the woman, after putting her hands to her blushing cheeks, made her way haltingly to the door and was gone.

'It's not like they spend a lot of time together.'

Jasmine turned her face at the sound of

the young woman's voice. At the next table sat three young women, all with firm throats and shiny hair. The one who was talking had dark hair the color of rich chocolate ganache. 'He says he's always working and that they barely have anything to say to each other.'

'It happens,' agreed the one with upper arms thinner than Jasmine's wrist.

'I don't know . . .' said the third, who wore a tidy blue suit above shocking purple Nikes.

'Well, I really want to be with him,' Ganache said as she shoveled a plate of shredded lettuce into her mouth. 'It's not like there's a lot of choice out there. I mean, guys our age won't commit. Plus who wants them anyway, they have no money. The ones in their thirties want women five or ten years younger so they can breed. These guys in their forties, they're a whole new group coming up available. For us. So some are already married . . .'

'Most,' prompted Tidy.

'And many are looking to get out.'

'And what does that say about them?'

'Sometimes people just grow away from each other, it's no one's fault.'

Twig Wrists nodded emphatically and jumped in. 'Divorce is not so bad. People are living longer and so people aren't meant to stay together for so long. Before, you know, like three hundred years ago, the age people died at was like forty, and now it's eighty, so you see people can have double lives now.'

'What are you going to do when you hit forty?' asked Tidy.

Ganache swallowed a mouthful of iceberg. 'I'll have a kid probably about nine. So I won't need a double life.'

'So what about her?'

'Her kid is sixteen. She's practically out of the house. And you know I'd make a great stepmom. And anyway, we'll have a couple of our own, so I'm not going to have much time for her. So it'll be good that she has her mom.'

'So he's really going to divorce her.'

'I wouldn't be the first trophy wife.'

Tidy snorted.

'You know what I mean.'

Twig Wrists nibbled a french fry. 'So are you going to have a white wedding or what?'

'No, I was thinking just a cream suit. And maybe just one flower. Like a calla lily tied with cream bow?'

'Ann Taylor is having a sale. I like their stuff.'

'Wanna walk by before we go back?'

'Or what do you think about red? Is that too . . . I don't know, too . . .'

They picked up their trays and left, leaving Jasmine shaking from head to foot. Her father had left her mother for another woman. Met her at work and three months later came home to pack his bags. At the time, Jasmine had assumed the marriage hadn't been strong enough, that somehow it had been her mother's fault. But at twelve years old, what the hell did she know. Now she knew that some days a marriage can be stronger than steel, others as fragile as a web. And if something sharp were introduced right at that moment, it would be wrenched apart. And in her parents' case, it was.

Her mother had been unusually philosophical. 'Happens all the time,' she'd say, sipping on her Bloody Mary, trying to avoid her daughter's accusing eyes. 'I don't know if it's preventable. It's like cancer. Some people live like monks and they still die of it. Others do everything wrong and they live forever, and more importantly, their man loves them forever.'

Things were looking up, thought Tina. Maybe this one was the one. Maybe this one was ready to take it to the next step. The man was obviously smitten. Constant phone calls.

Endearments. He was on the ledge, she could feel it. And this time she was going to close the deal. She was preparing her battle plan and the first piece of weaponry was a dress. A dress so spectacularly erotic that her lover was sure to forget his name, let alone the pesky existence of a wife. She stepped into Betsy Fischer on Connecticut Avenue and placed herself in the two sales assistants' capable hands. She tried on a tight knit fuchsia dinner suit that barely scraped over her protuberant pubis. She tried on a snug white silk dress with a slit up the back that threatened to split her in two. She finally decided on a brown clingy number that laced haphazardly up the back, turning her into a sweet chocolate surprise.

She chose her lingerie with care. Victoria's Secret, of course. A plum corset over a lacy French panty, black silk stockings, and shoes that could only be described as f-me shoes with a long black lace wrapping her shin from knee to toe. The makeup she left under-done, knowing her main trump was her still relatively (compared to his wife's) smooth face. A touch of mascara, a sweep of blush, a dab of deep mocha surprise on the pout of her lips. Her hair she left loose, thick and long. Ruffled a bit for that just-fell-out-of-bed look, that how-long-do-I-have-to-wait-

before-someone-tips-me-back-in-again attitude. She unwrapped a new pack of condoms and slid them into the drawer of her
bedside table.

Daniel, for his part, sat at the kitchen
table finishing the dregs of his wild mushroom soup, sweeping the rich creamy broth
around with a nugget of freshly made dou-
ble-grain bread. He had meant not to eat so
much, but the heavenly fragrance of the but-
ter-rich mushrooms had called to him like
sirens and he had ended up asking for a
second helping. He could already feel the fat
of the butter cling to his blood cells as they
passed through his stomach, hitching a ride
toward his heart and belly. His satisfied
stomach pressed against his pants, but still
he could not stop himself. He looked over to
his wife who held up the ladle again. His
eyes narrowed at her. What craven devil did
he live with? What cancer had he married?
He sucked in his gut impatiently and
nodded with the same self-loathing with
which a priest might reach for his altar boy.

As he renewed his slurping, he tried to
figure out how to step out of the house for a
couple of hours. He felt vaguely like a teenager trying to muster up courage to borrow
the car. Next to him, Careme sat in front of

her filled bowl, licking the soup off her finger with what Daniel thought was alarming sensuality. Jasmine sat ignoring both of them, staring out the window that reflected back her pensive face and the lights of the kitchen.

'So,' Daniel began.

Careme looked up, finger in her mouth. Jasmine didn't budge.

'I was thinking about going to Hechinger's, pick up some . . . nails.'

Jasmine's eyes turned toward him in disbelief.

'For . . . I want to put up some pictures,' he continued.

'There's a whole sack of nails in the basement.'

'Not the right size.'

'Not the right size,' Jasmine repeated in a daze, and returned to her staring out the window.

'So . . . I'll see you in an hour or so. Maybe two.'

'Jeez, Dad, you going on a date or something?'

'Ha, ha, very funny.' He stumbled over the chair as he left.

Daniel rang Tina's doorbell and hopped from foot to foot. It was freezing. He had lost weight since his cleansing and the wind blew through his body like a wind chime. Where the hell was she? He peered through the window. A trail of clothes led back to her bedroom. Messy girl, he thought. He banged on the door again. Then flipped open his mobile phone.

'Hello?'

'Open the door.'

'Where are you?'

'I've been banging on your door for a half hour.'

'I'm busy.'

'I'm freezing.'

'You can't just turn up like this.'

'Well, I just did.'

'Go home.'

'Tina.'

Click.

How do you like that, he thought. She was really turning on the juice. Trying to make him choose. This was just the latest ploy. She'd obviously been reading that Rule Book, that antifeminist crap about not putting out until he'd wrapped her in gold. She and all her other unmarried friends probably got together and made solemn promises to each other about how they were really going to stick to the course. This time. Well, she was pushing thirty, she had to be feeling the pinch. He could understand that.

But he wasn't budging. He wasn't the kind of guy to get pushed around like that. Because when it came right down to it, he knew she loved his bed act. And she would come back.

Daniel's throat caught and he leaned forward to cough his lungs out. He grabbed his side at the pain that seared through his body. He was tired. Dead tired. Drained of energy. His parked car seemed so far away now that he had no libido to thrust his walk. Maybe he was getting too old for this. Daniel brushed away the thought angrily. Never. He was fine. Just needed a nap. Just a little tired. And he felt empty. His bowels were empty. His heart was empty. He shuffled along the road, cold and miserable.

The next afternoon, Jasmine slid the last spoonful of rich vanilla ice cream into her mouth and let it slowly melt on her tongue. She closed her eyes and concentrated. She opened one eye to make sure her stewing plums were not overstewing, then closed it again and returned to tasting the spicy, fragrant cream. The flavor made her supremely happy and yet sad at the same time that it was the last bite, and she thought how like life it was, the fabulous so often hand in hand with regret.

The doorbell rang. Ah, the wine delivery,

Jasmine thought, as she padded out to the hall.

Troy stood before her as she opened the door. Jasmine blinked, then panicked.

'What's happened to Careme?!' she cried.

'Nothing. Nothing's happened to Careme. She's fine. She's at school.'

'Oh.'

Troy shifted to his other foot. Jasmine continued to stare at him, confused.

'I decided I wasn't going to go today. I mean, I'm a senior and . . . well, I got in early decision to UVA. So as long as I don't totally screw up . . .'

Jasmine clutched her sweater around her. 'I'm working.'

'On that Hazan article?'

'No, this one's on stewed fruit.'

'Really?'

He stood there, thin, waiting. She finally opened the door wider.

'You wanna come in?'

He slid past her in a flash.

In the kitchen, he examined her knives. 'Man, these look sharp.'

'They better be. I just spent a fortune getting them professionally done.'

'You can write it off though, right?'

'Eventually.' She returned to the stove, where her plums were bubbling. She fished around the pot, trying to remember if she had already added the cinnamon stick. She felt Troy behind her, watching her.

'That's a good color on you,' he said. She gazed down at her gray sweater, trying to figure out if he was joking. 'I mean,' he stuttered, 'a lot of people can't wear that color, but you've got a lot of color so it works.'

'Thanks.' She touched her hair.

She gave the plums a last stir and turned off the heat. He had retreated to the other side of the counter when she approached with the steaming pot.

'What do you do with it now?' he asked.

'Let it sit for about twenty minutes to let it cool down and then take out the vanilla pod and cinnamon and divide it into jars.'

'Hmmm.' His nose quivered over the steam. She eyed his strong hairless hands. His smooth, hairless chest that peeked from his shirt. His jaw firm as a nutcracker. She bit her lip and turned away.

'And in the meantime?' he said.

'Let's see.' She thumbed through her notes. 'Well, this wouldn't strictly be work.'

'No?'

'No. More personal.'

Troy leaned forward. 'How personal?'

'I'm trying to come up with something dazzling for my husband's birthday.'

Troy leaned back. 'Oh.'

'Is it too early for a glass of wine?'

Troy shook his head. Again Jasmine pulled out a bottle of red.

She raised her glass to him and took a long sip.

'What do men like to eat?'

Troy stared at her, waiting for the punch line.

'I'm serious.'

'Oh. Meat. Definitely meat.'

'That's what I thought. What kind?'

'Red. Redder de bedder.'

'Yup, but how?'

'BBQ?'

'Maybe, I was thinking a rich stew of some sort.'

'How old's your husband going to be?'

Jasmine hesitated as if she were divulging an embarrassing secret. 'Forty.'

Troy whistled.

'Happens to the best of us,' she said.

Troy reached out and laid his hand on hers. 'On you it looks good.'

'I haven't gotten there yet,' she said sharply.

He removed his hand. 'Maybe that's why you look so good.'

He continued to stare at her, his eyes on her lips. She flushed and pushed a plate of radishes toward him.

'Try them,' she urged. She reached out, took a radish by its leaf top, and dipped it into the softened butter. She then rolled it in the sea salt and popped it into her mouth. The crunch she made was so satisfying it brought tears to her eyes.

Troy brought one to his mouth and slid it past his sensuous lips. 'Oh, yes,' he said between crunches.

Jasmine's hands shook when she reached for another one.

Troy stood up. 'You've done a lot to this house.'

'A while ago. Not lately.'

'Can I have a tour?'

Jasmine suddenly felt sixteen and playing a game of 'tour my parents' house.' Here's the bedroom, here's the bed, here's my . . .

'Absolutely.'

At the bedroom door, Troy reached out and stroked Jasmine's back. A long purr erupted from her head to her toes. She sank down on the bed. He shuffled next to her, pressing his pelvis against her hips. Jack Sprat he ate no fat, his wife she ate no . . .

'Comfortable?' He reached under her shirt, her nipples stood at attention. And with them Jasmine's whole body jerked out of bed.

'I can't do this.'

Troy leaned back against the pillows. 'Why not?'

'Aren't you interested in my daughter?'

'She's really nice, your daughter.'

'But aren't you sexually attracted to her?'

He shrugged. 'Sure. But you know, girls that age, they don't really know what they're doing. I like experience.' He smiled up at her. 'And roundness. You've got boobs to die for.'

Jasmine straightened her back.

'But are you guys . . .' she persisted.

'No.'

'Oh.'

'I'm not into deflowering. Too much responsibility. Some guys, that's what they live for. You know, cutting notches into their belt. But me, I don't know. Maybe I like it a little more seasoned rather than all bland and tasteless.' He nonchalantly lowered his zipper. 'Plus, you know, I like a little meat on my women. The bigger the cushion the better the . . .'

'I think you should go now.'

'But I thought . . .'

'I was just showing you my house.'

'It's a nice house.'

'Thank you.'

He reached down, again as nonchalantly as possible, and zipped his jeans back up.

Jasmine stepped aside to let him pass

210

through the door, down the stairs, and out of the house. Jasmine collapsed in a heap on the bed. What on earth was she thinking? That delicious hard flesh could have been hers. She could have had him completely at her service, doing whatever she wanted. Ooo, the things they could have done together. Over and over again. With barely a hiccup in between. She breathed in the rich boyish scent that still lingered in the pillow. And she had said no. Well, for one thing, Careme would never, ever have forgiven her. And for another, she thought as she straightened her skirt, marriage vows were marriage vows. She had made a solemn vow to be true to Daniel and she was going to keep it. She stared up at the ceiling and sighed. He had been such a nice person to talk to. Maybe that's what she missed most of all.

Jasmine returned to her kitchen and pulled out her notebook. She had finally conceived of a recipe for Daniel's birthday. A venison stew with crushed juniper berries. She smiled. It had everything he loved: rich, meaty flavor, bright, tangy vegetables, and a puckering, fragrant sauce that would make him drool. A stew. Nothing like a lusty stew to bring out the primitive in us all. She was hoping it would bring out the primitive in Daniel. He had been entirely too civilized with her lately, falling into bed midsnore, waiting patiently for her to finish showering instead of barging in and joining her like he used to.

Stews, of course, were deceptively tricky. Bad stews ranked up there with shoe-leather steaks in Jasmine's book of culinary crimes against humanity. The secret to stew was treating it with the same respect as you would anything else you cooked. People got so sloppy with stews, throwing in potatoes gone soft, sprouted onions, old wine, everything but the dregs in the kitchen drain. And then had the gall to complain when they ended up with a cheap, fatty mess. When Jasmine approached a stew, she insisted on buying chuck roast, trimming it carefully, searing the meat in butter, sometimes bacon fat, pouring off the excess fat, then deglazing the pan with good red wine. She combined the freshest, crunchiest vegetables, bright herbs, and her best stock. While her stew simmered, she tasted for seasoning, checked continuously to make sure meat and veg were not falling apart, and at the last minute thickened the sauce with kneaded flour and butter. Stews, like family, deserved the very best.

Lisa and Alessandra deposited their books on the kitchen floor and scrambled onto the tall stools. Their fresh pink cheeks shone brightly in the recessed lighting.

'You sure she won't mind?' Alessandra whispered as if she were in a library.

'Please. We're drowning in food here.'

Careme opened up the refrigerator and pulled out a pan of lemon bars. They used to be one of Careme's favorite recipes, little cheesecakes topped with a lemony butter glaze. But now they were the work of the devil. Concocted solely to tempt her away from salvation: i.e., thinness. Alessandra's eyes, however, grew wide and reverent.

'I've never seen anything so luscious in my entire life,' she said.

'Except for Billy Green in Algebra Three,' Lisa reminded her.

But Alessandra was not listening; her eyes and the whole of her cerebrum were fixed on the yellow, glistening topping. As Careme deposited two on her plate, Alessandra hastily pushed her long hair behind her and coiled it into a large knot. Lisa glanced over at Careme and raised an eyebrow.

'Dig in,' Careme urged, refraining from giving herself one.

'What about you?' asked Lisa.

'I'm allergic to cream cheese.'

'You are not.'

'Am too.'

Lisa shrugged and bit into hers.

'This is so good. I wish I had a mother like yours.' Alessandra closed her eyes and relished the moment, her mouth full.

Lisa and Careme watched Alessandra eat with greedy eyes. She wolfed down the first and then savored the second, slowing down as she reached the last bite, drawing out the moment as if saying good-bye to a cherished lover. She finally swallowed and opened her eyes.

'Excuse me,' she said. 'I've got to go to the . . .'

Lisa leaned forward and grabbed Alessandra's wrists.

'We need to talk to you.'

'In a minute.' Alessandra wrenched her hands free.

'Now.' Lisa grabbed them again. 'Why do you have to go to the bathroom every time you eat?'

'I don't have to every time.'

'Every time.'

'I do not.'

'You do too.'

Alessandra rolled her eyes. 'That's sooo . . . you know, you don't know what you're talking about.'

'Are you throwing up?'

'What is this?'

Careme leaned forward and tried to pat Alessandra's hand before it was snatched away. After all, she was just trying to help. She saw that her friend was in need. Alessandra was hurting herself. All the magazines said so. The girl was an addict, addicted to throwing up. And this was a very popular method to break through an addict's defenses. Everyone was doing it. Jason Roberts's father had it done at work. She'd read the guidelines very carefully. They were going by the book.

'It's an intervention,' she said.

'A what?' Alessandra jumped up.

'You need help.' Careme was determined to keep the proceedings calm. 'You're a bulimic. And we are telling you as your friends, you need help. We love you . . .'

'I need help! Look at you, you're so skinny you could get a job as a scarecrow, and you,' she cried, glaring at Lisa. 'I don't even know where to begin, girlfriend.' She choked on the last word and grabbed her books.

'Hold her!' Careme barked. Lisa lunged from her stool and tackled Alessandra to the ground.

'Let go of me!'

Careme ran to the front door and flung it open. On the steps, Alessandra's mother stood back as two men in white coats dashed through. They grabbed her daughter by the arms and whisked her out to the waiting van. Careme's last vision of her friend was Alessandra's open, howling mouth.

'I'll never be able to thank you enough,' said Alessandra's mother, clasping Careme's hand.

'We just hope she feels better, Mrs Diaz.'

Afterward, Lisa hopped up onto the stool again and helped herself to another lemon bar. 'She's definitely got a problem.'

Careme nodded in agreement as she double-wrapped the lemon bars carefully in Saran wrap and scrubbed every inch of her hands.

When Daniel arrived he found Tina's door ajar. Nervous, he pushed it open slowly. It seemed like Tina had been avoiding him for the past week. He'd begun to despair. But suddenly an invitation. To her apartment. To talk. Tina's dog clipped up to him and sniffed at his feet. Daniel tried to step on its nose. The dog scurried back down the hall.

'Tina?'

'In here, close the door. Put the chain on.'

He slid in the chain and walked down the hall. As he rounded the corner, he heard snuffling and Tina.

'Stop it, Sugarfree. Shoo.'

He turned and stared at the vision before him. Tina lay on the hallway floor, naked, her legs coyly crossed. She raised her hand, slid her finger between her legs, drew it forth, and licked it with a long tongue. She smacked her lips and smiled.

'It's chocolate, wanna lick?'

Daniel was half polite, half curious as he bent down and untangled her legs. He wondered why they had to do this in the chilly hall but deduced that a certain abandonment was required. He licked tentatively and mmmed. Tina had raised herself on her elbows and was watching him like a mamma who wants her child to eat up.

'You like it?'

'Sure.'

'You like it or not?'

'It's a little cold here in the hall, isn't it?'

'Daniel.'

Daniel reached up and began to twist her nipples. She sank back down and the chocolate began to flow.

Afterward, Tina minced back to the bathroom to clean herself up. She dripped on the floor and cursed. Daniel lay back and picked hair from his mouth. He padded into her kitchen for a glass of milk. He spied a box of pretzels on top of the freezer and dug in.

'That wasn't exactly a star performance, was it?' Tina appeared at the kitchen door in a white terry cloth robe, her hair cocooned in a white towel. She looked very pretty like that, Daniel thought.

'I'm telling you this diet is killing me,' he said, his cheeks full of pretzel.

'It's because you keep cheating. You've got to go full hog. A day cleanse followed by a pretzel pig-out is useless.'

'I haven't been pigging out.'

'I find that hard to believe. You are such a cheater. You act like a monk here and then you go home and debase yourself at your wife's table. Which reminds me. I bet you haven't told her yet.'

'What?'

'You know. About us.'

Daniel slid by her into the living room, taking the pretzel box with him, and plunked down on the couch. He was dog tired. Tina stood before him, her arms on her hips. 'So what's the next step?'

'What do you mean what's the next step?'

'Well, we're obviously attracted to each other. We agree on the important things: nutrition, energy flow, systematic cleansing. I'm just wondering where you want to take this?'

'You're kidding me.'

'No, I'm not. What would make you leave your wife?'

'Leave my wife?' Daniel stared at her. Where did this come from? Talk about going from cold to hot. Tina leaned forward, peering deep into his eyes, almost as if he were a specimen. He wanted to say, 'I have no intention of leaving my wife,' but, nervous of an immediate boycott, shrugged instead. Tina extended her finger and drew a line down his chest toward his groin.

'How can you be so stubborn?'

'Have you had her cooking?'

'What?'

'She cooks like a dream.' He closed his eyes in ecstasy. 'It's erotic the way she cooks, her sauces, her roasts. When she takes out her roast lamb from the oven my knees actually go weak. I see stars.'

'Daniel!'

But Daniel couldn't stop, he was drooling. 'And I have yet to taste a beurre blanc that even remotely matches hers. Even at Jean Louis.'

'Will you stop it. The way she cooks is killing you.'

'Maybe,' he sighed. 'Maybe.'

'And besides, I can cook too.'

Daniel laughed. Tina kicked him in the shins.

'Ow! What can you cook?'

Tina paused. 'I can make a very nice salad. With everything you want in it. Just like a salad bar. And appetizers. I can make these little potatoes with yogurt and caviar.'

'What kind of caviar?'

'What kind of caviar? I don't know. It's black. They come in little jars in the Safeway.'

Daniel raised his eyebrows.

Tina stamped her foot. 'Who cares what kind of caviar? There's more to life than eating.'

'Is there?'

'Hello? Sex?'

'I consider that foreplay.'

'What is it with you guys?'

'What guys?'

Tina looked wary. 'Nothing.'

Daniel grabbed her hand. 'We're having a good time, aren't we?'

'We are?'

'You're not?'

'You're pulling me out of the Zone, Daniel.'

Daniel shrugged. Tina looked down at him with studied eyes. She sat at his feet, leaned forward so he could gaze down her cleavage at will, and took his hand.

'What can I do to make this better for you?' she said, looking deep into his eyes and smiling encouragingly. She'd read *Win-Win* and *Getting to Yes*.

Be ready and willing and then leave, Daniel thought.

'Give me more time,' he said.

'I'll learn to cook.'

Daniel barked out loud.

'Yes, I'll learn to cook better than your wife.'

'What's it gonna be, tofu and egg white surprise?'

'You don't like the taste of it because you're not committed.'

'I am perfectly committed.'

'I'll show you. It'll be delicious.'

Daniel shook his head.

The phone rang just as Jasmine popped a full load of mashed potato and cheese and freshly sautéed bacon and garlic spinach into her mouth. She picked up the receiver and grunted.

'Jasmine?'

She grunted again.

'Henry here.'

She swallowed.

'Henry?'

'Your agent.'

'My agent.' Jasmine laughed.

'What's so funny?'

Jasmine paused. 'Nothing, really,' she said honestly.

'Listen, I've done the most fabulous thing. I've got you on a TV cooking show.'

'Me? How?'

'Pulled some strings . . .'

'Someone cancelled.'

'Well, of course someone cancelled. You don't think you were first choice, do you?'

'Wouldn't dream of it.'

'Hell, that's gratitude for ya. I give you authors, for lack of a better term, the moon, and you all demand the galaxy.'

Jasmine dug deep and found a teaspoon of enthusiasm. 'That's great, Henry.'

'Damn right it's great. Of course they don't know about you and Garrett. I told them you were working on a sure-to-be bestseller, working title *Toxin-Free Tuscany*.'

'Henry, you didn't . . .'

'You want it or not?'

Jasmine hesitated. Briefly. 'I want it.'

'OK, so this is the story . . .' He told the details quickly, in shorthand. Jasmine barely had time to scramble up a pen.

'So that's it,' he concluded. 'You won't blow it, will you?'

'How would I blow it?'

'I don't have time to tell you how many ways you could blow it, Jasmine. You just

222

keep those fat ideas to yourself, you hear.'

'I promise.'

'How are those peonies?'

'Dead.'

'Damn shame.'

Click.

Jasmine replaced the receiver and sighed. It should be fairly simple. It was to be a quick segment. A little dash at the end of their cooking program on how to take away their guilt from overeating during Thanksgiving. They wanted one recipe, something short, sweet, and low toxin. Well, she thought, as she took another large bite of cheesy potato, they had come to the wrong person.

Chapter Ten

Daniel suffered. Emotionally if not physically. He lay on the hydrocolonics electric table in fetal position. Supine. Giving himself up to the comfort of the warmed rubber tube inserted into his rectum. All his badness draining from him. All his trials and worries flushing away with purified water. Claire, his hydrocolonist, held him like a pietà and manipulated the folds of his tummy. His body responded and the clear tubes grew dingy with his waste. Warmed sheets felt soft and silken on his body. A chamomile tea cooled fragrantly beside him. He felt as vulnerable as an unborn baby and as secure too. Womblike, that was the word. He was returning to the womb.

'You look like death,' Jasmine observed as she sat across from Daniel at their kitchen table. Daniel stared weakly into his high-fiber muesli, his teeth too sore to chew. 'Maybe you should see a doctor.'
'I'm fine,' he mumbled.
Jasmine tsk-tsked and resumed spooning

last night's apple crisp into her mouth. Her pink cheeks wobbled as she chewed and Daniel winced at the thought of all that refined sugar invading her body.

'Do you ever worry what that might do to you?' he asked.

'What?'

'That.' He pointed to her dish.

'No.'

Daniel nodded and wondered again how two such different people had ever managed to come together in matrimony in the first place.

'Daniel, do you still love me?'

'Where did that come from?'

'Just checking.'

'Sure.'

'Do you still find me attractive?'

'Sure.'

'Can I be honest with you?'

'Sure.' He thought a second. 'I guess,' he added.

'Your breath stinks.'

Daniel stopped midchew.

'I don't know what you're eating, but you're like a dragon these days.'

Daniel swallowed.

'I just thought I'd share that with you.'

She picked up her dishes, deposited them into the sink, and walked out the door.

Daniel slumped in his chair and felt the despair of middle age crush down on him like a geriatric hippo. How could his wife so misunderstand him? Here he was killing himself to extend his life and she had absolutely no sympathy. Maybe Tina had a point. Maybe Jasmine was killing him. All that cream and butter. How can a man live like that? Day after day, rich, delicious food. Oh, the monotony of it.

Careme turned around in class. Again Roger's eyes flicked away from her. What a geek, she thought. Definitely a member of the unpopular group. She pointedly rolled her eyes at Lisa at the desk next to her and returned her perfect profile to the front. Still, she thought in a pique, she'd better be nice. He was the smartest in the class and he did have all the notes from last week when she and Lisa and Alessandra played hooky to see the mall fashion show. She turned around again. She gave him a sideways glance and a flicker of a smile, just enough to keep him on her fishing line.

When the bell rang she pretended to fuss with a button on her shirt, waiting for him to walk by, which she knew he would like she knew the sun would rise the following morning. Roger picked up his books and with a slight hesitation strode along her aisle. Just as he was brushing by, his shoulders ever so slightly touching hers, she lowered her voice a breathy notch and said, 'Hi.' He jerked to a stop.

'Hi.' His voice came out too loud, his mouth all teeth and pink gums. Careme winced. Still, she had her grade point average to think of.

'I missed last class.'

'Yeah,' he nodded, an eager elf.

'And I was wondering . . .'

'Sure.'

'Great.'

She held out her hand. He fumbled with his notebook and tore out the notes in three short jerks. Her hand clasped around them like a spider.

'That's really sweet of you.' She moved away quickly.

'Um . . . ,' he said. But she picked up her pace, aiming for the door and freedom.

'Ah . . . ,' he persisted, and tapped her lightly on the shoulder before snatching back his hand as if burned.

She didn't stop, but for appearance's sake she half turned her head.

'Would . . . would you like to see a movie?'

'God, I've seen them all,' she said wearily, and was through the door and gone.

Jasmine sat in CBS's greenroom splashing lukewarm tea over her dress and watching Miranda Lane on the in-house monitor push chunks of goat meat around a studio stove.

Miranda picked up the pan and dumped it to the side.

'People ask me, Japanese-Jamaica: What's the connection? I tell them, there isn't any. That's the point. You've got to free your mind. Make new connections. Plaintains with Soy Sauce. Why not? It's delicious. That's why my book *Jamaica Going Japanesa* is such a hit. You'll find great recipes breaking new ground.'

Miranda poured a measuring cup of fish sauce into a saucepan.

'Here we go, oops a daisy. Never worry about a spill. Just part of the fun. Whee.' She brushed at herself and handed the spoon to an assistant off camera.

'Will you finish up, please?'

The assistant pulled off her headset, strode onto the stage, and began stirring the sauce. Miranda ran her fingers through her hair. She wore a bright turquoise-blue Japanese-cut dress, the small, tight collar cutting into her neck like a garrote. A huge dragon on the front looked like it was trying to delve into her crotch.

'And here,' she snapped her fingers, 'is the finished dish.' The assistant placed the platter on Miranda's fingertips. 'Jerk Goat with Fish Sauce. Isn't it beautiful? And so delicious too. And, not one bite over twelve calories. Can you go wrong? I don't think so.'

She flashed a dazzling smile. The cameraman waved off. The producer yelled, 'That's it.' The smile evaporated like steam off manure.

The assistant poked her head into the greenroom. 'We're ready for you.'

Jasmine nodded and put down her tea with a shaking hand. She followed the assistant out to the television studio set. Jasmine tried to shield her eyes from the bright chrome gleaming in the television lights. The producer, a young late-twenty-something woman in an awfully severe black suit for seven o'clock in the morning, addressed Jasmine without looking up from her clipboard.

'OK, this is the deal. Talk fast but not too fast. Big smile. And don't zip around. Slow, steady moves. Rushing doesn't look good on camera.

'Remember, it's not about food. It's about entertainment.' She cracked what she thought looked like a smile. 'And don't worry. I'm here to make you look good.' She hollered. 'Jenny!'

The assistant arrived with her own clipboard and took Jasmine by the elbow.

'I've had everything you requested laid out. If you need anything else just yell. Everyone else does,' she muttered, as she led Jasmine to the kitchen counter where Miranda was still gathering her notes.

'You were great,' said Jasmine.

'Ah, yes,' agreed Miranda as she stepped away.

Jasmine sweated under the TV lights. A trickle ran down the valley of her back and drenched the elastic waistband of her support hose. She glanced at her watch. Three minutes to go and she would have a captive audience to which she could lend hope. She made a last sweeping glance of the TV cooking counter to make sure all was in order. A sauté pan, a baking dish, utensils lined up as neatly as dental equipment. She held out one of the six little dishes filled with chopped ingredients.

'Need more shallots here. Two tablespoons, not two teaspoons.'

Jenny, the assistant, grabbed the jar on the run much like a ball girl at Wimbledon and disappeared into the back kitchen where the actual cooking was being done. Her dish had been cooked to three different stages, sautéed, baked, then broiled to a mouth-watering crispy crust. This was live TV, no time for real time. Jasmine had insisted, however, on real food being prepared. No mashed potatoes masquerading as ice cream for her.

No, her audience was going to get the real thing — real cooking, real tips, a full culinary experience of staggering proportions. She just wished she could pop her freshly baked treats through the lens of the camera and feed the world.

'Ready?' Jenny prompted.

'Oh, yes,' answered Jasmine.

Jasmine smiled confidently as the camera-man counted down the last five seconds with his fingers. But as she wrenched her attention from his fingers to the camera every thought in her mind turned to fuzz. She stared like a kangaroo caught in headlights. Precious TV time was being spent televising Jasmine's large pores. The cameraman's frantic gymnastics at the camera's sidelines made not one iota of difference.

'Jasmine.'

A hand alighted on Jasmine's arm and clutched it like a falcon's talon. Jasmine woke up to her producer entering her TV space.

'Jasmine March is a widely acclaimed cookbook author.' The woman was chatting to the camera, fighting, Jasmine could tell, the urge to look down at her notes.

'Take it away,' she concluded, her smile headlining, I'll murder you later.

Talk, talk, talk, Jasmine's mind screamed. Jasmine's mouth cracked open.

'Hello, America.' She waited a second as if expecting America to shout back, 'Hello, Jasmine!' She smiled encouragingly into the camera and flung her right arm straight back as if introducing someone.

'This is a kitchen.'

The producer rolled up her eyes like a rolltop desk.

Jasmine walked closer to the camera and peered into the lens. She stood back and put her hand to her chin as if in deep thought. The producer was about to appear again to rescue her floundering show when Jasmine began to speak.

'How do you all like being treated like sheep?'

The cameraman hid a horrified smile.

'No, I'm serious. There you are sitting in front of the television. Half of you think Mc-Donald's deserves three stars. The other half can't even boil a pan of water. And yet there you sit day after day watching chefs prepare meals you'd never in a million years cook for yourself. Why are you watching?' Jasmine waved away her audience and turned her back on the camera. 'Turn off the TV. Get out of the house. Do something. Sheesh.'

Two assistants looked at each other — there's been a meltdown on the set.

Jasmine jerked her chin around to regard the camera again.

'And those of you who do know how to boil water, don't smirk. Because I bet true as I'm standing here, you're forking over hundreds of dollars to some chef who's convinced you that creating a beurre blanc is akin to creating one of Einstein's equations. Am I right? Here, let me show you something . . .'

She waved for the cameraman to follow her and returned to the studio stove and counter. She grabbed a couple of shallots which had been placed in a bowl for show. She began chopping. 'I'm going to show you how to make your own beurre blanc.'

She paused midchop and looked up. 'Yes, I know I have everything already chopped up.' She showed off the little bowls of already chopped ingredients. 'Cute, no? But if

I don't chop it myself, I lose track. So I'm going to start from scratch. Bear with me.'

She continued to chop in silence, her tongue pressed neatly between her teeth.

Jasmine looked up suddenly.

'You know what I can't stand? I can't stand people who stare at recipes as if they've been written in Czech. Who stand limp in the kitchen as if they've just walked into a surgeon's theater. Who cry, what the hell does "frappé" mean? I say get a life. Better yet, get a saucepan and add your shallots, your white wine vinegar, dry vermouth, and lemon juice. Place it over a high heat and stir.'

She grabbed a pan, tossed in her ingredients and began to stir.

'Gently, you're not playing the congas, for God's sake. You have to give it time. OK, now look, see how it's almost all evaporated? OK, now in goes the cream. Yes, full cream. If you touch it with that albino piss they call skim milk I'll hack off your hands. All right. Now stir again, medium heat this time, until it's thickened.'

Jasmine stirred, staring into the pan with full concentration.

'Add four sticks of butter.'

Jasmine added the butter. Again the minutes ticked away. The producer stifled a bloodcurdling scream with her fist. Jasmine gave a last stir.

'And that's it. Voilà, a beurre blanc.'

She wiped her hands and took off her apron. 'I was going to show you how to make Monkfish Wrapped in Bacon with Goat Cheese and Basil to go with your beurre blanc. But who am I kidding?'

She pulled out the three modes of dish, quarter done, half done, finished product. 'We all know you have no intention of making this dish, so let's have a little chat.' She swiped all the dishes to the side and hopped onto the counter. She stared into the camera lens again as if listening to it speak. She nodded her head as if she understood its pain. She took a breath and began.

'Can I ask you something? When did big eaters become the culinary equivalent of sexual deviants? You know what I'm talking about. You're in a café or a restaurant and you've just ordered a huge ice cream or brownie à la mode and you're about to tuck in when you see them. Across the way with their diet salads and their wholegrain, no-butter bread looking at you like you've taken off your clothes and are fiddling with yourself right in front of them. Am I right?

'What is it with people today? Everyone's defining themselves by what they don't eat.

"Oh, I don't eat meat." "Oh, I never touch fat." "Oh, I am lactose intolerant." Well, you know what? I am lactose-intolerants intolerant. When did food become about what it's not? No fat, no salt, no cholesterol, no preservatives, no nuts, no wheat. Food has become a substitute for politics. People aren't Democrats or conservatives or anarchists anymore. They're vegans or strictly organic or rabid food combiners.'

Jasmine wiped a bead of sweat from her brow.

'And you know the latest? Breatharian. They don't eat, period. My daughter's one. She looks like death.'

Jasmine stopped to take a long sip from her water glass. She nibbled absentmindedly from the monkfish platter.

'Eating now is like taking drugs,' she continued, delicately licking her fingers. 'I see them in the supermarket. They say, "I need a pound of vitamin A, I mean, tomatoes. And some magnesium, so how about throwing in some almonds. And let's see, I'm deficient in phosphorus. Got any good crab legs?" Now everything is protein and carbohydrates. "How many carbohydrates have you had today?" And "Damn, you're not going to eat that baked potato with the steak, are you?" And then they look at their watch. "You can't eat protein for another two hours!"

'What happened to the simmering of pork in honey and soy sauce and buttered fried onions? Or pan-frying juicy rib-eye steaks and serving 'em up with a big pat of garlic butter just 'cause it tastes heavenly? Or stuffing a baked potato with butter and blue cheese and crisp bacon and topping it off with a dollop of sour cream? And then eating it and savoring it and holding the taste in your mouth before swallowing and sighing and starting all over again?'

Jasmine grinned at the thought.

'Isn't it time we look at food again for what it is: sweet sustenance? Of the body and the soul. I say we give food a break. Stop laying such a trip on it. After all, it's not Jesus, it's not your therapist, it's not even your mother. It's just your dinner.'

The lights flicked off and Jasmine was left as drenched and agitated as a dunked chicken. Within seconds two strong arms held her in a lock, threatening to crack her windpipe. It was the producer, pressing her note board painfully into Jasmine's back.

'You were sensational. The phones are ringing off the hook. You are a hit!' She shadowboxed her. 'Albino piss. I nearly died laughing.

'Now,' said the producer, clicking back to business. 'We're going to want some copies of that book for our telethon, helps bring in subscriptions. Tell your publisher to send up a dozen, will ya?'

Oh, yes, Jasmine thought. That book. What was she going to do about that book?

She stopped on the way out to shake hands with the cameraman.

'Thank you for your help,' she said.

' 'S all right,' he said. His hand was still trembling.

Chapter Eleven

'Jasmine dahling, yes, that's it, chin to the left, fabulous. You're a natural. Now pout. Just for fun. See where it goes. We're having fun. Are you having fun? Great laugh, Jasmine. Love it. Love ya.'

The magazine photographer whirled around Jasmine with the lightness of an elf. Jasmine, bedecked in a new fire-engine red dress, took turns preening and looking embarrassed. For this particular article, it appeared they were marketing her as a fat sex goddess.

Daniel stood with his arms crossed at the back of their living room, which the photography crew had taken over. His wife, the celebrity. He still couldn't believe it. Her television spot had been such a success the TV telephone lines had broken down with the onslaught of phone calls clamoring for more. Women weeping with relief, men proposing marriage, *Time* magazine begging for an interview. When the TV producers had gathered around her in celebration, they'd been a little taken back when she finally admitted there was no new cookbook about toxins. A tight smile, a cough, then a wave of the hand. Well, they cried, toxins were so passé now anyway. They offered her her own show called *Tell It Like It Is, Jasmine*, which featured her ideas of food and fat. She now had her own personal makeup woman, a new wardrobe, and a chauffeur to whisk her to the studio.

Garrett, of course, had completely changed his tune and begged her to give him the manuscript of her masterpiece *Really Good Food*. Henry sold it instead to Doubleday and Daniel had stared at the check in wonderment. And now people everywhere were falling over themselves, straining to hear everything his wife said, laughing at her jokes, eyeing her when she passed by them in the street. Jasmine, who had never asked for anything more dramatic from life than a little kindness, was now star of the show. Even Missy Cooperman, the food editor, was calling, begging for articles. Daniel shook his head and smiled. He was proud of his wife. She had stuck to her guns and had won. He was happy for her. He was. But he couldn't resist it; sometimes a bubble of envy seared his blood like hot chili sauce.

Two large hands grabbed Daniel by the shoulders and eased him back further from the proceedings. The photographer's assistant was showing him the door. 'Could you give your wife a little space, please? That's it. Thank you. Another cappuccino, Jasmine?'

'The notes are back home,' Roger said. He was ready this time.

Careme's eyebrows knitted together in a perfect pout. She cocked her head, stumped.

'You could drop by for them after school,' he said. 'I live just down the block from you.'

Careme gave her tongue a good chew. If any of her group knew she was actually contemplating going to the house of one of the undesirables she would be drummed out. But she'd always been a stickler for good grades. 'OK,' she finally said.

'We could take the bus back together.'

Careme flinched. Roger knew he'd gone too far.

'Oh, no,' she said. 'Lisa drives me home.' He saw her pause a second, realizing the polite thing to do, the only really acceptable thing to do was to offer him a lift as well. He waited.

She blinked quickly, her beautiful brow overheating.

'And she . . . has to bring . . . a lot of stuff, and people and stuff back too. Not a lot of room . . . otherwise, you know . . .'

'So I'll see you back at my place.'

'Your place.'

'OK. See ya then.'

Careme gave him a sickly smile and Roger walked away feeling like a king. He was getting Careme March to come to his door, come into his house, his bedroom, his . . . Jesus, he thought, his mother better not be there.

'I can't believe how hard it was to get in touch with you. Who is that man who answers your phone?' asked Missy Cooperman as she settled back into the banquette at Galileo's, *the* Italian restaurant in town. Jasmine looked around in rapture. The last time she had seen the inside of this place was ten years ago when Daniel had splurged for her birthday. And that had been the present, no bauble, no scarf, no book, just four delicious courses at her favorite restaurant. So when Missy called begging for lunch, well, she just couldn't say no. Jasmine took a deep sniff of the heavenly scent coming from the restaurant's kitchen.

'You mean Daniel?'

'Well, he guards you like the Secret Service. I mean, I kept saying *The Washington Post. The Washington Post.* And he kept saying yes, I know, but she's still not available for two weeks. You should really have a talk with him. You have to be firm with these assistants.'

Jasmine stared at the handwritten menu, trying to decide between the white truffled quail and the sea bass with balsamic vinegar. She had had coffee, cake, and a plateful of cookies just an hour earlier at the radio station where they were now broadcasting her in a regular show, but she was still starving. The waiter sidled up and gave her a knowing smile.

'Signora March, what an honor it is to have you here.'

Jasmine hesitated. Or perhaps the beef Firenze for two? But before she could decide, Missy closed her menu with a snap. 'I'll have the salmon carpaccio. No olive oil. And she'll have,' she continued, nodding at Jasmine, 'the minestrone soup. Hold the croutons.'

She handed both menus back to the waiter, who stared at Jasmine in disbelief. Jasmine shrugged apologetically. Missy waited until he passed out of earshot.

'I'm doing a story about the place. Don't say a word. I'm incognito.' She shielded her face with her hand and took a sip of water. She moved the small, delicate complimentary Parmesan nibbles to the side of the table, out of the way, and leaned forward, all business .

'So let's hear your ideas.'

'Well, like I told you on the phone, Missy, I'm not sure my ideas . . .'

'Oh, stop being so modest. Just give 'em to me. I want your name top of the fold.'

'Well, in that case . . .'

Jasmine held up her hand to the waiter and pointed to the beef. He smiled and bowed. She reached forward, grabbed a handful of cheese nibbles and tossed one into her mouth.

'. . . I was thinking of doing an article about lard. Its history, its uses, its secrets.'

Missy blanched. 'That sounds nice,' she said weakly.

'We could have a sidebar on how it's good for you. The benefits of lard. A natural energizer. The wave of the future.'

'I see. Well, you would know.'

'And then, of course, lots of recipes: Lard Burgers, Lard Stew, Lard Ice Cream. And my favorite: Lard Cream Pies. They're covered pies filled with lard, whipped cream, peanut butter, and marshmallow. Delicious.'

Missy stared, unable to move.

Jasmine took a deep pull of her Barolo. She finally leaned over and patted Missy's hand. 'I'm kidding.'

'Oh.' Missy stared down at the notes she'd been taking and scratched them out. 'Of course you are. Ha. Ha. I knew that.'

Later, at the supermarket, Jasmine interviewed the lettuce, squeezing each head, ruffling their leaves, demanding of each one, what would you bring to my salad? A final jab with her thumb and she placed the lucky applicant into her basket. Really, the choice these days, she thought, is of a much inferior class. Now the tomatoes. She stared down at the mealy, pale orbs, all color leached from them. She palmed one in her hand and compared it to a rubber ball. Her salad was turning out to be a limp, tasteless mixture of lame textures. She stopped in her tracks and returned the vegetables to their ranks. She was not going to compromise.

Especially now that she had a public to serve. A hand pressed her shoulder.

'Excuse me,' the hand was attached to a young woman. Jasmine sized her up. Skinny. Hard cheekbones like the backs of tablespoons. Hair the color of smashed pumpkins.

'I noticed you were putting the tomatoes back.'

Jasmine eyed her suspiciously. Was she giving Jasmine a hard time? She'd seen young women like this before. So full of self-righteousness that they attacked everyone in sight. The kind who wanted to hand out black marks for every senseless thing you did that day: Ooh, came the impatient click of the tongue behind you as you reshoved your card back into the ATM, 'Don't you know how to work a cash machine?' Or 'That's the pickup line, this is the ordering line. Can't you read?' They were worse than meddling old women because they had more energy. They had the nerve to tell complete strangers how to live their lives. It was impulsive, uncontainable, completely beyond their control. They were Tourette's syndromes in miniskirts.

The girl scratched the side of her face nervously. 'They look so awful I was wondering if you knew whether I could use canned tomatoes instead.'

Jasmine raised an eyebrow. 'What are you cooking?'

'Stew. Beef.'

'Yes, you can. Plum tomatoes. A pound can will give you about seven tomatoes. Which equals one cup pulp.'

'Oh, thank you.'

Jasmine nodded, about to carry on, when

the hand caressed her shoulder again.

'You're Jasmine March, aren't you?'

Jasmine smiled involuntarily.

'God, I can't believe it! Jasmine March!' The young woman stuck out her hand to shake but Jasmine's hands were full so she clasped her own hand.

'Gosh. This sounds silly, but I was wondering if you did any private teaching.'

'No. I'm afraid not.'

'Or classes. That I could come to . . .'

'No.'

The woman waved her hand before her eyes as if one more second and she would faint at the horror of Jasmine's negative answers.

'It's my boyfriend, you see.'

'Hmm,' Jasmine murmured politely as she glanced at the cheese behind her, pondering maybe a little cheese course tonight. A little Brie. Maybe a St Nectaire . . .

'He won't marry me unless I learn to cook.'

Jasmine blinked back to the girl. 'Oh, honey,' she said.

'And I try. I really do. But he's so hard to please.'

'Maybe . . .'

'I know what you're going to say, get a new boyfriend. But I love him.'

The anguish in the girl's eyes touched Jasmine to the core. And really, was the man so unreasonable? Food, meals, dinner. It was the staff of life.

'What do you have to learn to cook?'

'I was thinking a stew.'

'Yes, a good choice.'

The girl watched Jasmine's eyes for a break. 'D . . . do you think he'd like that?'

'Oh, yes. Men love stews.'

The girl breathed a shaky sigh of relief, comforted that at least she was on the right track, even if she knew she couldn't deliver.

'You wouldn't have a couple of tips, would you? I know I shouldn't be doing this. I'm so sorry. You must get stopped all the time. I . . .'

Jasmine peered down at her watch. If she was going to get cooking she'd better get going. The decision seized her.

'I'm making one this afternoon. Why don't you come join me?'

The girl looked stunned, as if Jasmine had just offered her her left kidney.

'No. Really? Oh, no, you're so busy . . .'

'I insist.'

'Really?' The girl clasped her hands to her heart. 'Oh, would you? Really? Oh, God. That's . . . Oh, thanks so much. This is so great.' The girl jumped up and down, on legs longer than a high jump, Jasmine noticed.

Careme stood on Roger's doorstep, hopping from toe to toe.

'Come in,' he said, opening the door wide.

Careme quickly looked behind her, praying no one she knew could see her standing on Roger Johnson's doorstep. 'That's OK. I've got to get home. Study. You know.'

'They're upstairs.'

Roger left the door open as he ran up the stairs. Careme peered around the door and made a hesitant step into the hallway.

'Oh, man,' Roger cried, returning to the top of his stairs. 'You've got to see this.' He turned immediately away and disappeared.

'What?' Careme called, but Roger didn't answer.

Careme glanced around and, pulled by curiosity, stepped slowly up the stairs.

'In here,' he called from a room down the hall.

At the threshold, Careme beheld a teenage boy's bedroom: three posters of BMW motorcycles, two of Duke Ellington, and curiously, one of Henry VIII. The screen saver on his computer was a photo of an aborigine pissing on a tin can. Behind the door, Roger was peering down into a glass tank.

'Check it out, he's molting.'

A bright red snake with black stripes lay on a gravel bed. Its eyes were opaque, almost pearly. The skin around its head had loosened and was peeled back like tissue paper. Careme gave the snake a cursory glance.

'Mine molted last week,' she said.

Roger looked up in disbelief. 'You have a snake?'

'Mmmm.'

'What kind?'

'A reticulated python.'

'Wow, that's so . . . so cool.'

'My mom's making me get rid of it when it reaches three meters.'

'What's it now?'

'Two and a half. A couple more inches and it would be strong enough to strangle me in my sleep.'

'Cool.'

'And then I'm going to get a king snake. It eats rattlesnakes.'

'Yeah, that would be cool.'

'Yours is from the Colubridae family. Did you know that?'

'No.'

'It is.'

'Really?'

'Yes.'

Roger's mind worked quickly to provide his own bit of interest. 'A cobra can spit venom straight into the eyes of the victim. In India it kills over a hundred thousand people a year.'

'I heard ten thousand.'

'Maybe. But it's still a lot.'

Careme didn't respond. She just brushed the hair from her face in one long, flowing movement. She licked her lips and arched an eyebrow. 'Did you know a grass snake feigns death? One of its main lines of defense. Also from the Colubridae family. And you know, of course, about the glass snake.'

'Yeah.'

'What?'

'. . . I don't know.'

'It's a legless lizard.'

'Really?'

'Uh-huh.'

'What family?'

Careme hesitated, she didn't know. She looked at him coldly.

'I've got to go.'

Roger gazed at Careme with open wonderment. She was better than he thought. She held out her hand. He was about to clasp it when his brighter mind reminded him of her mission. He grabbed his notes from his desk and handed them over. She turned on her heel.

'It needs extra vitamin E right now. Good for the skin. I pierce a gelatin capsule and leave it on the leaf. See ya.'

And she was gone.

Roger fell back on his bed overwhelmed.

At home Jasmine unwrapped her package. Meat. Jasmine loved meat. She licked her lips at the luscious words: loin, leg of lamb, shoulder and butt, rump roast and brisket. Meat loaf, minced beef. Pork smothered in honey and thyme. Stewed rabbit. Pot roast. Ribs: Honolulu style with ginger, honey, and chili sauce; Texas short with brown sugar, ale, and hot green chili. And steak. Oh, yes, steak. A perfectly grilled porterhouse steak, lightly charred, red-pink and juicy, could leave Jasmine in salty thankful tears.

Jasmine had bought the meat at her local butcher's. She loved walking into that shop, the tangy smell of blood in the air, the red splatters on the butcher's white-wrapped belly, the unfortunate carcasses hanging from the meat hooks. Talk about survival of the fittest. Jasmine knew her place in the food chain. She would glance over the homemade sausages, plump and pink in their milky-white casings, admire the scarlet cuts of filet mignon, the shimmering garnet of a veal kidney. But this time she had gone for Daniel's birthday stew. A trial run. Two pounds prime venison, if you please.

Bert Gerry was the kind of butcher who knew what each of his beasts had for breakfast the day they died. He was a small man, tidy as a linen closet. He changed his apron at least three times a day. No portion was too small, no cut too difficult for Bert Gerry to handle. He was the consummate professional, precise, gracious, and entertaining. If there had been tables and chairs in his shop, Jasmine would have sat down for the afternoon, sipped a cappuccino, and watched.

'Two pounds for you, Mrs March.'

He always handed her the package as if he were offering her a tray of champagne, with a slight bow, hand behind his back. One afternoon, when she had asked for a special cut, he had given her a tour of the back room. There the bodies of cows hung from chains, covered with white fat, heads still attached, looking like ghosts. He chose one and with a huge electric saw buzzed downward between the legs to split the carcass into two. She had stood there, entranced, in a white coat with her hair in a plastic hair cap, fingering the canister piled high with deep-red beef hearts.

Jasmine now picked up the thick chunks of stew meat between her fingers and pressed lightly. They were juicy and springy. Perfect. If brought up before a judge, she thought, stews would have to plead malice. They take forethought, ingenuity, a ritualistic attitude. And a certain deftness with a knife.

Jasmine smiled at the young woman standing next to her. Nothing pleased her more than to help a young couple in love. Ah, yes, food and love. So entwined, so well mated. Jasmine gave the woman a quick side glance. Her name, she'd learned, was Tina. An actress. Nice looking. A nice girl too. Pity about the boyfriend. Really, the things girls put up with these days. Still, the girl seemed to have never seen the inside of a kitchen before.

'Oooh,' Tina said, 'what a nice stove. Look, it's got four burners *and* a grill.

'Oooh, aren't these cute,' she said, waving Jasmine's many varied whisks in the air. Jasmine retrieved her whisks. The girl dug into her large bag and pulled out a microphone. She balanced it against the scales.

'I have to tape. Can't remember a thing.'

Jasmine returned to her cooking position. Tummy against the counter, feet a salmon-width apart, knees loose. Tina leaned against the counter backward on her elbows, looking like she was trying to pick someone up.

'OK,' said Jasmine, 'you start with the chopping of the meat.'

Tina nudged the microphone closer.

'Now they have to be uniform. I suggest about the size of a marshmallow.'

'Marshmallow,' Tina repeated.

'Now in browning you don't want to put too many in the pan at once. You don't want them to steam.'

'I don't?'

'No, you want them to sauté.'

'Sauté, not steam,' Tina murmured into the microphone.

The way she said it, Jasmine wondered if she was going to look up *sauté* and *steam* in the dictionary later.

'Yes, you want them nice and caramelized.' Jasmine's mouth salivated spontaneously at the rich meat searing. She gazed down at the pan with utter devotion. She browned and turned with exemplary Zen concentration, shaking the pan in between to loosen the chunks of meat. She fussed over them like a grandmother. And then, when she ascertained their perfect doneness, she scooped them from the fire and laid them gently on a paper napkin. From the corner of her eye she noticed Tina stifle a yawn.

'Now the onions,' she said. Jasmine's hand hovered over her selection of knives a fraction of a second. She then pulled out her double-handled mezzaluna. Tina spied the array of photos stuck to the refrigerator. She leaned forward.

'Is that your daughter?'

'Yes.'

'She's pretty.'

'Sometimes.'

'And your husband.'

Chop, chop, chop. Jasmine splayed the onion against the cutting board. Tina sucked in her breath. The onion lay emasculated, cut tightly into short, thin sticks. The onion juice wafted up and stung Tina's eyes. Jasmine shoved the cutting board toward her.

'Here. You add them to the pan.'

Tina looked around helplessly.

'Just use your hands.'

Tina stared down with ill-concealed horror.

'Touch them?'

With a delicate pair of fingers Tina nudged the onion sticks one by one into the pan. At the first sizzle, she backed away like a hostage, her hands still in the air. Jasmine wiped her greasy hands on her apron and pulled open her pantry door.

'Wine?' Jasmine offered.

'Oh, I don't want to be any trouble.'

'No trouble.'

Tina perched herself on the bar stool away from the stove and abandoned herself to hospitality. She swung her long leg back and forth, carefree, as if she were at a tiki hut in Bali. Jasmine had half a mind to shove a paper umbrella into her merlot.

Tina dug deep with the paper towel to remove the imagined onion grime from under her fingernails. 'This is so nice of you to help me.'

'My pleasure.' Jasmine pulled out a chicken neck from her refrigerator.

'Oooh.' Tina leaned back.

'I'm going to add it to this water and red wine mixture to increase the flavor and then pour it over the stew. It's the name of the game, adding flavor.'

Tina nodded, her eyes avoiding the limp neck dangling from Jasmine's hand. She swirled the blood-red wine in her glass.

Jasmine lifted her own glass and toasted the young woman. 'There's no sight on earth more appealing than that of a woman making dinner for someone she loves.'

'You got that right,' Tina said, taking a big gulp.

'Thomas Wolfe said that. Must have been a real gourmet.'

'My boyfriend is a real gourmet. Won't leave his wife till I learn how to cook.'

The neck of the chicken bones cracked under Jasmine's pressure. She stopped to stare at Tina.

'He's married?'

'Yup.'

'Kids?'

'One. Teenager.' Tina lifted the back of her hair to cool her neck, stretching her large bust high. She gazed at her boobs appreciatively. 'Of course I don't think of him as someone's husband.'

Jasmine tossed the broken chicken neck into a pan.

'How convenient.'

'Maybe because he doesn't mention his wife.'

'That would be a mood breaker, I imagine.'

Tina hunched her shoulders one by one to release the tension in her neck. 'Not as much as you think. What we have is very strong.'

'What they have is a child.'

'Almost grown.'

'I wouldn't call a teenager grown. They're more mature at three.'

Jasmine shook the sautéed cubes into a stew pot and added the onions. She doused it with a good shake of red wine vinegar and a handful of crushed juniper berries and tucked the pot into the oven.

'Lesson over,' Jasmine said.

'Fine.'

Jasmine surveyed the young tart with her hands on her hips. Tina stood by the counter and fussed with the crease in her pants. She hiked her huge bag over her shoulder.

'Thanks for the wine.'

'You forgot something,' Jasmine said.

Tina turned back.

In one smooth motion Jasmine swung open the refrigerator and pulled out a can of whipped cream. She, of course, never used the stuff, but Careme, in a fit of culinary disloyalty and rebellion, had insisted on bringing the sacrilege into the house and had stashed it in the refrigerator where it had stayed, unused, until now. Jasmine pointed it at Tina and pressed down the button for all she was worth. The cream flung itself over Tina, dolloping her in soft white peaks.

Tina screamed. She clawed at her face to wipe the foam away from her eyes.

Jasmine tapped at the canister as if astonished. 'Gosh, I'm sorry. This thing has a mind of its own.'

'What are you doing?' The masculine

tone was unmistakable. They both looked up. Daniel stood at the door.

'Oh, Daniel,' Tina whimpered.

Oh Daniel stood speechless at the sight. The two women in his life, drenched and spitting. It was a delicate moment.

'What happened?' he said, trying to address the room in general, as if hoping perhaps the pots and pans would have a solid explanation.

Tina rushed into his arms. It was horrible, just horrible, she cried, sobbing onto his shoulder, unaware, or was she, of the exchange of looks flying over her heaving shoulder.

Daniel's arms remained at his side, so Tina burrowed closer, hip to hip, nudging, bruising, until Daniel finally clasped her by the waist to pull her off. She let go reluctantly and stood hunched and mewling in front of him, blocking out the vision of Jasmine, for which Daniel was grateful until Jasmine dislocated Tina with a shove and stood large in front of him.

'Oh, Daniel?' she said.

Chapter Twelve

'What the hell were you doing?'

Tina grinned and bit into her bacon, avocado, and blue cheese club with relish.

'Pretty fancy footwork,' she said, blue cheese crumbling on her lips.

Daniel took another gulp of coffee to ease his frazzled nerves. His forehead was a mop of sweat. He had seen his whole life collapse when he had walked into that kitchen. He had looked into his wife's eyes and seen the abyss. His stomach had lurched with the violence of that knowledge. With the fear. He had put it all up for ransom. His marriage, his wife, his daughter. For what? This protein-scarfing vixen.

'This can't go on.'

'This can't go on,' Tina mimicked him. 'You sound like a bad radio drama.'

She picked an insufficiently chewed wafer of bacon from her mouth, examined it, and then tried again.

Daniel looked away. 'You wanted to break us up.'

'No, I wanted to learn how to cook.'

'From my wife? The reigning queen of clogged arteries?'

'I was just going to replace all the fat with Pam and all the carbs with egg whites. It would have been delicious. But your wife went schizoid on me.'

'You were going to replace the butter with Pam?'

'Yeah.'

'And you think it would have tasted as good?'

'Honey, you can't taste the difference. Says so on the can. I eat all my rice cakes with it. One spray of Pam. Mmmm. Deelish.'

Daniel put down his coffee. She was worse than he thought. He glanced around for anyone he knew. What a vision they must make, a man with sweat dripping from his forehead like a hose leak and a young, expertly made-up woman with whipped cream on her head. Luckily, Kramer Books was quiet at this time of day, gearing up for the evening onslaught of hopeful singles bumping into each other in the self-help aisles. Tina pulled the menu toward her and flipped to the desserts. The whole affair seemed to have whetted her appetite. Daniel jerked the menu from her and slapped it on the table.

'We can't do this anymore.'

'OK, fine.' Tina shrugged, picking at the crumbs on her plate with an apricot-colored fingernail. She brought the crumbs to her mouth and sucked. She looked up at him with her finger in her mouth, sucking. He stared at her sucking lips.

'I mean it.'

She smiled.

'Are you done?' he said. It came out in a croak.

'Uh-huh.'

He propelled her toward the door and back to her apartment, his hand placed the entire way proprietarily on her ass.

How close to death we are, thought Jasmine as she stood alone in a trance in her kitchen. She'd never touched a person in anger before. What strength in hands. She examined her long fingers. Her nails ragged from near misses of the knife and grater, stained around the cuticle from gravy and red wine. Her gold ring dulled by salt and continuous scrubbing. She had read once that of all the professions it was cooking that contained the most murderers. Why was that? More tools at hand? An ease with dismembered anatomies? Or just an intrinsic reliance on death for a successful outcome?

263

She looked around the room. A torture chamber, really. Instruments hanging in waiting. The knives, of course, but also the less obvious: meat thermometers, rind peelers, blenders. Cooks had to have an ease with skinning vegetables and fruits, dismembering dumb and often barely dead animals, then gathering their precious blood in a saucepan with the one-mindedness of a witch. Cooking, after all, was a heartless endeavor. Better your life than mine. Very few prayers were said anymore over the body of the brave beast. Now cooks were more likely to poke and prod and turn up their noses at its offending layer of, well, until recently, life-preserving fat. Diners now pushed morsels of someone's leg or buttocks discontentedly around their plates. Worse, they tossed their uneaten death into the waste bin. Because, after all, to give life is to murder. Or is that too harsh? Certainly to cook is to instigate murder. Something. Someone.

Jasmine pulled out the bean salad she had made yesterday, when she had carefully roasted the red peppers and crisped the bacon before mixing them in with cannelloni beans and a mustard vinaigrette. She didn't bother with a plate, just picked up a fork and dug in. The oil and salt of the bacon revived her. She took another bite, poking around for a large sliver of red pepper to marry with the rest. It slithered satisfyingly down her throat, earthy and rich. The oil began to gather in a large drop at the end of her chin and still she kept eating, methodically, almost in a trance, her concentration complete on the many varied flavors in her mouth. She reached for her pepper mill and then a bit guiltily for the salt shaker. It wasn't necessary, she knew, but her state of mind required overindulgence of every kind. She brought the well-salted beans to her mouth and chewed, swirling the gooey nuggets around her tongue with satisfaction. As the bottom of her bowl drew near, covered in a thick inch of oil, the front door slammed and Careme sauntered into the kitchen. Jasmine ignored her and dug into the last three beans, anchoring them down with her finger to foil their escape.

'What's this mess?'

'Ask your father.'

'Where is he?'

'I have no idea.'

Careme was silent, her teenage mind whirring.

'You ate that whole thing?'

'Oh, I'm sorry, did you want some?'

'Yeah, right.'

Jasmine stared dully down at her bowl.

'You've got grease on your chin,' her daughter informed her.

'I'd like to be alone now, if you don't mind.'

Careme clicked with her tongue her disgust, her exasperation, her complete disinterest, and dripped out of the kitchen. Jasmine finally raised her hand to dab at the oil at her chin. But instead of wiping it off she began smearing it upward toward her cheeks. She reached into the bowl for more oil, splatting it on her face and creaming it in wide circles. She let it drip onto her chest and then dribbled it between her breasts. Her T-shirt darkened with the oil but she continued, dabbing it behind her ears as if it were perfume. She then leaned forward and lapped at what was left like a cat. As the last film of grease slipped down her throat, she leaned back and gave a huge, variegated burp.

'Mom!' Careme exclaimed, horrified, from the next room.

Jasmine put down the bowl. She took off her apron. She pushed a carton of eggs off the counter. She poured a carton of milk over the cracked yolky mess as if the floor were a bowl of cereal. She turned off the stove. She unhooked the refrigerator. She wiped her hands on the towel and let it float to the floor as she walked out of the kitchen.

Upstairs she shrugged off her sweater, shimmied out of her pants. She dropped her bra to the floor and slid under the cool sheets. She piled an extra duvet on top of the blanket and squirmed until she was warm. She turned and lay on her side like a fetus and closed her eyes. That was it. She planned to sleep for the rest of her life.

Later, Daniel tiptoed out after rearranging the duvet over Jasmine's bulk.

He had taken a while to return home, he said, because he had taken the girl for a cup of coffee to explain the situation. And then wouldn't you know it, he was on his way home when he remembered they had blocked off Key Bridge. Haven't they been working on that thing forever? Anyway, he had to go right around, over Wilson, added, what, another half hour? Jesus.

Daniel had sat down and stroked Jasmine's hair. He had told her that this Tina was not an actress but one of his students, a secretary trying to be an actress, and that in his opinion she should hang it up. Too old. But you know how actresses can be, he had said, holding Jasmine's hands tightly. Their small sliver of reality. And he hadn't wanted to say anything. He hadn't wanted Jasmine to worry. But this one. Well, this one had taken a bit of a liking to him. He thought he could ignore it. He had tried. But he didn't think they should press charges. Did she? It was up to her, of course. Though the woman didn't do anything. Except watch Jasmine cook. And wasn't it Jasmine who attacked her?

But it was Jasmine's decision. Whatever she wanted to do. He would drop the girl from the course. That went without saying. If he could. At least he hoped he could. There might be legal ramifications. Anyway, they would sort it out. How was she feeling? Any better? What a shock. Yes, what a shock it must have been. But it was all better now. Now she must sleep. Sleep. It would all feel better in the morning.

'Love you,' he had whispered.

She did not respond.

Jasmine wondered what too old was. Late twenties? Mid-thirties? Acting was a cut-throat business. She was happy her ambitions had never lain there. She felt sorry for the poor thing. Trying to catch a break. She wondered if the young woman had a family to support her, to help ease the rejections. Or whether she was one of those haggard beings who had to support themselves in dead-end day jobs before finally giving up and taking the promotion to office manager, which would give them better benefits, more responsibility, and a chance at a solid credit rating. It was so sad really. Daniel was right. What a shock it had been. And she knew just what she had to do about it.

Careme knew it was her fault. She shouldn't have told Roger she had a snake. She shouldn't have admitted they had something in common. That's what Lisa always drilled into her, 'Never give the masses an inch'. Still it was pretty cool he had a snake. None of her friends did. In fact, Lisa always raised her eyebrow at Medea, giving Careme the distinct idea that snake ownership was *très* white trash.

Careme clicked impatiently at the phone.

'OK,' she finally said. 'I can come over for about ten minutes. I've got lots of homework to do.'

'Great, thanks,' Roger said.

When she arrived, Roger was waiting in his coolest Gap shirt and black jeans. He led her up to his bedroom again like a worried parent.

'I don't know what's going on. He's turning all these weird colors.'

'What kind of colors?'

'Red, green. Some yellow stripes.'

'Really?'

Careme leaned over the cage and peered in. She let out a bark of laughter. The snake was covered with stripes and dots of different colored Post-it notes. Careme picked off the Post-its and patted the snake maternally.

'There, there,' she said, 'all better now.'

Roger batted his forehead in fake amazement. 'Wow, you're an amazing doctor. Have you thought of veterinarian school?'

Careme shook her head, grinning wide.

'Have you had dinner?'

Careme's smile disappeared.

'Come on, I just want to talk. Talk about snakes and stuff.'

'I'm not hungry.'

'OK, you talk, I'll eat.'

She looked at her watch.

'Come on,' he pleaded. 'I've never met a girl who had a snake before.'

Careme was silent, flattered. But Roger took it as rejection and went on the attack.

'You scared what your friend Lisa is going to say?'

'No!'

'I hope not. She's got the biggest mouth in the Mid-Atlantic area.'

'She doesn't have a big mouth.'

'Oh, please. Nothing is sacred with that girl. Nothing. She does better press than her mother.'

'Stop it.'

'Everybody heard what you did to Alessandra.'

Careme flushed. 'I thought it was a good idea.'

'You did?'

'Well, I just didn't want to not do anything. You know, so many people, they just look away when someone's being weird or sick or something. And they pretend it's not happening. And I didn't think that was right.'

Roger shrugged. She had a point. He looked down at his feet, a bit shamefaced. 'I guess you don't want to stay now.'

'No. I mean, no, I do. Sure. You know, for a little bit.' Careme suddenly didn't want to leave. She felt relieved to finally talk about something other than clothes or boys or what position everyone's father had.

'Come on then.'

In the kitchen, Roger pulled out a vanilla Slim-Fast shake. He poured it into a tall frosted glass, topped it with an umbrella, and set it before her.

'Oh,' Careme said.

From the oven, he drew forth a four-cheese Lean Cuisine lasagna, bubbling hot and bursting with creamy cheese and only 267 calories. Careme caught her breath. Roger waggled his eyebrows like a comic and set down a lightly tossed salad of iceberg, thinly sliced radishes, and shredded no-fat, no-salt American cheese. Careme placed her hand at her throat and stared down at the food, speechless.

For himself, Roger extracted from the same oven a medium-size pepperoni and cheese Stouffer's pizza. With a tall glass of Coke in hand he sat down before the stunned Careme and dug in with gusto. He nodded toward her meal. 'I hope you like it,' he said. She nodded, almost touched to tears. She gazed over her 275 calories at Roger and smiled. Roger nodded and smiled back. He was in like Flynn.

The doorbell rang. Tina glanced at her watch. Back already? The guy's insatiable. She padded down the hall, shooing Sugar-free, who tangled herself between her legs.

'Who is it?'

'Jasmine March.'

Tina stopped dead in her tracks.

'Hello?' Jasmine prompted.

'Just a minute.' Tina raced back to her bedroom and threw off her sweats and T-shirt, skimming into a flowing silk robe. She shook her hair free. She wanted to rub the woman's nose in it.

On the doorstep stood her . . . well, she would say competition, but the old goat wasn't actually up to the job, was she?

'What do you want?'

'I'd like to speak with you.'

'Now?'

Jasmine said nothing.

'Look, I'm very busy. I've got an audition . . .'

'Won't take a minute.'

Tina stumbled back as Jasmine breezed by. In the apartment Sugarfree came racing around the corner in full yap, her little claws clicking on the hardwood floor. Jasmine neatly stepped back so that when the terrier jumped up it fell forward onto its nose. She turned to face Tina and smiled sweet as icing.

'I'd love some coffee.'

'You're kidding.'

'Can't have a girls' chat without coffee.'

Jasmine followed Tina into her kitchen. As Tina fumbled about with a cup and coffee, Jasmine's hands found the Ajax and a rag and began to wipe down the counters. After a few swipes she washed out the grimy cloth at the sink and undertook a thorough scrubbing behind the faucet, her cloth picking up months of dead vegetable and juice bits. She shook them expertly into the sink and rinsed the cloth out again. Tina watched mesmerized, Jasmine's coffee cooling in her hand.

'As you can imagine, I was pretty angry,' said Jasmine.

Tina smiled smugly.

'And when Daniel said you were too old . . .'

'What . . . ?'

'. . . I wondered what too old was. Acting is a cutthroat business. Here you are trying to catch a break. What pressure it must be to wake up and see every new wrinkle and watch your marketability take a nose dive. Wasting hours in classes and rehearsals. Before finally giving up. I've seen it happen a million times. Have you thought about applying for office manager?'

'Listen, lady . . .'

'Ooh, you have to be careful with mildew, dear. Once it starts the next thing you know you've got rats in the cupboards. Have you ever been married?'

Tina stared with horror at her cupboards.

'It's a strange thing, marriage. You think that it's everything. That if only you could get hitched it would make everything seem right. So you wait and scheme and shave your legs religiously until finally you're married. But suddenly you're in a whole new game. Like a computer game. Only it's the next stage up times a hundred. And all the enemies are coming at you from all directions. They come so slow you don't see them. And that's the trick. You have to be able to see the movement of an invisible snail, because as it moves toward you it's eating grass and crap off the ground and growing bigger and bigger until you look up one day and you've got this huge gelatinous sticky smelly bag of slug in your living room. Or in my case, kitchen.'

'I'm not looking to marry your husband.'

Jasmine peered at her closely 'Really? Why not?'

'Why are you cleaning my kitchen?'

Jasmine stared down in surprise at her cleaning hands.

'It's filthy.'

'I think it's time for you to leave.'

Tina strode to her front door and opened it.

'I couldn't bear the thought of you sitting here alone.' Jasmine stood at the kitchen door. 'You see,' she said, 'I know about obsessions.'

Tina took in the plump middle-aged

woman in her kitchen with the rag in her hands and laughed.

'I think you should go back to your husband. He must be wondering where his little hausfrau has gone.'

Jasmine poured a mountain of soap on the rag and started on the stove rings. 'Daniel's my obsession. Been so since I met him. He's what they call a taker. You name it, he takes it. And I give it. And together we're a perfect pair. When we first were sleeping together, I'd get this overwhelming feeling. It would start in my belly and it would spread. I nearly crashed once just thinking about him. I had to ban myself in the car. I think it was his perfect row of upper teeth. The bottom aren't so great. But the top teeth, they look like they were put into his gums by a master craftsman. You must think I'm crazy, but I've got a thing about teeth. Anyway, the point is, you shouldn't make someone else your obsession. It ends up all wrong. I mean, in the end, who can live up to an obsession? You got to find something that doesn't talk and doesn't have the ability to say no to you. Like food. Food never says no. It says yes. It says more. But a person. A man. Recipe for disaster.'

'Why are you telling me this?'

Jasmine paused to rinse out petrified spaghetti crud.

'Well,' she finally said, 'you seem like a nice girl and I don't want you wasting your time on someone who's not interested in you.'

'Your husband and I have been fucking regularly for the last three weeks.'

'Have you talked to anyone about this fantasy?'

'He's got a thing about ears. Chews on mine like they're some kind of appetizer.'

Jasmine dropped the rag. She swayed back against the counter. Tina stepped forward to try to steady her. 'Look, why don't you sit down?'

Jasmine wrenched her hand away. 'When, where?'

'Sit.'

'Here?' She slapped the counter. 'Like in that movie.' She grabbed a knife from its rack and began pounding on the counter.

Tina backed away from the flailing knife.

Jasmine brushed by her and strode down the hall to the bedroom. She flung open the door and stood next to the futon, gazing down as if Daniel were still there but the size of a gnat which she had to discern from the flowered pattern on the duvet.

Tina stood at the door and watched her.

Jasmine looked large and cumbersome in the feline room.

'It didn't mean anything to you that he was married?'

Tina shrugged. 'What am I, the marriage police?'

'I never did it. Oh, I got offers, but you know what I thought? I always thought that if it happened to me and I had slept with a married man I couldn't really get good and mad. And that's what you want to be able to do, get really good and mad.'

'That's a stupid reason.'

'Is it?'

Jasmine brushed past Tina out to the hall. Tina hurried after her.

'My knife,' she called.

Jasmine gazed down at the knife, weighing it in her hand.

'This is an expensive knife. It must have been a gift. Am I right?'

'Maybe.'

'It can chop, slice, core, and, if I press really hard, it will crack through bones. You should sharpen it every day. You have to start at the base and work in long, smooth movements. The key is quick and often. Keeps it sharp.'

Jasmine leaned forward to show her the knife's point.

'What are you going to do, kill me with it?' Tina snorted.

Jasmine laughed. 'Oh, God, no. Killing is the easy part. I could hit you on the head, run you over, I could drown you, push you off a cliff . . . No, the hard part is disposing of the body. Because with no body, no conviction.'

Jasmine slipped the knife into her bag and walked out the door. 'That's what I'd use the knife for.'

Jasmine sat in her car in front of Tina's apartment and beat herself up. How could she have been so stupid? So blind. What an idiot she was. What a cliché. She rested her head on the steering wheel. He nibbled on that tramp's ears. He had nibbled and chewed and sucked that tramp's ears. And all this time she had thought it was her ears that drove him wild. Her clean, moisturized, beautiful ears. Jasmine cupped her hands over them protectively. Oh, the time she had taken with them once she realized what turned him on. And now they had been replaced.

She slumped in her seat and thought about the smug, slim young woman she'd just left. How Daniel had kissed her, had fondled her, had . . . Jasmine scrunched her eyes shut.

The very thought stabbed her in the gut. Her bones felt weak. A dark moon rose in her sky and her whole world was plunged in loneliness. Oh, God, she thought, he wasn't going to leave her for that woman, was he? Jasmine sat very still as the thought passed through her chilled body.

Then a new thought flashed its edge. Careme. Oh, Careme. What would she say to Careme?

Jasmine brought down her hand on the horn and leaned. The violent screech sounded like a sorrowful elephant. She finally flung herself back exhausted. Well, she was damned if she was going to let that tramp make her daughter's life, as unpleasant as she could be, one iota more unpleasant. She was not going to let her turn her daughter into a statistic. She was not going to have her daughter's emotional life ruined by this. She was a pain in the ass, her daughter, but she was a secure pain in the ass and in two more years she would be out of adolescence and she would be sane again, human again, and they could be friends again. Jasmine could see the future. Her daughter would come home from college and they would go shopping and have frozen yogurt and Careme would tell her about all the impossible course hours she had and the weird kids and all about her dorm and Jasmine would listen, spooning her chocolate/vanilla swirl into her mouth and never letting her gaze fall from her daughter's eyes.

But if Tina had her way, Careme would be pushed into a grownup world she wasn't ready for yet. She would internalize the idea that a man could grow tired of her, discard her. She would approach boys with world-weary eyes, with claws sharpened like a tomcat, with a jagged sexuality. Their trips to the mall would be full of silences, full of disclosures, Careme knowing things about her father and his new love that Jasmine didn't know. Their talks would be faulty and evasive and silent.

She clutched at her chest. The affair had to be stopped. Something had to be done. Something drastic, something final. But first, before anything, she needed . . . fries. Yes, fries. McDonald's fries. No other fry would do. Not even her own. She needed greasy, salty, blistering fries. She envisioned shaking out her large order over her tray and then grabbing the fries, three, four at a time, dipping them into the ketchup which she had swirled on the paper tray lining in a mad Jackson Pollock and stuffing them into her mouth. Never just one fry at a time, it had to be at least four, best five, so that her mouth could champ down in a hot, salt crunch and then suck the smooth potatoey mash. Jasmine was always methodical, concentrating solely on salt and grease and the divinity of fries.

Jasmine drove straight to the nearest McDonald's and parked askew. She ran in, rushed up to the counter, and said in a loud, firm voice, 'Two jumbo fries, please.'

The pimply girl with the EMPLOYEE OF THE MONTH button on her bulging breast clicked in the order and looked up.

'Would you like an apple pie with that today?'

'No,' said Jasmine.

'How about a drink today?'

'No.'

'Burger?'

'No.'

'Salad?'

'No.'

Click, click. 'That will be four-oh-eight.' The cashier removed a carton from the conical stack protruding from the wall and approached the great fryer where the short, thin fries glistened with oil and salt. She reached down and scooped the fries with two short, expert jerks. Jasmine eyed her, willing her to dig further, longer for just that extra fry. She watched disappointed as two fries dropped back to the fryer when the cashier placed the carton on Jasmine's tray.

Jasmine leaned forward. 'There were two that got away.'

'Excuse me?'

'Two. See. They fell when you lifted it. Can you put them in?'

The girl looked back at the fryer.

'See. Next to the rim.'

The girl stared back at Jasmine.

'Am I not speaking English? There were two fries that fell out when you scooped. Can you put them back in?'

The girl nudged her supervisor. The supervisor with small eyes set on a fast-food career path turned his attention from the till to Jasmine.

'Can I help you?'

'I just want the two fries.'

'What two fries?'

'The ones that were in my container but fell off when she scooped.'

'They fell off.'

'Yes.'

'A lot of fries fall off when we scoop.'

'I'm sure they do. But you see, they looked especially tasty.'

'Are you trying to give my employee a hard time?'

'No. I just want . . .'

'Because we have a policy against that. See?'

He pointed to a plaque. VIOLENCE WILL NOT BE TOLERATED.

'I'm not about to hit anyone for two fries. But if you wouldn't mind . . .'

'Could you step away from the counter, ma'am?'

'What?'

'I said step away from the counter.'

He tipped his chin down toward his chest and murmured into his clip-on mike.

'Decon at f-con. Decon at f-con.'

'You've got to be kidding me.'

'That's affirmative. Aggressive white female with large bag. Need backup. Do you read me?' He held out his hand to her. 'Ma'am you're going to have to hand over that handbag.'

Jasmine turned the color of Styrofoam.

When Daniel finally arrived at the police station, Jasmine was sitting on a visitor's bench, staring down at her shoes, her hands neatly cupped around her purse. She said nothing as Daniel signed her out. Nor when he escorted her elbow out the door. Nor when she sat in the car beside him. She stared straight ahead like a pious sphinx. The traffic was thick as they drove from

Arlington back into Georgetown and they had to sit through several light turns on Key Bridge. Jasmine gazed out the window down the Potomac River.

It was thirty-five degrees outside and yet Daniel's upper lip was slicked with sweat. He jammed repeatedly on the brakes and glanced over at the back of Jasmine's head. His tongue scraped like sandpaper against the roof of his mouth.

'Look, Jasmine . . .'

'How many times?'

'How many times what?'

She turned to face him, her eyes cold. His eyes flicked back to the windshield and its crust of broken and gutted flies.

'Not that many.'

She presented the back of her head again. The car in front of them jerked to a halt again and Daniel slammed on the brakes.

'Asshole.'

'You found her attractive?'

Daniel didn't answer, just leaned on his horn. Jasmine stared out the window and shook her head in disbelief.

'Why is skinny so attractive? It just means less of her is there. Is that why you wanted to sleep with her? Because she takes up less space? What kind of reason is that? Is that why everyone is dieting? They're thinking, hey, baby, you're gonna want me bad because I am compact. I am an environmentally friendly human being. And when you've used me up, you can toss me in a landfill. And guess what? I take up less space. Biodegradable too. See? Says so on my tag. Whereas this model here,' Jasmine points to herself. 'Look how big she is. They sure didn't worry about space when she was being made. Heavens, better throw that one on the scrap heap.'

'I didn't throw you on the scrap heap.'

'That's right. You kept me. Anyone would think you had a two-car garage.'

Jasmine examined Daniel's impassive profile.

'I thought we had something.'

'We do,' Daniel whispered.

'What? What do we have?'

'We have Careme.'

'Is that all? Is that all that's tying us together?'

'No.'

'What else?'

Daniel was silent.

Jasmine held her breath and then finally released it as if letting go of all her hope.

'You're going to have to leave.'

'Never again, Jasmine.'

Jasmine folded her arms and stared out at

the impending rain. 'Do you know how hard it is to love someone when they no longer want it? Every morning hoping that today, maybe today you'll smile at me like you used to. Kiss me like you used to . . .'

'Please, Jasmine.'

'Well, think of yourself in my shoes. Would you have it any other way?'

'No, Jasmine . . .'

'You can stay until your birthday. Careme has been looking forward to it. So let's have one last happy birthday. Happy, happy birthday . . .'

The driver in front flicked on his hazard lights and jumped out of his car.

'What the hell are you doing?' Daniel bellowed out the window.

The man flipped him off as he strode across the other side of the road and made for the end of the bridge. Daniel jerked around his seat like a trapped animal. He glared behind him at the car jammed up against his rear, where a woman stabbed at her horn in frustration. Daniel shoved open the car door, nearly getting it taken off when the lane next to them suddenly began to move. He pulled at the locked door of the car in front of them. He then rocked the whole car back and forth, back and forth like a cradle. Jasmine settled back to watch, the meltdown of her husband in harmony with the meltdown of her heart.

So this was what it all came down to, Jasmine thought as she stepped into their home. She dropped her purse on the chair in the hallway and without a word to Daniel made her way upstairs. He tried to follow her but she closed the bedroom door in his face.

She looked about the room and took a deep breath. So. Her husband was having an affair. He had been having sexual intercourse with another woman. Jasmine, who knew each nook and cranny of that forty-year-old body and who had lovingly catered to its every need since she first met him seventeen years ago, had been replaced. Well, that was life. Now Jasmine was about to enter a new phase. Just as that woman said . . . what was her name, big-bucks author, something about passages . . . no matter. It was just another passage. Birth, marriage, indifference, death. She must enter each one as gracefully as possible.

She stripped to bare skin and crawled between the sheets of her bed. She lay back and thought about love. Such a weathered thing, love. Battered and bruised. Maligned. Did it gain a patina? Did it intensify the longer it was on the fire? Did it even exist?

After all, weren't they all just animals? Wasn't love just another word for survival of the fittest? Maybe it was just the by-product, the fallout of competition. Love certainly propelled you to do things that you wouldn't otherwise do. Was love need? She didn't really need her husband. Because after all, Daniel wasn't as rich and warm and delicious as that first taste of bouilla-baisse. He wasn't as seductive or perfumed. And yet she had accepted him, whereas he obviously had not returned the favor.

She brushed away the tears which pooled in the hollows under her weary eyes. Her body heaved a drawn-out sigh. Her spirit, once so resilient, lay flat out as if decked.

The truth was, she didn't want her husband to leave.

For one thing, she loved him. Passionately. Wholeheartedly. Unconditionally. Maybe others would find this hard to believe. What a loser he was, what a shit he was, they'd croon. She could hear them now rallying in her head. Get rid of him. The bastard. How could he do this to you? String him up, hang him high. Jasmine smiled as she mentally hung Daniel from her pots-and-pans hook. But immediately she saddened again. That would be so easy, wouldn't it? Just to say that's it.

But life was more complicated than that. And truth be told, she didn't think it was the worst thing he could do to her. The worst would have been an emotional withdrawal. The belittling she saw from some husbands. Like Betty's, for example. A day-by-day chipping away of the wife's sense of self until nothing remained but an apologetic shell. Daniel had never done that. He had always been enthusiastic about her powers and had always stood firmly behind her. Even when he became Mr Jasmine March, standing at the back of demonstrations and holding cocktail napkins, he had smiled with humor. And when he was so inclined he still made Jasmine's toes curl. You don't give up on something like that. No, you don't.

And besides, what on earth was she going to do with all that food in the house? All that food she had planned to cook for Daniel. Both freezers filled with joints and chops and mince. Meals planned way ahead for his pleasure. Who would taste her recipes with as much enthusiasm? And joy. And discernment. Who would understand the difference a half teaspoon of salt could make? The unpleasant mark on the tongue a heavy hand with vinegar could leave? The man had, she had to admit, an exquisite palate.

Still, he couldn't be allowed to get away

with it. Jasmine settled back against the pillows and let her mind wander. What does one do when one's husband dines on another's cuisine, so to speak, gorges on another's victuals, partakes of another's fare, sups at another's . . . oh, stop it, Jasmine. What does one do?

Chapter Thirteen

Careme flicked closed the *City Paper*, the headline of which screeched: CELEBRITY COOK IN THE SOUP. A very accurate photo caught her mother coming out of jail, her hair wildly askew, her large form bulkier than usual in the wide-angle lens. Careme looked up to find the whole class gawping at her and giggling. She spied Lisa staring straight ahead trying very hard not to laugh. And she knew immediately who had placed the tabloid on her desk and who had told the entire class.

Careme held her head high. To think that she had called up Lisa to moan about her mother being splashed like spilled tea all over the paper. She had been so embarrassed. And Lisa had been so nice on the phone, assuring her that nobody she knew read the *City Paper*. Careme had hung up almost believing that her classmates would never find out. Roger was right. Lisa couldn't be trusted. Careme had never called her on it before because she didn't want to be ejected from the popular group.

After all, what would she be if she wasn't popular? A freak? A druggie? A Goth? The sad possibilities were too numerous to contemplate.

Careme walked over to Lisa's desk carefully, as if walking on crushed bones. The crowd around nudged each other in glee. Dissent and intrigue in the royal court. All for their viewing pleasure. Lisa looked flustered, having clearly not expected confrontation. Not in front of everyone. Careme spoke clearly.

'You showed them.'

'Some of them had seen it anyway.'

'You told me you wouldn't.'

'It's not a big deal.'

'You promised.'

Lisa's fluster turned to annoyance. 'Well, Little Bo Peep, why don't you go blow your horn?'

Her crowd giggled again. What a witty thing to say.

Careme stood her ground. 'It was a really mean thing to do.'

'Can I help it if your mother is a fat jailbird?'

'Shut up!'

Lisa threw her Coach bag over her shoulder and stood to her full slender height. 'Oh, come on. Look at it this way. Maybe your mom will see the light. Maybe she'll finally lose some weight.'

'That's none of your business.'

'Porky. Porky.'

'You're such a bitch.'

'Me? You're the one who always calls her that.'

Careme looked away. Lisa was right.

Lisa smirked. 'I know. I know. I forgot. You can. She's your mother. Lucky you.' As Lisa retreated to the hall, her pack followed her, hands over their grinning mouths.

Careme's hands itched to scratch out all their eyes. Imagine them laughing at her mother. Her mother, who had more talent in her burned fingertips than they had in their whole horrible bodies. And was a hell of a lot nicer too. She sure wasn't a snob like most of their parents were. Lisa's mother was the worst. Always in a rush, always name-dropping, real slick. Kind of like Lisa, actually. Whereas Careme's mom was always warm and inviting and . . . well, it had never occurred to her, but the best thing about her mother was that she could trust her. Oh, she could be really annoying sometimes, but never in her entire life had Careme's mother ever let her down. Her mother would never tell anyone any of Careme's secrets. Ever.

Careme thought about that as she waited with Roger and the rest of the geeks in line for the bus.

Betty sat in the corner of the library and wept with relief. She had discovered something. She had been perusing the shelves of her library trying to find one book she hadn't read on diets when her hand alighted on it. *Fat Power*. It was as if it had been waiting for her, just for her, tucked behind *Fab Abs and Better Buns*, which she had read a dozen times already. The small green volume went on for 240 tight pages about the horrors of diets. Now that was something Jasmine had been telling her for years. But there was something about the way these women wrote and looked, the fat packed around them like armor, their smiles grim determined lines in a pillow of flesh that made Betty sit up and pay attention. Fat. You are fat, they said. And for once she was not horrified. The way they put it was as if she had scaled the mountains to join a very special club. A club that had been maligned and sidelined and made a scapegoat long enough. A club that was ready to fight back and take what was theirs. Fat Power. Maybe it was the answer. Her salvation. Plus, she thought, as she peered closely at the pictures, these fatsos made her positively look like a stick.

Betty glanced up and saw two young men at a library table eyeing her and grinning. The two boys nudged each other and looked away quickly. Betty's eyes narrowed and she returned to her book.

Start with the kitchen, the book ordered. Throw out anything remotely to do with low fat. Stock up on high fat like a survivalist waiting for the end of the world. It's time to eat with attitude. Pack in those calories and wear the weight like a shield. You have entered a new millennium, it promised. The millennium of the Big Bad Girl. Time to Pig Out. Betty shut the book and shivered with excitement.

Roger had it all prepared. The Lean Cuisine again. The iceberg lettuce. The grapefruit salad.

He had also showered, shaved the light fuzz from the left side of his chin, sprayed aerosol deodorant in every crevice of his body, and applied extra antifungal cream to his toes. He stood in the middle of his bedroom holding his box of condoms, pondering where to put them. Under the pillow? In the top drawer of the nightstand? Slipped in the elastic of his boxer shorts? He had practiced the night before putting them on. He was ready.

Careme was coy as she walked in. She licked her lips and wove in and out of Roger's personal space. She and Roger shuffled around each other in the hall before he led her into the kitchen.

'How's it going?'

'Fine.'

'Snake's good.'

'Yeah?'

'Yeah.'

'Good.'

'Hungry?'

'Sure.'

He held out a choice: Lean Cuisine Broccoli Cheese or Vegetable Lasagna.

'Lasagna.' Careme was quick with her decision. She too was ready. Showered and shaved with three packs of condoms hidden deep in her zebra-skin bag.

As the lasagna nuked in the microwave, the two gazed at the kitchen floor. Roger's mind clicked along with the seconds on the microwave. He hesitated, then leaned over toward Careme's mouth. She tilted her head back helpfully. Their teeth met and they dissolved in a tongue and saliva fest that would have drowned a lesser couple. Roger pulled back for air. He grabbed her hand.

'Come on,' he mumbled and led her upstairs.

Careme did not demur.

As he closed the door to his bedroom the microwave dinged. Connected at the hip, they gyrated to his single bed and fell heavily on it. The scene set, the body procured, Roger frowned with concentration as he went about his business.

Careme yelped and scrambled up.

'What are those?'

Roger felt light-headed from the sudden shift of focus.

'What?'

Careme pointed a shaking finger at his chest. Two rings pierced his pert red nipples.

'Haven't you ever seen them before?'

Careme shook her head.

'A lot of kids are wearing them.'

'No.'

'Yeah.'

'Don't they hurt?'

'Not now. They feel great.'

Careme scrunched up her nose.

'Really. They're about control.'

'You get control by poking holes in yourself?'

'Better than dieting yourself to death.'

Careme was silent. Roger shrugged his shoulders. 'You do what you do.' He reached out and caressed her bony shoulder.

'You should try them.'

'No way.'

'Maybe start smaller. A nose or tongue ring.'

Careme laughed but was in fact pretty turned on. She reached out and delicately touched the left ring. Roger closed his eyes.

Two minutes later Careme smirked over Roger's shoulder as he fumbled about. She was within seconds of womanhood. She was thinking she couldn't wait to see Lisa's face when she told her. Then she remembered; she was no longer speaking to Lisa. Just as she felt the smooth barrel of rubber between her legs the door opened and a large woman stood red-faced at the threshold. Betty Johnson stared into Careme's eyes a split second before opening her mouth and bellowing, 'Roger! My baby! What are you doing?'

Tina trotted into the café on Eighteenth Street. She was fifteen minutes late. She wore the self-satisfied look of a woman who had just picked up a Christian Dior brassiere for half price.

As she sat down in a cloud of perfume Daniel had never smelled before, he poured them both a large glass of wine.

'What is all the urgency, Daniel? I told you I'm really busy today.'

He set her glass before her. She pushed the glass away and hailed the waiter.

'Can I have a glass of ice water please? No ice.'

Daniel took a gulp of wine and studied Tina.

Tina shifted uncomfortably. 'What?'

Daniel said nothing, just stared at her, reducing her to her sum parts. He tried to use Careme's dismissing mind and regarded the tarnished gold chain around Tina's neck. The chipped brown fingernail polish on her left hand. The whisper of mustache above her purple lips. But it all looked enticing. He gazed to where her breasts struggled to break free, where the thin material of her skirt filled to bursting with her muscled thighs. He swallowed hard.

Tina's strong neck pulsed as she drank her water down in one go. She touched her lips with two fingers as she set the glass back down.

'Why did you ask me here anyway?'

'I didn't want a scene.'

Tina laughed. 'You're not going to break up with me, are you?' She stopped laughing, then stood up abruptly. Daniel grabbed her wrist.

'Sit down.'

Tina's eyes flicked over to where another clandestine couple sat two tables away. She took in the woman's diamond earrings and cashmere dress and sat back down.

Daniel fumbled with his pants pocket and drew out a small jewelry box. Tina's eyes opened wide like flower petals. He pushed the box across the table to her. She accepted the box with an incredulous grin, as if she'd just won the jackpot. She took a deep breath and opened the box. Her smile dimmed as she saw the ring. A trim one-carat diamond.

'Wow,' she said politely.

In a quick, self-conscious swoop, Daniel settled in front of her on one knee. He took her hand. He was doing something he would never, ever, in a million years, as he would have declared, have done. Kneeling in front of a woman, a credit card receipt for a jeweled ring in his pocket. Jasmine had had to make do with a Mexican wedding ring, three gold bands of different-colored silver. No diamonds. He was not that kind of man, he told her. They were not that kind of couple. They were above all that. But Tina made him do things beneath himself and he reveled in it.

'It's been great. But I've got to let you go. This is a token of my appreciation.'

Because in the end, after a night of unlimited depression, he realized not only was he a cad and a heel, he was, above all, a man who loved his wife. A man whose life, for all his complaining and insecurity, was exactly how he meant it to be. He had stayed in Washington to be with Jasmine. He had started a family with her because he couldn't imagine anything more rewarding. He loved her because she was who she was. He had wronged her. Now it was time to set it right.

'Don't take it too hard,' he said.

'Wow,' Tina said again.

Daniel's knee began to throb, so he stood back up. Tina continued to stare down at the ring. Daniel had never broken with a mistress before and wasn't sure of the protocol. He wanted to be a gentleman about the whole thing. He didn't want to be cheap. Plus he knew how hard she was going to take it. So he had thought something sparkly might soften the blow. But within ten minutes of entering the jewelry shop the owner had worked him so smoothly he had put down two months' salary. Daniel took the box and began to disengage the ring, but Tina pried his fingers away and shut the box. She handed it back to him.

'What?'

'I should have told you before this,' she

said. 'You're not the only man I've been seeing.'

She drew from her purse an identical jewelry box. She opened it to show him the ring inside. A ring encrusted with three diamonds, all three double the size of his one solitaire. She tilted it carefully so that the woman at the other table could see.

She then snapped the box shut and buried it back into her purse. She stood up and hiked her bag over her shoulder. She held out her hand.

'I too have very much enjoyed our relationship, Daniel. I was going to have to break up with you but you've saved me the trouble.'

Daniel was not computing. He stood with his eyes and his mouth slack. She tried to push past. He blocked her exit.

'What are you telling me?'

She stepped back.

'That you were not the only one.'

'Who gave you that ring?'

'Someone I've been seeing. It started before you. So I wasn't exactly cheating on you. Him, maybe. In fact, it wasn't only you two. A girl has to keep her options open.'

'But I thought . . .'

'He's buying us a new house in Potomac. A six-bedroom colonial. Marble foyer, his and hers bathrooms. We're eloping to Rio tomorrow. Well, we're leaving, anyway. He still has to get a divorce.'

'But what about us?' Daniel leaned forward. 'What about . . . you and me? I mean . . .' Daniel was at a loss for words. 'What about our dietary commitment?'

'Oh, Daniel, you said it yourself, there's more to life than food. Besides, you're a director of a failing theater. Why on earth would I marry someone like you? You have no money, no pizzazz. You're a has-been. Well, I'd say you were a has-been, but in fact, baby, you never was. Can you please move, I'd like to leave now.'

'But you wanted to learn to cook for me.'

'I was just trying out my ultimatum on you. A rehearsal. See how it would play. I needed to get my lines right.'

With a sharp elbow, she shoved the speechless Daniel to the side and walked out the door. He stumbled after her.

'Tina.'

She turned. Outside the sun was too bright. It hurt his eyes but whipped her hair into a luminescent strawberry cotton candy. Daniel swallowed hard. Tina softened a slight second. She came forward and kissed Daniel tenderly, regretfully on the lips. She was enjoying her scene.

'Good-bye, Daniel,' she said, and walked away, taking her sweet ass, her big tits, and her dietary rules down the road.

Daniel couldn't breathe. His body was numb but his mind was buzzing with humiliation. 'A never-was.' His blood seared through his veins. That no-talent was calling *him* a never-was. *Him.* Daniel opened the ring box. Well, she knew her price. A house in Potomac with a marble foyer. He laughed harshly. She'd be staring out of the society pages next. Or those back pages of *Regardie's* where all the rich and bloated show off their parties for the camera. She wouldn't last long. She'd be scarfing down refined flour canapés and forgetting to eat her protein and in two years he wouldn't recognize her. She'd come back to him, bored with her moneymaking husband who couldn't get it up, and she'd be begging Daniel for it, grabbing at him, promising him anything. And he'd brush those grasping hands of hers off his body and say, 'Man, you look old. Haven't you had a good crap lately?' Ha. He slammed his hand against the lamppost. Ha. Ha. Ha.

Really he thought, as he slumped home, the women in his life were completely impossible. Desdemona, he thought. Now there was a woman. Strong, beautiful, ethical. Dead in the end. But then most heroes are. Desdemona. How long did it take for her to die? What did she think of? That's what an actor has to think when she plays her. What was she thinking when she died?

Careme thought long and hard about what she had just seen. Her father kissing another woman. It was as if she'd seen an alien step off a spaceship with Gucci shoes and her brain was still trying to figure out the new look. Her father kissing another woman.

Careme sat hiding behind a small menu of the café where she had gone to recover from the shock of Roger's mother coming in and ruining her sex life. The woman's screams still rang in her eardrums. Oh, why, oh, why had she decided to lose it with the son of her mom's best friend? She might as well have broadcast it live on national TV. Everyone knew what a gossip the old goat was. And Roger, a wimp for all his mettle, had just buried himself under the covers while Careme dashed around the room trying to find her clothes. She would never speak to him again. Maybe Lisa was right after all. Maybe losing it just wasn't worth it.

Careme peeked over the menu, but her father and his tryst had separated. The woman was sauntering away down the street, her father watching her go. He then swung his head around in the direction of the café. Careme dropped to the floor, her no-fat, sugar-free muffin toppling onto her head. She waited. When she stood up again, wheatless crumbs covering her head, her father was gone.

Of course he was kissing another woman. What did her mother expect? Walking around looking like a trussed-up hog. That was cruel, she knew, but her mother had to face facts. The wolf was at the door. And the little pig had better build herself a nice strong façade. And go on a diet. That's all she needed. And a little makeup. Careme would take her shopping. Some plum and mulberry colors would suit her perfectly.

Careme took a long sip of her double cappuccino and thought about the other woman. She'd always heard about them but had never seen one in person before. And frankly, she wasn't impressed: fake gold jewelry, shag hair, Hit or Miss suit.

Well, her father had better shape up. Because Careme had no intention of turning into a statistic. She was not going to be one more child of a broken home. She had her future to think about. This was a very delicate time for her. Her adolescence. The timing was all wrong. She had college to get into. College her father had to help pay for. He couldn't be off spending money on some floozy. No. He had to restrain himself. She still had her virginity to lose, damn it. She had to get married, find a career, have children. And she was not about to shuffle her kids from his and his new wife's house to her mom's on Christmas morning. No, this had to stop. It had to stop right now. Someone had to stop it.

Chapter Fourteen

There were two options for Jasmine to choose from. She could demand an immediate divorce or she could forgive and forget. As Jasmine was not prepared to accept either of those options, she had found her own more individualistic response to Daniel's philandering. Like a great recipe it would take skill and careful planning. Similarly, like a great recipe the reward would be luscious if brief in duration. The aftertaste would depend, Jasmine knew, on her artistry.

Jasmine ran upstairs to make herself ready. As she undressed, she smiled into the mirror. Her full form looked delicious, her mounds of flesh tantalizing. It was so much more fun preparing oneself for the ravenous and she knew this particular man was greedy for her. All she needed was a quick shower, a black lacy dress, and an open mind. Because half of what he wanted was all in here, she reminded herself, tapping her forehead. At the sound of the doorbell, she added a hint of her perfume — two dabs of truffle oil behind each ear — and ran downstairs breathlessly to open the door.

Again he wore the jeans and the white oxford shirt with the sleeves rolled back.

'I'm glad you changed your mind,' Troy said.

'Come in,' she whispered.

Troy looked both ways before entering. In the hallway he reached for her. But she sidestepped him neatly. She planned to lengthen their ecstasy.

'This way.' She led him into the kitchen.

'Wherever you like,' he said.

'It seemed appropriate.' She nodded toward the kitchen table.

'Here?' he asked, amazed.

'Hungry?' She sidled up to the oven.

'Oh, yeah,' he said, watching her bend forward to open the oven door a crack. He stepped forward to manhandle her, but the aroma that escaped stopped him in his tracks.

'Oh, man,' he groaned with pleasure.

'Sit down.'

His eyes sparkled. A dominant woman. He collapsed into the nearest chair.

'Close your eyes.'

Troy hesitated.

'Go on. I won't hurt you.'

Troy closed one eye, then reluctantly

closed the other. Jasmine stepped behind him and tied a large napkin around his neck. She placed both her hands on his shoulders.

'You listening?'

He nodded eagerly. She breathed into his ear.

'I have not asked you here to make love to you.'

Troy's eyes popped open.

Jasmine shut them gently with her fingers. She paused. She gazed down at this young man so eager to receive what she had to offer and her eyes filled with sorrow at what could have been with Daniel. She shook herself. She would not retreat. She caressed the soft curls at the top of his neck.

'I have asked you here to cook for you. My husband no longer seems to be interested in what I have to offer, so today I am turning to you. Every fiber of my being is in this meal. I have researched it, tested it, and honed it. I have dreamed about it. This is the best that I am capable of. And I knew you would appreciate it.'

Unable to help herself, Jasmine caressed his shoulders, lingering on the hard muscle at the top of his back. Her fingers itched to massage down that back until they reached his perfectly rounded . . .

'Stop it,' she blurted to herself.

'Excuse me?'

She took a deep breath. 'After the meal is over I never want to see you again. Is that clear?'

'Why?'

'Because sometimes in life, once *is* enough.'

Troy was silent as he thought this over. Finally he nodded.

'Good,' she said. 'You can open your eyes now.'

Troy gazed up at the woman before him with a mixture of want and fear. Jasmine popped open a wine bottle and poured the straw-colored liquid into a crystal wine-glass.

'We'll start with a '95 Kistler-Dutton Ranch.'

She poured one for herself and tasted. Ah, yes, she thought. Intense and lively with layers of pear, spice, vanilla, and nutmeg. And a hint of honey, if she wasn't mistaken. She smacked her lips. Her foray entered into, she was relaxing and beginning to enjoy herself. She grinned with glee as she wrapped herself into her oversize apron.

'As I am a culinary orphan, I have chosen dishes from a wide range of influences. We're starting with classical French. In France, to begin, they often offer you what they call *amuse bouches*. Amusements for the mouth. Here are yours.'

She set before him a platter filled with baby profiteroles, little puffs of pastry sliced in the middle and filled with a surprise.

Troy reached out and brought one to his lips. His face flushed with pleasure as he bit into the creamy filling.

'Yes,' she said. 'Finely chopped cooked lobster mixed with finely chopped cooked mushrooms sautéed in lobster butter. All bound with hot béchamel sauce. You like?'

Troy grunted with reverence and reached for another.

Jasmine smiled and returned to the stove, where she stood at a large pot swirling with a long wooden spoon. She tasted, added a pinch of white pepper. Tasted again. Thought a second and reached for the salt. She counted out six grains and added them. She poured two bowls and carefully wiped the edges clean. She placed a bowl in front of Troy.

'Oyster bisque. Cajun style. It's got a real bite to it.'

She sat down at her place and took a sip. She puckered her lips in concentration. Rich and creamy with just the right touch of red pepper heat. She nodded with approval. Troy still held his first sip in his mouth, reluctant to release it.

Jasmine patted his hand. 'There's plenty, Troy, let it go.'

He swallowed. He had tears in his eyes.

'Attaboy.'

In silence they sipped through their soup, occasionally pausing to lick the back of their spoons. Troy ate two bowls, mopping the bottom clean with crusty bread. Jasmine had to gently release the bowl from his hands.

She reached for the main course: the stew.

'This is a nod to the northern woods where deer run free . . . for a while.' She brought forth from the oven a large earthenware dish, steaming and bubbling. The rich brown juices crusted at the edges. She set it on the table.

'Smell.'

They both brought their noses close and breathed in the aroma.

'The essence of venison, thyme, Madeira, and juniper berries.'

She spooned Troy a generous helping, adding a succulent baked tomato and perfectly roasted potatoes. She served herself and sat down. She poured a deep, lush '94 Opus One Silver Oak Cabernet Sauvignon into their wineglasses. She held up her glass. The wine glowed like an exquisite garnet.

'Happy birthday Daniel,' she toasted.

Troy held up his glass. He didn't know what to say, so he didn't say anything. Instead he took a small sip. He closed his eyes and held the bouquet, big, ripe, and dark, in his mouth, his senses acutely aware of the woman across the table from him, knowing even in his tender age that this moment was going to be with him, a cherished memory, till the day he died.

When Daniel opened the front door, the aroma hit him between the nostrils like a left hook. He stumbled. Saliva sprang like a leak inside his mouth. His head pounded with desire. He stopped a moment to collect himself. Damn, he thought, the old girl could still do it to him, still fan his flames. He wondered, though, why she was cooking now. His birthday wasn't until tomorrow. Still, Daniel wasn't about to complain. As he approached the kitchen, he rubbed his hands in anticipation.

At the door, he stopped and stared. Jasmine, a spoon in her hand and a radiant smile on her lips, turned to him.

'There you are, Daniel, you're just in time for dessert.'

Daniel looked past her to his vision of hell, a young man eating his birthday dinner. Eating it with virile gusto. He watched as the strong white teeth tore through the lumps of meat, as the lips smacked at the rich dark juices, as the strong neck worked its way through this most majestic of meals. Had Daniel a sword he would have drawn it. He would have run the upstart through the heart up to the hilt. He would have looked deep into the brazen dying eyes and uttered but one word: 'Mine.' As he only had his gym bag, he tossed it to the ground with fury.

'What's going on here?' he bellowed.

'I hope you saved room, Troy,' Jasmine said as she stood up and pulled out their dessert.

'It's one of my own recipes: peach crème brûlée with a brandy crust.' She paraded it past Daniel's eyes. 'See,' she said, 'I made your favorite. Of course I've perfected it considerably these past few weeks.' She kept walking and deposited the dish in front of Troy. She poured over it a good douse of brandy, then rummaged in her apron and drew forth a long match. One flick and the brûlée ignited in a crown of blue flames. Troy's eyes widened with childish pleasure.

'Here you go, my big man.' Her spoon crunched into the caramelized topping and reemerged with rich, creamy, peachy dessert. On the plate, the velvety brûlée glistened with delicious, crackly caramel.

Jasmine pushed forward a glass of Robert Mondavi's luscious Moscato d'Oro.

'Bon appétit.'

Daniel stepped forward. Jasmine's eyes flicked over at him dangerously. He stopped. And stood helplessly as Troy savored each bite. Jasmine dug in and savored too, eyes half closed in rapture, lips turning and twisting with pleasure. Daniel sat down abruptly on the corner kitchen stool. Every ounce of energy sapped from him. His eyes drooped, his hands fell limply by his sides. The blood in his veins slowed to an imperceptible crawl.

Finally, Troy and Jasmine set their spoons back on their empty plates with a clatter. They drained the last of their wine and reclined in their seats silent and happy. Troy let out a long sigh.

Daniel let out a long groan.

Jasmine leaned forward and patted Troy's hand. 'I think it's time for you to go now.'

Troy glanced over to where Daniel sat mute with despair, then stood up heavily and stared with the greatest respect at Jasmine. He leaned down, took her hand in his and kissed it. In two hours she had gone from possible lay to icon. She was the most desirable and satisfying woman he had ever met. He made a vow to himself that when he figured out what he was going to do with his life he would dedicate what he did to her. Troy opened his mouth to speak, but Jasmine gently placed a finger on his lips.

'Good-bye, Troy.'

Troy walked past Daniel out the door.

Daniel turned on Jasmine. 'That was my birthday dinner!'

'So it was.'

'How could you?'

'How could I? How could I?' Jasmine barked a laugh so loud it made Daniel jump. He scowled at the table as if it were an unmade bed. He suddenly reached out and swept all the dishes to the floor. As the clatter and crash cascaded around them, a black jealousy surged through Daniel's body.

'All that work you put into it,' he accused.

'Yes.'

'So personal. So . . . so intimate.'

'Yes.'

'For him.'

'Yes.'

'Damn it, why didn't you just screw him! It would have been more understandable, more tit for tat. But by giving all that . . . that . . .'

'Love?'

Daniel put his hand to his head and tried to collect himself, but his eyes were blinded

318

by pain. By bestowing all that cooking on another man she had raised the stakes to a stomach-churning high. Jesus, all he had done was have sex with Tina, a simple friction-based sensation, a bodily function, as satisfactory and nonemotional as a sneeze. But Jasmine, she had offered her very soul. She had cheated on him absolutely.

'Why?' he moaned.

'You know why I did it. I want to know why did you do it.'

'I don't know,' he sniveled.

'That's bullshit.'

'I thought it was my last chance.'

'For what?'

Daniel hesitated. He hung his head and finally mumbled.

'To have sex.'

'Why? Are you dying?'

'I thought maybe no one will have sex with me . . . later.'

'When?'

Daniel's voice dropped to a whisper. 'When I'm old.'

'I will.'

'Yeah.'

'But that's not enough, is it?'

'Sure it is.'

'What do you want, Daniel?'

'I want us. Like it was.'

'When you were cheating on me and me not knowing about it.'

'Before that.'

'When you had stopped talking to me.'

'Before that.'

'Like in the beginning.'

'Yeah.' He reached out. 'Please, Jasmine. I'm sorry.' He drew her close. He lifted his hand to her neck and began to stroke her.

'No!'

Jasmine pulled away. She was amazed at the shock of anger that still ran through her. 'I'm sick of this. I'm sick of being the cheerleader around here. Everyone else walking in and out with their moods, doing what they please, while good ol' Jasmine is always smiling, always trying.'

'But that's wonderful.'

'Oh yeah? Then why did you go off with that . . . that what's-her-name . . .'

'Tina.'

'I don't care what her name is!'

'OK. OK.'

'She shows her face around here one more time, she's dead meat.'

'It's over.'

'Why should I believe you? You lied before.'

'What can I do to prove to you that it's over?'

'Oh, her head on a platter would be a good beginning.'

'Jasmine . . .'

'You know what was so wonderful about that boy who just left?'

Daniel's eyes grew wary. He didn't want to know.

'He was so grateful. He was so grateful to receive everything I gave to him.' Jasmine paused then smiled. 'And it was my pleasure to give him pleasure.'

Daniel stared at her. The pulse in his cheek beating with anger.

'You have gone too far,' he hissed, and walked out.

Tina packed a small suitcase. Anything bulky they could buy when they got there. She surveyed the smallness of her apartment. Good-bye to this, she thought. Hello to luxury. She took a long swig from the bottle of Cordon Rouge she'd bought to celebrate. Because for once she'd won. The wife lost. For once it was going to be the wife who cried alone in her bed. Well, that's life, babe. Maybe you shoulda kept your paws out of the chocolate bonbons. She smiled, slightly guiltily. But not much. She'd really worked for this one. She had tantalized, teased, and enticed until she was green in the face. Some days she'd felt she was like that man in *The Old Man and the Sea*, reeling, reeling, reeling. Thank God this time the damn line didn't break off. Because frankly she'd run out of steam. If this one didn't bite she didn't know what she was going to do. Because it sure didn't look like she was going to make a splash out of acting. Some nights she would dream that she was sitting at a cluttered desk behind the plaque OFFICE MANAGER, and she'd wake up screaming.

Tina took a huge gulp of champagne to steady her nerves.

Imagine that creep Daniel telling her to get lost. As if she'd hook up permanently with some guy perched on the poverty line. Of course, he was pretty delicious between the sheets. She laughed ruefully and raised her glass. Well, good-bye to that too. It was to be pretty standard fare from now on. If she was lucky.

She threw in her makeup case, two teddies, three bathing suits with their matching sarongs, and clasped the suitcase shut. Well, what else do you need in Rio?

She placed the suitcase by her bed, then padded off to her kitchen in search of some protein. Wow, she thought. He was really doing it. He was really going to leave his wife and marry Tina. Of course he could still pull out. Which was why she was driving to his house the next morning bright and early and escorting him personally to the airport. Not waiting breathlessly by the gate only to have him not show up. No sirree. Been there.

Daniel stood in the moonlight under the awning of his theater. Litter skidded gently across the deserted street. Cobwebs of steam rose from covered manholes. He leaned against the darkened door and watched the clock on the 7-Eleven tick away. Tomorrow it would be December 12. Tomorrow he would turn and forever be at least forty years old.

So it was pretty official. He had reached the deadline. That deadline which told you in a flat, unforgiving voice, 'You didn't make it.' He was not going to be celebrated or rich. He was not going to be spied at in restaurants by strangers nudging each other's elbows. He was not going to get a front-page Style write-up. He was not going to be able to whisk his family off to the most expensive hotel in Venice as a surprise. Or show up in front of his parents' house with a brand-new Mercedes just for them. He was never going to feel that smug satisfaction of great universal acclaim.

Tina was right. He was a never-was. A never-would-be too. So there was really only one thing he could do. It was time to grow up. To put passion away. To start again. To mellow.

Jasmine collected the dishes and stacked the dishwasher. She wiped and mopped away every sign of Troy. She then pulled out another mound of venison meat. She had decided to make Daniel another birthday dinner and invite a few guests. The meal the next evening was going to be a simpler affair. Just stew, a side salad, and dessert. A suitable truce.

For Jasmine had decided to forgive, forget, and get on with the business of life. She was never one to hold grudges. Too acid a life for her. Instead she preferred to carry on through thick and thin and hope such a recipe turned out. Naïve perhaps. But Jasmine was a woman fully aware that life was not perfect. She was not going to waste time trying to make it so. She preferred to spend her precious moments enjoying what it had to offer. And so far what it had had to offer was pretty delicious. The affair had been bitter. No doubt about it. But she had retaliated and now as far as she was concerned the story was over. It was time to return to tasting life's pleasures. She hoped deep in her heart her trust in life's banquet would not be dashed.

Plus she had discovered the perfect new recipe for Daniel: Son of a Bitch Stew. A little known Texas specialty that would fire off the top of your head if you were not careful. Pint of chilies, a splash of Worcestershire, and enough garlic to fend off a flock of vampires. Again she sliced juicy morsels of venison but this time marinated them in two cups beef stock, two cups Worcestershire sauce, a glass of red wine, a cup of red wine vinegar, a good splash of olive oil, twelve, yes, twelve minced cloves of garlic, two bunches fresh oregano, and the real touch, ten red chilies, crushed.

She turned the meat over in the marinade and slid the dish into the refrigerator. She then whipped up a batch of her special double-chocolate brownies, Daniel's second favorite dessert. She covered the cooled brownies with tinfoil and went to bed.

Chapter Fifteen

It was the blood Jasmine saw first, coiling toward the refrigerator. She thought she had left meat out to defrost and it had dissolved in the warm morning light. But as she stepped forward to investigate, Tina's body came into full view, pale, limp, and askew in a dress entirely too young for her. Jasmine's shadow loomed forward and covered Tina's remains completely, even the brownie. She leaned down in a halfhearted attempt to feel for a pulse. But no, she quickly ascertained, the wafer-thin lover was definitely dead.

Jasmine surveyed the vivid crime scene. Blood pooled at her feet in a rich raspberry hue. Tinfoil balanced askew over the plate of Jasmine's homemade brownies. Her special marble rolling pin lay six inches from the girl's bashed temple. Jasmine stood very still. She had done this as a child when she had woken in the night to find the dripping jowls of a monster leaning over her bed. And it had always worked. When she opened her eyes a second time the monster would have transformed itself into an open closet door. She opened her eyes. Tina still leered up at her.

Jasmine stared back mesmerized. She'd never seen a dead human body before. What was it doing here? Who had done such a thing? Her mind jarred, it could not compute. She waved her hands before her eyes. Police. Yes, police. She must call the police. Jasmine reached for the phone. But then dropped it. Her breath caught in her throat as the horrific realization dawned on her.

Jasmine's knees quivered and she suddenly collapsed into a chair. She couldn't believe he had done it. He had really done it. She had asked for her head. And here it was. Well, more than the head. The whole kit and caboodle. Jasmine covered her blushing cheeks with her hands. How romantic. How passionate. She looked down again. How ghastly.

How could he have done such a thing? Jasmine's brain whirled like a blender. Well, obviously with all the strain of the last few weeks her husband had become unhinged. He was sick. Temporarily, she was sure. It was the lack of food. Lack of sustenance. All that cleansing and detoxing had snapped his mind. He would never have done it after a proper meal, with a full gut. The hollow bowel defense. That's what she would call it.

But would the jury agree? Probably not. As meager and pinched as the rest of them, they would certainly show no mercy.

Jasmine clasped the edge of her chair. It was all her fault. She shouldn't have been so cruel. She was responsible for this maniacal act. But what should she do? She couldn't let them take her husband away. No. She would have to help him. She had to save her family. But how was she going to do that? She had a full-grown body splayed on her kitchen floor. A skinny body at that. Hardly any meat on her at all. Jasmine paused at this. Of course, she thought.

Jasmine jumped to her feet. She would have to work quickly. She leaned down and gingerly retrieved the brownie from the girl's mouth. A worrisome touch, she had to admit. Jasmine then reached for her knives. After all, she thought, a good cook can cook anything.

In her bathroom, Careme washed the blood from her face. She watched it curl toward the drain like a red whisper. How on earth was she supposed to explain this to her parents? She could imagine her mother's horror, her immediate conviction that it was all her fault. She could see her mother raising her hands to her heavy chest, slumping over like a doll and beseeching, 'Where did I go wrong?'

Her father she was less sure about. Maybe he'd think it was cool. Maybe not. Probably not. But he'd be silent about it. He'd be white and still and Careme would be terrified. What was the punishment for something like this? They couldn't exactly ground her. Maybe they could, but it would be a pretty shitty thing to do. Oh, the pain. The pain. And all the blood. She hadn't expected that. But it was done. Finally done. She examined the front of her silk DKNY shirt and gritted her teeth. It was ruined. But it was worth it. It was time she grew up and took control.

In the living room, Daniel lay back on the couch where he had slept the night and sighed deeply. It was a sigh of relief. The fever had broken. The turning-forty fever had broken. Men, in his opinion, should be locked up for the six months prior to their fortieth birthdays. As much for their own safety as for the feelings of those around them. What a cad he'd been. What a jerk. God, he hoped he hadn't gone too far. Yes, Jasmine was pissed off. He didn't blame her. She had every right to chuck him out. He was at her mercy. He hiked himself up on his elbows and gazed about the room, blinking rapidly and letting everything come back into focus. It was all so clear now. This was his home. And tucked inside was his family. And he loved them very much. Oh, Auntie Em, he grinned, there's no place like home. He swung his legs over the side and made for the bathroom.

As he pissed a strong stream toward the back of the toilet he turned philosophical. So he was turning this number today. It was a number like any number. A day like any day. And if he didn't have to tell anybody no one would notice. No one would stop at the sight of him on the street and screech, 'Oh, my God, you're forty. Jesus God. What happened?' Above all, his dick was not going to fall off. Those friends of his in L.A. making it. Ha. Didn't they know he was the one who had made it? He was the one with a woman whom he loved and who loved him, who he hoped still loved him. And what he had was a marriage. A work of art in progress. Imperfect, perhaps. But in the end that was the thing of which he was proud. And he was damn sure at this he would not fail.

He just hoped he hadn't completely screwed up. He just hoped that she would find it in her heart to forgive him. He would do anything to win her back. Anything.

Luckily, Jasmine thought as she wielded her electric saw, the best thing about Daniel's birthday stew was that it was so versatile. You could use any meat you liked, as long as it was red: beef, venison, lamb . . .

She had thought quickly and now it was all planned. The bowl of meat she had prepared the night before was already marinating in the refrigerator. This meat, or to be more precise, Tina, would marinate in another bowl downstairs in the second refrigerator away from everyone. If the cops came they would think this bowl was just extra. Jasmine gasped when she saw the oven clock. She had to hurry. She placed the meat into a large Tupperware bowl, added the beef stock, wine, vinegar, garlic, and chilies, mixed well, and rushed the bowl downstairs.

When she returned to the kitchen she jumped. Tina's head still sat on the far kitchen counter. She gazed at it and shuddered. What was she going to do with it? Her nerves were wearing thin. She scanned her cookbook shelves. Surely they would give her an idea. She took down Mrs. Beeton's. Head cheese? How about a head *en croute*? *Tête en sarcophage*? That was more like it. She opened her well-thumbed *French Provincial*

Cooking. Mmm. Fairly simple. She would do a French pastry adding whole egg so that the dough would be more pliable and hold its shape better. She needed it to keep until she could figure a way to dispose of it.

It took just a few minutes to mix the flour, butter, eggs, oil, salt and cold water together. With quick, deft movements she patted the dough about and stood back to admire her work. A swipe here, a pinch there, and it looked just like the Doughboy. She then whisked it to the downstairs refrigerator to set.

Upstairs, Jasmine blanched. Was she really doing this? She took a deep, steadying breath. Yes, she was. She couldn't let them take her husband away. She couldn't let them lock him in some small institutional cell devoid of Jasmine's roasts and minces and crème brûlées. It would kill him. And life without Daniel, well, that was unimaginable.

Jasmine wiped her hands, then hefted the three trash bags of leftover detritus over her shoulder and hurried them to the car. She arranged them in the trunk and firmly closed the tailgate.

As Daniel walked into the kitchen, he heard a car door slam. He glanced out the window and saw Jasmine shove herself behind the wheel of their Toyota and drive off. He smiled indulgently, wondering where his dear bat out of hell was flying to. He surveyed the room, scrupulously clean. How unlike Jasmine. Maybe she was turning over a new leaf for his birthday. Was it too soon to start drinking? Absolutely not. He padded down to the basement. He opened the refrigerator door to find the dried bust staring out at him. Daniel gazed back trying to figure out if it was supposed to look like him. A present from Careme? He peered closely. The poor girl had less talent than he thought. Luckily she was good looking. He pulled out his Stella Artois and shut the door. There was a thump inside the fridge. He opened the door again and the bust fell to the floor and cracked open.

Daniel did not move as he stared down at Tina's head. Broken dough lay like shattered white glass. Long red hairs still clung to the temples. Daniel laughed out loud. What a great joke. What a wicked birthday present. How did Jasmine find such a likeness? Did his wife have a sense of humor? Or did she have a . . . Daniel shrieked as his fingers touched the skin.

He tried frantically to wipe off the feel of cold flesh from his finger. He then brought his hand to his throat to protect it. He wanted to swallow but his mouth had dried to a bone. Daniel clamped his hands over his face in horror. He opened his eyes to peek and gazed into the bony face he had . . . no, not loved . . . cherished . . . well no, that wasn't strictly true either. How about cared for? Nnnnn . . . Oh, all right. Lusted after. The face with those lips he had hungered for. Not to mention those ears. Damn. Jasmine had obviously not gotten over it.

He reeled. After all, this was his wife. This was the woman he slept with every night. This was the woman he so lovingly loved. She had . . . she had . . . Jesus, what had she done? He frantically pulled out the freezer compartments looking for the rest of the body. He rummaged through pork chops and rib roasts, minces and whole turkeys. All frozen solid. He peered into the bowl of marinating meat. Then shook his head forcefully, rejecting the idea. No. Absolutely not.

He was on the verge of short-circuiting when the banging started at the front door. The whole door frame quaked with its violence. Daniel's heart stopped. Oh, God, she's been caught. They've come for her. His eyes narrowed. Well, he would not let her go. This was just another hiccup in their marriage. Well, perhaps a bit more than that. More like a gargantuan belch. But it was a private thing. They would seek counseling. They would work through it. They would survive this. The marriage would survive.

After all, it was all his fault. If he had been a better husband . . . but it was too late now. Now, he had to save her. He grabbed his old motorcycle helmet from their sports rack, shoved it over the head, and set it back on its platter in the refrigerator. He dashed up the stairs and opened the door.

Betty stood weeping on the doorstep.

'How awful,' she wailed. 'So awful!' She stood with her large arms crossed over her breast, clutching her sides, as though if she didn't hold herself in she might explode before his very eyes.

'Betty.' He choked with relief.

She lunged at him and held him in a tight grip, burrowing her head into his chest.

'What's wrong?' he asked, trying to keep his balance around her rotund belly.

'You don't know?' She blubbered over his sweater.

'No, what?'

'Is Jasmine here?'

'She just left.'

'Where was she going?'

'I don't know.'

She peered around him into the house. She wiped the excess tears from her eyes, rubbing mascara deep into the creases around them.

'It was so awful.'

'What?'

She glanced behind her. 'Can I come in?'

'It's not a good time.' He backed away.

But she had pushed forward and stood cowering in the hall, her hands over her face.

'I'm so thirsty,' she mumbled, and stumbled toward their kitchen. Inside, she lifted her face and stared around the room as if she'd never seen it before.

Daniel poured her a glass from their filter jug. His hands were shaking. Betty accepted the glass, which she held like a small bird she didn't want to let loose. Daniel popped open a beer.

'You feel better now?'

She nodded. They continued to stand in silence, Betty staring at the floor, Daniel leaning back against the counter, swigging his beer. As suddenly as she had arrived, Betty set down her untouched glass, nodded to Daniel, and shuffled back to the front door. She opened it, took one last look at Daniel, and left. Daniel put down his beer and began to shake.

'Daniel.'

Daniel looked up. Jasmine stood at the kitchen door. Her face was ashen. Her hands trembled at her coat. Daniel stared slack-faced at her.

'Don't worry,' she said. 'It will be OK.'

'Th-th-the refrigerator.'

'You saw,' she whispered.

Daniel was silent.

Jasmine's hands trembled against her coat. 'I had to do it.'

He nodded his head. He wanted to take Jasmine in his arms, to console her. This poor woman, what had he driven her to? And yet he stood frozen in his tracks, he couldn't move. He was confused. Horrified. And, of course, there was a small voice in his head that was screaming at the top of its lungs, 'Run!'

She stepped forward. 'The car. It's broken down.'

He stepped back. 'Where?'

'In the middle of the intersection. Wisconsin and Q. They're all beeping. I didn't know what to do.'

She stepped forward again. 'Daniel, what should we do?'

Daniel took a deep, steadying breath and pushed his wife toward the door. 'Lead the way,' he cried.

At the intersection, the cars were indeed beeping. But they were managing to push their way around the stalled car. The language flying out of their windows was strong. Some of it so raw, Jasmine had to blink. There was a long, jagged scrape against the door and the side mirror was gone.

As Jasmine let out the clutch, Daniel leaned into the passenger door and pushed the car around the corner onto Q Street. He massaged his aching hands.

'That should do it.'

'The trunk,' Jasmine said. Her eyes were as big as hard-boiled eggs.

He opened the trunk. It was filled with trash bags. When he felt one, it gave to the touch of his fingers like a bag full of meat. Daniel slammed the trunk shut. His eyes met those of Jasmine above the car.

'What are we going to do?' she whispered.

It was at that moment that Daniel noticed behind Jasmine, up behind the gas station on the right corner, a police car. Jasmine turned to see where Daniel was staring. The cop, feeling no doubt the two gawking at him, glanced their way. Jasmine and Daniel jerked their heads in the other direction.

Daniel glanced at Jasmine from the corner of his eye. Here was his chance. If he had any brains, he would turn her in and hire a good lawyer. But his heart pained at the sight of his wife, so bulky, so vulnerable.

He shook his head. They were going to survive this. This marriage would not fail.

'Let's just leave the car.'

'It's no parking after four. What if they tow it, what if they look inside the trunk?' Jasmine said. Already the cars were starting to clear from the road.

Daniel gazed up and down the cross street.

'Dumpsters,' he said. 'These restaurants have dumpsters. How many bags?'

'Three.'

'You take them and start down that alley. I'll wait here and guard. There's a Thai place, about five down. Don't let them see you.'

The cop car pulled up behind them. Its door opened, the words TO PROTECT AND TO SERVE swinging toward them like a threat.

'Is there a problem?' came the words above the swagger.

Jasmine coughed with fright. The cop skimmed the car with his eyes.

'Breakdown,' Daniel blurted. 'Waiting for AAA.'

The cop examined Jasmine, whose plane of sweat threatened to splash down over her lips like Niagara Falls.

'How long?'

'They said twenty minutes.'

'You got fifteen.' The cop gave them a last look and sauntered back. Daniel waved his hand as the car passed him. Jasmine reached into the trunk and grabbed the bags.

'Watch out for blood dripping,' whispered Daniel hoarsely.

'It won't. I cooked them.'

'You what?'

'I cooked the bones. Well, nuked them. So if anyone found them they wouldn't think . . . they'd just think it was, you know, beef or something.'

Daniel stared at his wife. 'Good idea.'

Jasmine nodded. She looked both ways before trotting across the road with her three Hefty bags. She looked like a common housewife taking out the garbage.

Daniel gasped for more air. He rushed to the side and threw up at the curb. He wiped his mouth and closed his eyes.

'Dad, what are you doing?'

Daniel opened his dripping eyes. Careme balanced behind him on her bike. Daniel took in her bright face, her innocent eyes, her fragile figure. Words in no apparent sequence tumbled out.

'I, um . . . the car . . . broke down . . . waiting . . . soon . . .'

'Need help?'

'No! No. See you back at the house.'

'You're white.'

'Not feeling so great.'

'Is Mom home?'

'She's . . .'

Jasmine appeared at the edge of the alley. The front of her blouse was wet where the sweat was pouring in rivers down her face and neck. At the sight of Careme, Jasmine stepped back into the alley, but then, realizing what a wrong move that was, tried to correct it by walking as nonchalantly as possible across the road.

'Hi, dear,' she smiled.

Careme glared back and forth at her parents. 'What are you guys doing?'

'Errands,' answered Jasmine crisply. 'You ready for tonight?'

'Yes, I'm ready for tonight.'

'Good, because we're having a bit of car trouble. Can you be a peach and go home and put the stew in the oven? The meat is marinating in the refrigerator. And could you set the table? The green tablecloth. You know the drill. We'll be back as soon as we can.'

As Careme rode away she glanced back at her parents, who stood in a trance by the side of the road.

'Can you believe it?' she said to herself,

sticking out her newly pierced and swollen tongue. 'All that worry and they didn't even notice.'

As Careme rode away, her parents watched her go.

'Do you think she saw?' Jasmine asked.

'I don't know.'

'Do you think she'll say anything?' Daniel asked.

'No. No, she won't.'

They looked at each other and knew that really they had no idea. That if they were betting people the odds would be that their daughter would tell someone. Because she had morals. Her morals were a teenager's morals: primitive, bedrock, intolerant. Good and evil flashed in her mind like neon lights above a 7-Eleven. To Careme, you were either one or the other and you had to choose very carefully because this was it. Everyone said so. If you screwed up now and chose evil over good or vice versa, you were stuck. Never would you be able to back up or do a U-ie on the path chosen. Careme had chosen. She had chosen good. The good were better dressed, for one thing. And they had much better stock options. So to their daughter, Jasmine and Daniel would be criminals. Didn't matter that they had spawned her. Didn't matter that they had nurtured her, coddled her, bought her that damn hair-sprouting jive-talking Barbie for her twelfth birthday. They'd done their deed and were replaceable. Parents were always replaceable. It was a horrible state of truth.

Daniel stared straight ahead.

'Why did you do it?' he asked.

'Because I love you.'

He nodded. She held out her hand. He took it and gave it good squeeze. Then he placed a note on the car to the parking Nazi and they walked as quickly as possible back home.

Careme locked her bike and let herself in. Her parents had outdone themselves in weirdness. Why her mother had to get rid of her leftovers in the public dumpsters and not leave it by their own curb like any other mother was beyond her. And why had they looked so guilty. Were they having sex in that alley? That was so gross.

But she had more important things to think about. What to do with her tongue, for instance. It was so swollen she could barely talk. She glanced at her watch. Only an hour before guests were to arrive. She needed to get ready. She needed to shave and moisturize, she needed to wash and condition, she needed to clip and pluck. She needed to blow-dry and gel. And then she had to set the table. Jeez, her parents never thought about her responsibilities. It was always what could she do for them. You know, she was an adult, after all. Almost. And she had things to do. But first she needed ice to suck on. That would bring the swelling down. Careme trotted down to the basement to where they kept bags of ice and opened up the second refrigerator door.

Careme lifted the motorcycle helmet and beheld the head of the other woman. Her blood, already on the cool side, chilled to absolute zero. She grimaced as she took in the woman's cold clogged pores. So that's why they were acting so strangely, she thought. They had gone and gotten rid of the mistress. Why her father couldn't break up with her like anybody else's father was beyond her. But then again her father was a drama teacher.

Careme was shocked. She didn't think her parents had it in them. They had struck her as more of the sweep-it-under-the-rug- and place-the-coffee-table-over-it kind of couple. It was gratifying to see that they were handling their differences head on.

Careme clamped her hand over her

mouth. Fear replaced the respect. A searing clutch of fear. Her tongue. What would her parents do if they found out Careme had pierced her tongue? Obviously her parents should not be pushed over the edge. Careme began to sweat through her mint and elderflower natural deodorant. She would take the stud out immediately. She would shape up. Yes, that's what she would do. She would become an impeccably well-behaved teenager. Who cares if that was an affront to nature. She would defy the elements. And she would start by doing exactly what her mother said. What was it she'd ordered? Something about a stew. Oh, yes. There it was. Behind the head. Careme took out the bowl of marinating meat and brought it up to the kitchen. She transferred the meat into a casserole and slid the dish carefully into the oven, making sure not to spill any of the juices. She then ran to set the table.

As she lay the last piece of cutlery on the table a new thought came over her. She would help her parents. That's what she would do. And then maybe they wouldn't be so mad at her. First thing was to remove the evidence. What were they thinking leaving evidence in the second refrigerator? It was probably the absolutely first place cops would look. They probably walked into houses and asked right away, 'Where's the second refrigerator?' People aren't going to dump bodies in the first refrigerator. One, it's too full of milk and juice and diet Coke and Crystal Lite. No, they're going to place them downstairs, out of the way, until they've had time to think. Careme sighed. Must she do everything?

She ran downstairs again and slid out the large platter. She then chose her mother's largest cleaver and brought that and the head up to the sanctity of her room. As she chopped and watched her snake feed, she thought about how much she loved her parents, as klutzy as they sometimes could be. They always did their best. She had to give them that. Careme smiled as she remembered the Barbie they bought her for her twelfth birthday. It was so last year's model. But they did work hard to send her to that expensive school. And they did bring her up in a hot air balloon for her fourteenth birthday. That was really, really cool. And now this, working to keep the family together. Careme sat back on her haunches, watching Medea yawn happily through her meal, and made the vow that from now on, she would be much nicer to her mother.

Daniel and Jasmine barely spoke as they

returned home. Daniel held the door for Jasmine and let his hand run down her back as she strode past him. She rubbed his leg as she went by. 'Thank you,' she murmured. They had switched into polite mode. It was a mode they had used when first married and realized they didn't know each other as well as they thought they did. It had gotten them through some rough patches. She switched on the coffee maker. They both could use a pick-me-up.

She sat down at the table and folded her hands.

'Any ideas?'

Daniel sat down across from her. He too folded his hands. He puckered his eyebrows. He fiddled with his lips. He hunched his shoulders one by one to relieve tension. He placed his hands on the table in front of him.

'No,' he finally said. He had no idea of how to get rid of the head.

Jasmine nodded in agreement.

'Well, let's have a look. Maybe it'll come to us.'

Again Daniel stood back and let Jasmine pass first through the door. They made their way downstairs and stood in front of the second refrigerator. Jasmine took a deep breath and opened the door.

'Well,' Jasmine said, and closed it again.

Daniel was white.

Together they walked up to the only place the evidence could be.

When they walked in, Medea was just swallowing the last of her supper. She lay around the bottom of her cage, lumpy and satiated. Careme leaned in and stroked her distended scales.

'Careme,' Daniel said, clearing his throat, 'we'd like to talk to you.'

Careme motioned to her bed like a hostess. Jasmine and Daniel sat down side by side, their knees almost touching.

Daniel leaned toward Careme.

'We all have moments of weakness and your mother . . . has had hers . . .'

Jasmine jumped. 'Me?'

'It happens to the best of us . . .'

'I didn't do this.'

'Well, maybe not this,' he waved at the snake.

'I didn't do any of this.'

'You didn't do any of this?'

'Why would I do this?'

Daniel looked at her, almost disappointed.

Jasmine cleared her throat. 'I thought you . . .' She began but stopped.

'What?'

'Never mind,' she mumbled.

348

Jasmine and Daniel looked at each other and saw their other half. The half they had first been drawn to and now were often repelled by. The other half over which they had no control yet which they kept hoping would someday stand up and amaze them. But each day it had just lain limp and unyielding, completely predictable, completely unchanging. Jasmine held out her hand. Daniel accepted it tenderly in his fingers. For once, they correctly read each other's faces: humility, regret, forgiveness, and then panic.

They swung their heads to regard their daughter. Careme put up her hands as if to say 'Don't look at me.' She didn't say it because upon taking out her stud her tongue had swollen until it fitted her entire mouth, snug as a snail.

The doorbell rang.

'Oh, God, they're here.' Jasmine stood up and smoothed out her skirt. 'We'll just have to talk about this later.'

Daniel gave Careme a last, piercing look before walking out the door. Careme gazed back impassively. She wanted to tell them that she knew they had done it. That all the playacting in the world wouldn't pull the wool over her eyes. That they didn't have to worry. Because Careme, for one, knew how to keep a secret.

★ ★ ★

Betty was the first to arrive, bearing a large Cobb salad piled high with sliced cheddar cheese, crumbles of blue cheese, and chunks of ham and turkey. There was no sign of any lettuce. The bowl nearly slipped from Daniel's sweaty hands.

'Where's Richard?'

'Who the hell knows?'

Daniel peered at her. Very unlike Betty. Usually she took her husband's absences more stoically.

'Drink?'

'Double,' she said.

He filled two scotch glasses to the rim and handed Betty her drink. Betty was a nice woman, he reflected as he eased back into his chair. Warm, fleshy. Not much going on upstairs, he'd always thought, but easy on the nerves. The air waves didn't move much when she came into the room. The Bettys of the world rarely left a cosmic wake. Betty, for her part, settled herself on the deep blue couch, flicking the folds of her ample skirt around her shins.

'Where's Careme?' she asked.

'Upstairs, I think.'

'Hmmm,' Betty said, and took a long drink.

'Smells gamy,' she noted.

'Hmmm,' Daniel agreed.

They sat in silence, drinking quickly, steadily, Betty calculating the number of calories in each swallow, Daniel calculating the extent of his horror. They had gotten rid of the head. They had gotten rid of the bones. Where was the rest of the body? Daniel sniffed again. The smell was unlike anything he'd remembered eating. His eyes grew wide. Betty looked up from her stupor.

'What's wrong?'

'Nothing. Nothing.' Daniel hunched down in his seat. The bones in his body were beginning to ache with the strain. He wasn't sure he believed Jasmine when she said she hadn't done it. In fact, he was positive he didn't believe her. They would have to talk about that when they went to the marriage counselor. Trust. It was a big issue for them. That and the unmentionable he'd found in their second refrigerator. Daniel settled down to drink long and hard, too terrified to return to the kitchen.

More guests arrived: JD and Sue Ellen with their latest vintage, then Jasmine's mother, Linda, who wore a long flowing tunic and a necklace of human teeth. Daniel did a double take. Actually they were dried corn kernels. Soon the room swelled with noise and Betty, who loomed so large, began to shrink until she was nothing but a small blob perched on the couch nose deep in her fourth double scotch.

In the kitchen, Jasmine tried to collect herself. If she could just maintain her sanity until the end of the evening. She heard a creak behind her and jumped. She looked over to find Careme standing at attention behind her. Jasmine patted her pounding heart.

'What are you doing?'

'Wouth you like anything elthe?'

'Anything elthe?'

'For the parthy.' Careme smiled politely, her hands clasped neatly in front of her like a waiter. Jasmine eyed her suspiciously.

'What is going on?'

'Nothing.'

'Do you feel OK?'

'Yeth. How are you?'

Jasmine sat down. Her daughter was asking her how she was. Unprecedented.

'I'm fine.'

'I'm glath. May I go now?'

'Sure.'

'I'll be in the living room entherthaining the gueth.'

Careme gave her mother a slight bow and walked backward out the door. She stopped.

'Thith ithn't one of your ecthperimental dinnerth, ith it?'

Jasmine sniffed, her large porous nose flickering like an otter's. What a strange smell. What on earth had gone wrong with the stew? Jasmine ran to the oven and pulled out the stew. It was nicely browned and bubbling. But it smelled like . . . she ran to the refrigerator and opened it. There on the top shelf sat her Tupperware of marinating venison meat. Jasmine slowly turned her eyes back toward the oven.

'Come on, where's the grub? I'm starved!' JD poked his nose into the kitchen.

He spied the huge dish. 'Ah, there it is. Jesus, you made enough for a football team. Need a hand?'

Before Jasmine could move, he grabbed two pot holders and picked up the earthen pot. 'Come on, let's get this show on the road,' he cried, and carried it out of the kitchen.

Jasmine stood alone in her kitchen. She was horrified, dismayed, and fully aware that her dish was a disaster. For one thing, it was going to be on the tough side. Not to mention the seasoning was all wrong. She just wouldn't have used oregano. It was too sweet. With this kind of meat, you need something more robust, earthy, sage, perhaps. Jasmine sighed. She had to remember that not everything was edible. But if she took it back now she would have to explain. There would be suspicions. And right now those suspicions would fall smack onto her shoulders. Who else had a motive? Why else would she have tried to dispose of the body? It didn't look good.

Jasmine's blood chilled. How many years would she get? Far too many. And when they finally let her out Daniel would have grown old or worse. Jasmine might never see him again. Oh, Daniel. Poor Daniel. Who would cook for him? Who would lovingly feed his tired and often cranky soul? Well, her guests would just have to eat it. Because after all, Careme needed a mother. Didn't she? Jasmine wondered sometimes.

Jasmine unwrapped her apron and approached the dining-room table. The stew pot sat in front of her place. JD banged his fork and knife on the table in anticipation. Sue Ellen smiled limply. Betty downed another glass of wine like grape juice and waved the empty glass around for another refill.

'Do you mind?' she said vaguely in Daniel's direction.

But Daniel didn't answer. His eyes were fixed on the stew pot as it seemed to almost levitate itself over the table.

Jasmine held out the spoon. 'Daniel, would you like to dish up?'

'No!'

Everyone at the table peered down at him. He regained his composure. 'You go ahead. You're much better at this.'

'Alrighty,' she said with a tight smile.

'Smells . . .' JD's nose flickered uncertainly. '. . . great.'

'Venison.'

'Ah,' he said. 'That explains it.'

'I hope so,' said Jasmine. 'Mom . . .'

She held out her hand for Linda's plate.

Linda sniffed suspiciously. 'Does it have any wheat in it?'

Jasmine contemplated the bubbling stew. 'No,' she finally said. 'No wheat.'

Next was Betty's turn. Jasmine lifted a spoonful onto her plate. She hesitated.

'Give it to me,' Betty slurred. 'I'm starved.'

They passed the mounded steaming plate down to Betty. Daniel never took his eyes off of it.

'Sue Ellen?'

'Just a smidge.'

'Of course.'

To make up for his wife's paucity, JD demanded extra.

'Load it up.'

'Here you go,' Jasmine said with an indulgent smile.

Without a word she filled Daniel's plate. And then her own. The steam curled like a ghost around her nose.

Jasmine lifted her glass. 'I'd like to propose a toast. Happy birthday, Daniel. To many more.'

Daniel smiled sickly.

'Whath abouth me?' asked Careme, holding up her fork.

'I made you a salad, sweetheart.' Jasmine passed down a small tossed salad.

Careme looked at the salad then pushed it to the side. 'I want thtew.'

'Eat your salad.'

'I'm hungry. I promith.'

'No, you're not. Eat your salad.'

'But . . .'

'Eat your salad.'

'I . . .'

'It'll make you fat,' Jasmine hissed.

Careme dropped her fork.

'Mmmm, damn, this is good,' groaned JD, who had already tucked in. 'Yup,' he said, 'Happy fortieth, big guy. Hope you're enjoying it, 'cause it's all downhill after this.' He laughed and began choking. He clutched at his throat. His wife leaned over and thumped him on the back. He kept on choking, turning a bright sunset shade of red. No one moved except for JD, who pointed frantically at his throat.

'Help him, somebody!' Sue Ellen screamed.

Daniel jumped up and, pushing Sue Ellen out of the way, seized JD around the chest. He pumped and pumped and pumped. Finally the chunk of meat discharged from JD's mouth like a small cannonball and fell into Careme's lap. Careme screamed. JD slumped forward dribbling.

'That stuff's a killer,' JD croaked.

'That's my JD, always a joker.' Sue Ellen patted his sweating head. Daniel stood up suddenly. He motioned at the half-empty bottle on the table.

'More wine,' he gasped, and disappeared to the kitchen.

Jasmine smiled at her guests. 'Looks like I forgot . . . something.' She followed her husband.

In the kitchen, Daniel leaned forward breathing heavily as if just finishing a marathon. The two of them stared at each other.

Daniel cleared his throat. 'Jasmine . . .'

'What?'

'Where is the rest of her?'

There was a knock on the front door.

Betty's husband, Richard Johnson, stood at the door. He was a big man, six foot two. He had that well-oiled beaver look of a corporate player, always dressed in starched white shirts, bright ties, and imported wool suits. Jasmine had never liked him. Tonight, however, his tie hung around his neck like a noose and his shirt was wrinkled and sodden with what looked like sweat. And he had two men with him. One was young and tall with a jaw like a meat cleaver. The other was pushing fifty and, frankly, bordering on obese. His stiff new raincoat pitched around his body like a tent. They both nodded at Jasmine and flashed police badges.

Jasmine found her voice. 'Richard. What a surprise.'

'Is Betty here?'

'I sure am.' Betty had followed Jasmine to the door and now stood in the hallway, stew juice clinging to her chin.

'Betty, dear,' her husband began.

'Don't "Betty, dear" me, you asshole.' Rage cut through Betty's inebriated blood like vinegar.

'Can you give us a moment?' Richard smiled a commanding corporate smile at Jasmine. He and the two cops walked into the hall. Betty held out her hand to Jasmine, who grasped it and encircled Betty's shoulders with her other arm.

The fat cop pulled out a slip of paper. 'We've never received a confession by e-mail before,' he began.

Richard took the paper and addressed his wife. 'Is this true?'

'I don't know. But I think it'll probably be something that catches on. It's so easy, really. Comfort of your own home. Just a click away . . .'

'I mean the e-mail, dumb head. What you wrote. Is it true?'

'Oh, I see,' Betty paused, then went on the attack.

'Why are you asking the questions? I should be asking the questions. For example, how long has this been going on? When were you going to tell me? Were you just going to call me from a hotel room, saying "Betty, dear, this is Richard, I'm leaving you. I'm with my tramp now and I'm leaving you . . ." '

'Ma'am . . .' The fat cop tried to cut in.

'I bet you're still looking for these.' She pulled out two airline tickets. 'Rio, damn it. You know I've always wanted to go to Rio!'

The young cop placed a strong, tan hand on Betty's shoulder. 'Ma'am!'

Betty looked over at the two cops as if just noticing them for the first time.

'Yes?'

'Is the confession a real one?'

Betty pushed her hair coquettishly back from her face.

'Why, yes, Officer. Yes, it is.'

'Can you tell us where Miss Sardino is now?'

Betty was silent a moment.

'Well, Officer, no. No, I can't.'

'Why not?'

'She seems to have moved.'

'You mean she's not dead.'

'Well, she looked pretty dead to me. I mean, I really gave her a good whammo. You see, I saw her this morning . . .' Betty's eyes shone. She looked around to find the rest of the guests out in the hallway and every one of them riveted by what she had to say. So unusual. Usually people's eyes glazed over when she spoke. She patted her hair and continued. 'I looked out the window and I saw her waiting in her car in front of my house. And I realized she was waiting for my husband. And it all just fell into place. The late hours. The airline tickets. The whole shebang. So I ran down, opened the car door, and dragged her out. I tell you, I had steel in my arms. Well, she ran like the scared cat she is. Was. And I chased her. And she ran straight for this house. I couldn't believe it. Right through the front door like she'd been here before. So I raced right after her and cornered her by the counter. And I gave her a good whammo.'

Betty smacked her hands against each other and grinned. The fat cop scratched the back of his head with his pen, leaving a long blue line above his collar.

'Why?' he asked.

'Why?' Betty laughed. 'Isn't it obvious?'

The fat cop looked up from his notes.

'No.'

'Well, look at me.'

'I'm looking at you.'

'Yes, well, you don't look at me like she did. She looked at me like I was some low form of insect that had just crawled out of the linoleum crack. Like I was the lowest of the low. And you know what she says to me? She says, "I know an excellent nutritionist who would do wonders for that body of yours." She didn't leave me much choice, did she?'

The fat cop raised his eyebrows in grudging agreement. 'Where did ya leave her?'

'If you would follow me.' Betty turned to lead the way but, fearful of exposing her backside, twisted her body around and walked backward into the kitchen.

'I left her right there.' Betty pointed to the black-and-gray-checked slate that covered Jasmine's kitchen floor. Jasmine froze. Under one of the stools the brownie with Tina's teeth marks remained in clear view.

'See, there's the brownie I shoved into her skinny mouth,' Betty cried, pointing. The fat cop moved quickly. But Jasmine moved quicker. As he moved the chair to look, Jasmine gave the brownie a swift kick and it went scuttling under the deep recesses of the refrigerator.

'I don't see any brownie,' the fat cop said, disappointed.

Betty leaned over. 'It was right there. I saw the brownie. Didn't you see a brownie?' She turned shining eyes to Jasmine. Both cops looked at Jasmine. Jasmine was in a dilemma. She wanted to back her friend, but in this instance she thought it wise to keep quiet. She shrugged. The young cop took Richard aside. He turned his back to Betty and murmured quietly.

'Has she had these delusions before?'

'She's one elephantine delusion as far as I'm concerned,' Richard said loudly.

Betty sat back into a kitchen chair and scratched her heavy belly.

'The problem with you, Richard,' she

sighed, 'is that you've never taken me seriously.'

'A big fat zero,' Richard continued. The fat cop turned his eyes to Richard.

Richard stopped. 'I mean, no offense or anything . . .'

The fat cop made some more notes on his pad. He drew a double line underneath. He looked up and examined Richard again. 'When did you say you last saw Miss Sardino?'

'I told you. Two days ago.'

The fat cop began to take notes again. 'And did you guys have a fight?'

Richard turned his eyes to the young one. 'What is this?'

The fat cop licked his lips. 'A lovers' quarrel?'

'Why would we have a lovers' quarrel?'

'You guys were lovers, weren't ya?'

'I don't have to answer that.'

The young cop stepped forward. 'Maybe we should take this down to the station.'

Richard snatched the airline tickets from Betty's hand.

'You guys go ahead. I've got a flight to catch.'

'You'll have to go alone.' Betty smirked.

Richard shoved the tickets into his jacket pocket. 'I doubt that.'

The fat cop cupped Richard's upper arm with his hand. 'You're going to have to come with us.' Richard jolted back.

'Why? I'm not the insane one.'

'No, you don't look insane to me.' The fat cop blew a fat pink bubble and let it collapse onto his fat pink lips. His wet pink tongue neatly protruded from his mouth like a slug and Hoovered the pink bits back in. Betty watched, mesmerized.

'What about me?' she said.

'You too, Mrs Johnson. Making up confessions is a very serious offense.'

'Can I get my purse?'

'Yeah, I'll wait.' The fat cop followed Betty into the hallway and stood a little taller as he helped her into her coat.

The young cop stayed to examine the premises. He shooed the guests back to the dining room and insisted they return to their dinner.

'Looks delicious,' he said as he closed the door.

In the kitchen, he swept the room with his eyes. Jasmine, Daniel, and Careme stood nervously behind him.

'Do you have a second refrigerator?' he asked.

Jasmine and Daniel stiffened, but Careme

smiled. 'Yes, this way Officer.'

She led him down to the basement and stood back while the man gave the second refrigerator a good checking. He rummaged through the pork chops and rib roasts, minces and whole turkeys. 'That's it?' he asked.

'That's it,' she answered.

'What's this?' he pointed to two drops of blood on the inside shelf.

Careme hesitated, then stuck out her tongue. The young cop recoiled.

'I needed ice,' she explained to his back as he hurried upstairs. At the top he shook his head to clear the sight of the mutilated tongue before asking to see the rest of the house.

Upstairs, Daniel followed nervously as the cop stalked the bedrooms. In Careme's room the cop peered over the edge of the cage where Medea lay dozily digesting.

'Nice snake.'

'My daughter's.'

'Kinda lumpy isn't it?'

'Big dinner.'

'What do you feed a snake?'

Daniel thought a moment. 'Whatever you can lay your hands on.'

The cop's eyes canvassed the room, then lighted on Daniel's white face.

'Why do you look so stressed?'

'It's my birthday.'

'So?'

'I'm forty.'

The young cop whistled in sympathy.

At the front door, he held out his hand to Jasmine. 'Sorry to bother you, ma'am, but we have to check these confessions out. As crazy as they might be.'

'I completely understand,' said Jasmine, smiling up at his jaw.

'Good-bye, Mrs March.'

Jasmine returned to the kitchen and leaned back against the closed door. What on earth was she going to do? A young woman had died on her kitchen floor and yet Jasmine would never be able to admit it to anyone. If she did she'd go to jail for accessory to murder. At the very least for unregulated abattoir standards.

Jasmine bowed her head. Such a lonely death. Such a misguided, lonely girl. Of course the only decent thing to do would be to have a small ceremony. Some type of memorial. Yes, after the guests had gone home, she would dispose of the leftover stew appropriately. She'd sprinkle it with rosemary for remembrance. And add the flowers from the table. Yes, that's it. Perhaps tie the trash bag with a black bow. And say a few words.

Daniel could. He knew the girl better.

Jasmine nodded. It was the best she could do. Tina would understand. After all, Jasmine smiled, she knew all about fudging the rules. Jasmine then straightened her shoulders, smoothed her skirt, and reached for the plate of her special homemade brownies. She returned to her guests, holding the plate high.

'Dessert, anyone?' she offered.

A Note on the Author

Nina Killham was born in Washington, D.C., and lived overseas much of her childhood. After graduating from the College of William and Mary, she wrote about food for *The Washington Post*, wrote about travel and lifestyle for national magazines, and worked as an assistant at Columbia Pictures. She lives in London with her husband, an Australian who is a senior lecturer at the London School of Economics, and their two young children. Her husband does most of the cooking.